SERALYNN LEWIS

Cassie's Secrets

Women of Worthy Series – Book 1
A Second Chance Romance

Seralynn Lewis

Contents

Copyright © 2020
TimiDio Press, LLC
All Rights Reserved

First paperback edition September 2020

Edited by Carla Rossi
Book cover by Qamber Designs
Formatting by Polgarus Studio

ISBN 978-1-952953-00-2 (paperback)
ISBN 978-1-952953-01-9 (ebook)

www.seralynnlewis.com

"To be a Christian means to forgive the inexcusable because God has forgiven the inexcusable in you."
C. S. Lewis

Chapter 1

Cassie Verano leaned against the gray cement block wall and pulled out her phone. Where was her new friend, Mia? Tardiness was not in her friend's vocabulary and for sure not on an important day like today. She eyed the Worthy Gym and Dance Center's banner above the door, marveling that this small Ohio town actually had a gymnastics center and glad she was back in the southern part of the state. Even if it was early on a hot Saturday morning.

The lobby throbbed with excitement. Coins jingled in the beverage machine next to the reception desk. Groups of little girls in purple leotards stood in clusters with their hair drawn tight in braids and buns. A few girls sipped from juice boxes and crinkled their candy wrappers. Others performed ballet poses and spins. Eagerness for the pre-season gymnastics meet vibrated through the room.

A child rushed through the double doors with tears streaming down her cheeks. Cassie ran to her, squatted, and daubed the seven-year-old's face. "Where's your aunt Mia, sweetie?"

Her daughters became gym friends with her friend's two nieces. Mia was the caregiver for her widowed brother and in turn they had become great friends.

Tina Nardelli hiccupped, struggled with the words, and sniffed. "She's sick. Daddy did my hair, but it keeps falling out. Can you fix it?"

Mia repeatedly volleyed for her to meet her handsome brother and continually showed her photos of him with his daughters. Not even her less-than-interested comments dampened Mia's enthusiasm for them to meet. And her luck had just run out, but there was no way she'd let this sweet child suffer. All she ever wanted to do was to write and raise her daughters with no drama. Her ex-husband provided more than enough drama and she could do without another good-looking man in the mix.

The child's loosened braids fell apart in Cassie's hands. She spritzed the girl's head with a water bottle she pulled from a massive bag, then cupped a hand around Tina's face to prevent spraying her eyes. She brushed the dark tresses until they turned sleek, and re-braided them.

She patted the child's head and gave her a wide smile. "There you go. All's good now. You and your sister go join the team."

Thin arms wound around her neck and she held Tina for several seconds and enjoyed the child's closeness.

"You're the best!" The child yelled and rushed to join her team.

"Where's your daddy, Tina?" She called after her.

"He's right here." The low timbre of the masculine voice resonated through her. Still on her haunches, she almost failed to maintain her balance.

"I'm Steve Nardelli. You must be Cassie Verano." He extended his hand to assist her.

She recoiled and sprang to her feet, then adjusted her shorts and camisole. "I am."

Confusion stained his features, and he pulled his hand back. He didn't seem overjoyed to meet her but, then neither was she. She'd avoided an encounter. Until now. But she would make the best of it, if for no other reason than he was the father of her daughters' best friends.

"Tina cried about her hair, so I fixed her braids." Her voice wavered, and she darted her gaze from his chest to his mesmerizing bright blue eyes to beyond his shoulder. "Where's Mia?"

"Stomach bug. She should be up and about soon."

Cassie picked her bag up and her long ponytail flipped over her shoulder. She threw her purse over her arm and stared at his computer case.

"We should go in." She nodded toward the closed doors. "We don't want to miss anything."

Despite the air conditioner's hum, the gym didn't feel cool. In fact, the air stifled her. Or maybe it was the man who strode to keep pace behind her. She stiffened her spine and moved through the throng of parents who milled around the bottom benches.

When she got there early, she snagged a seat at ground level so she could handle any issues with her daughters. Not today. Thankfully, seats were still open near the top.

Climbing ahead of him, she stowed her bag under the seat and settled in. He scaled the stairs two at a time and jiggled the accordion-style bleachers, then folded into a seat a row below her and to her right.

She was glad she wouldn't spend the entire gym meet trapped next to him. Or worse, have to make conversation with him. But she positioned herself at an angle to keep an eye on him. Would he work while his daughters competed? *Forget about him and focus on the meet.*

The opponents, dressed in black and red leotards, were a stark contrast to the purple of her daughters' team. Both groups huddled around their coaches for last-minute instructions. Their daughters high-fived one another for the start of the meet.

Judges sat on opposite sides of the spring floor with scorekeepers ready nearby. In the far corners, the girls stretched and warmed up.

Out of the corner of her eye, she frowned when he pulled out his laptop. He kept his focus on the screen shutting out all the commotion going on around him. Unlike a soccer match or softball game, he wouldn't have to pay attention all the time. But it still bothered her that he would try to work at a meet. Practice, sure. Even she did some writing while the girls were at practice. But meets? No. It was their time to shine.

All four girls waved and gave a cursory glance at him. She responded with a grin and a silent thumbs up. When the girls returned to stretching, she glanced his way. He caught her gawking and raised an eyebrow. Heat rose on her neck, and she hurried to look away.

She hadn't dated since college. Her one and only boyfriend became her husband. And now, she was a single mother and had no intention of getting involved with any man. Her children were her focus and there it had to remain until they were grown and on their own.

His eldest, Stella, was on floor with her eldest daughter, next in the rotation. The girls seemed to have become immediate close friends. "Go, Stella!" Cassie alerted him to when his girls or hers were on beam or vault so he'd get his eyes off the computer screen and onto his daughters where his focus should have been.

Stella flashed a broad grin, took her place on the floor and saluted the judges. Canned music blared from the speakers. Her high leaps and graceful pirouettes showed she had made progress from summer practices. And she nailed her tumbling passes.

When the first half of the meet ended, the scorekeepers posted the tallies. Her daughters checked their rankings and dashed up the bleacher steps and halted in front of her. Her youngest daughter, Bella, begged for a juice box and goodies.

His daughters plopped next to him, and their chests heaved as they wiped sweaty faces. Cassie leaned toward them. "Would you like a drink and a snack?"

His mouth tightened, but he nodded to his daughters. He didn't appear to be happy she had offered. Too bad. The girls needed a drink and a snack. She wanted to glare back, but it would send the wrong message to the children.

The girls scooted over to accept her offer. "Thanks, Mrs. V."

"You're welcome, ladies. You're all doing terrific."

"Daddy didn't know to bring snacks and drinks and Aunt Mia sometimes forgets, but you always remember." Tina's lips gripped the straw, and she shrugged.

Cassie sneaked a look at him but he was frowning at his daughters. Maybe he *was* upset with himself that he didn't bring snacks. She wanted to give him the benefit of the doubt despite her experience with her ex-husband, but she struggled with her own pre-conceived ideas about men.

With a soft smile, she pulled Tina's braid. "Well, we all forget sometimes, right?"

Tina nodded and Cassie's younger daughter, Bella, mirrored her.

"We can't wait for camp to learn new tricks," Stella said.

Little heads bobbed in agreement, and Cassie smiled. The upcoming gym camp right before school started would be the highlight of their summer.

Her older daughter, Gabby, arose and hugged her. "We need to get back to the team."

She smirked and shook her head. They'd left their trash on the seat for her to pick up.

Toward the end of the meet, Steve closed his laptop and stuffed it in his bag then scooted closer, turning to face her. "The kids are doing well today, aren't they?" Shifting his gaze from her to his daughters, he had a slight smile on his face.

The pride she saw on his face made her happy for his daughters. Maybe he wasn't as bad as she thought, but still.

"Long hours spent at the gym and dance studio are paying off," she said, her voice quiet. Uncomfortable with Steve's attention, she fidgeted. It had been years since she'd been in the company of a man whose mere presence and gorgeous eyes set off alarms. More handsome in person than in his photos, she was unprepared to have a conversation with him, even if it was about the girls.

All four girls placed in all their routines. They raced up the bleachers to show off blue, red and yellow ribbons, and chattered with every step.

He hugged his daughters and glanced at her over their heads.

She descended with the kids in front of her and she could smell Steve's aftershave wafting behind her. A woodsy scent she knew would fill her nostrils long after she went home. She'd heard the sense of smell is strongest and she didn't doubt it.

He touched her arm when they reached the gym floor, and she shivered with goosebumps. "I wanted to thank you for the snacks." His smile seemed genuine. "Why don't you and the girls come to our house for lunch and a dip in the pool?" She frowned, but he continued to smile, staring into her eyes. "To celebrate their success. And I insist."

Her eyes widened. She hadn't expected an invitation for lunch. And he insisted? Biting her lip, she held back a sigh. He'd made the offer in earshot of the girls, who now squealed their delight. She wouldn't be able to stop the tide. Why had he made the offer? Was he aware his sister had been pestering her to meet him? That she shared family pictures of him and his daughters? She hoped not.

Her voice elevated as the girls danced around them. "We have to go home first to get their suits. It'll be about thirty minutes."

He gave her a half smile. "Don't worry. We'll wait for you."

Her stomach churned. Like it or not, she committed to lunch and his sister would have a field day with this news.

Steve flew through the kitchen door and dropped his bag on the counter. "We're back."

His family's long-time housekeeper, Fiona, bustled around the kitchen and prepared lunch while sunlight poured through the windows above the sink and made the stainless-steel appliances and the subway tiles gleam.

"Laddie, ye gave me a fright." Fiona's colorful accent grew pronounced when something startled her. Wisps of gray-streaked hair fell from the bun she always wore.

He puckered his brows and sniffed the air. "Sorry. We're having company. Do we need to order pizza or something?" Fiona had whipped up her famous cinnamon cake and he could almost taste its spicy richness. The scent permeated the room, and his stomach rumbled.

"Och. Dinnae fret. There's plenty."

He snagged a handful of chips she placed in a bowl and crunched them, then licked the salt from his fingers.

She crossed her arms. "Ye'll spoil yer lunch, laddie."

Fiona scurried around the kitchen with her ever-present apron tied around her slim waist and her blue eyes danced. "Now who might the guests be?"

He chuckled. "Will you ever call me by my name? I'm thirty-six years old. Way too old for you to call me laddie."

"Ye dinnae answer the question, laddie." Well, that didn't work. She'll ferret out the information, regardless.

"Cassie and her daughters. I'll check on Mia and change clothes. I'll be back in a few." He needed to get out of there before the inquisition started. The invitation had popped out of his mouth before he could stop himself. Whether it was the kids' excitement or his own curiosity, he couldn't say.

Snatching his bag, he escaped Fiona's surprised look. His brown leather Dockers made no sound on the pristine wood floors. He strolled into his home office and put the computer case on his father's old desk and gazed about the room. The 1920s colonial had been his boyhood home. He'd renovated rooms and added a pool that changed the old place into a better space for his family.

Through the open window, he stared at the aqua water and thought of the green-eyed woman who held his attention at the meet. What was wrong with him? He should have been focused on work, but no. Every time she rooted for his girls or hers, she pulled at him. He'd have to handle lunch with care. Fiona and Mia would be marrying him off to her if he let them and he had no intention of putting himself into another relationship. Once was more than enough.

Racing upstairs to get away from his thoughts, he tapped one knuckle on Mia's door and turned the handle.

Drawn shades shut out the summer glare and produced a gloominess that would help Mia rest and sleep. Nothing changed in here since they were teenagers. He wanted to renovate when she returned home, but Mia refused and moved into the over-the-garage apartment. But because she was sick, Fiona insisted she come *home* so she could look in on Mia.

He tiptoed in, perched on the edge of the bed, and brushed loose hair behind her ears. "How are you feeling?"

Mia rose from the mounds of those awful purple pillows. Her voice was a mere whisper. "I'm better. How was the meet?"

"The girls won ribbons on all their routines, but I didn't do much work."

She sat up and cocked her head. "You took your laptop?"

"I've invited guests for lunch." He hoped to distract her from giving him grief over working when he should have been more engaged with his daughters. He'd make it up to them in the pool.

He grappled with the biggest deal of his career and wanted to partner with a provider in Australia that would move his family-owned electronics manufacturing business up a notch in the world of technology and make the firm a global enterprise. His father had worked toward this achievement until his death. If he could make it happen, that is. He sighed. Mia understood nothing about the business. Nor did she want to.

She leaned forward. "Who?"

With a calm touch, he pushed her into the fluffy softness. "You stay in bed. I've got this."

"What exactly is *this*? More important, who did you invite to lunch?"

"Cassie and her girls," he said, keeping his expression in check.

Why had he invited them? Because he hadn't remembered the snacks and drinks? Or because he lacked the skills to be a top-rate dad? He couldn't rescind the invitation even if he wanted to. In some small way, he wanted to see just why his sister was so gung-ho on this woman.

Cassie was short, curvy and had eyes a guy could drown himself in, but he couldn't go down that road again. His dead wife had caused too many heartaches and her lies almost wrecked him, his daughters, and his business. He'd heard about Cassie from Mia. His girls had thrust pictures of her and her daughters in his face, but he hadn't really looked at her. He didn't want this irrational curiosity to lead him down another thorny path.

"She must have swayed you somehow." Mia beamed despite the paleness of her skin. "About time you two met."

Convincing her of something he himself was unsure of grated on his nerves. "Hold it right there, Mia. I invited Cassie *and* her daughters to repay her kindness and to celebrate my girls' first meet. Nothing more. Nothing less. It was spontaneous," he muttered.

A defiant look swept over her face, and she crossed her arms.

Stiffening his spine, he lowered his voice a few notches and frowned. "Stop with the matchmaking, Mia. Just because you live here and take care of the girls, doesn't give you the right to meddle in my personal life. If I want female companionship, I'm more than capable of finding my own."

He had to get away from this conversation or he might say something about Cassie he'd regret later on.

"We're twins. I know you better than you seem to know yourself. Laura has been gone for years, Steve. You can't judge every woman based on your dead wife. I just want the best for you and help you get on with your life. And unless I push a woman right under your nose, you practice blindness and selective hearing." She blew out a wisp of air that ruffled wayward strands of hair and turned her exasperation on like a light switch.

Such an annoying habit.

"Why would you imagine I'd be remotely attracted to her? She's not my type. Even if I were interested. Which I am *not*." He regarded her through the gloom and thought about how he could steer his sister in another direction. "She already has two children to keep up with. Her plate's quite full without adding two more to the mix. What makes you believe she's interested? Besides, she isn't interested in me, nor am I interested in her. Case closed."

"Methinks you protest too much, dear brother."

He raised his hands in surrender. "You're impossible! The Veranos will be here any minute. I need to change. Stay in bed." He stood. "And that's an order," he added with more force than intended. He stepped to the door without a backward glance. "And don't stick your tongue out."

In the hallway, his shoulders slumped against the wall, and he closed his eyes. Colossal mistake inviting Cassie and her girls. The girls were fine, but Cassie spelled disaster in giant capital letters.

Chapter 2

Steve heard the sound of a car stopping in the driveway. He tugged on his swim trunks and threw on an old college t-shirt, then raced down the steps and out the back door. Scattered puffy clouds and a summer floral aroma filled the air while the kids raced from one end of the yard to the other.

He spotted Fiona in a conversation with Cassie, and it put him at a disadvantage. Outnumbered two to one with the matchmaker twosome in his household. Not good. His shoulders jerked, and he resolved to keep his distance. He'd focus on playtime with the kids.

Stella ran to him and hopped from foot to foot, excitement coursing through her little body. "Can we go in now, Dad."

"Go ahead."

Splashes in the pool and squeals of delight pierced the air when all four girls jumped in the pool. His daughters sometimes shared a dip with him in the free-form pool after a brutal day at his office. The gentle waterfall at the pool's far end soothed him and the concealed hot tub washed away the weariness of his harried days and long commutes to Columbus from Worthy, Ohio, the small town where he was raised. The backyard had become his oasis.

Their antics in the pool resurrected childhood memories of vacations spent with his parents and sister. Contentment. Something he'd not had in forever, it seemed. Examine that sentiment? Not happening. His eyes drifted from Fiona to Cassie as he strolled toward them.

Steve stepped on the gray flagstone patio and placed his phone on the glass table. He passed Fiona, who winked on her way into the house. What was that for? Memories of his dead wife crushed any thoughts of happiness with another woman. Would he ever forget or forgive the pain she caused him and his daughters?

He pushed those thoughts aside as he gave Cassie a quick once-over. "You made it. Looks like the kids are enjoying the water."

"They are. I'm glad Mia's better and is sleeping."

Before Steve had a chance to respond, a wall of water drenched him from his head to his well-worn boat shoes and missed Cassie by inches. He scanned her shocked expression, winked, and toed off his shoes and jumped in the pool. Clothes and all.

With water streaming down his face, Steve's eyes lingered on Cassie as she dropped her bag on the chaise. What was so special about her that his sister insisted they meet? He'd admit she seemed to be a kind person, cheering for his daughters as well as hers, but he wasn't interested in developing any kind of relationship with her.

Stella and Tina jumped on him, and he splashed all four girls. He lifted each of them and threw them into the water on the pool's other side. The girls chortled with glee and returned for more. More fun than weightlifting at the gym.

Her daughters were cute little things, and they resembled their mother, but he detected a hint of sorrow in their eyes despite the frolicking. Why? Reminded him of his own daughters after his wife died.

"Last one out is a smelly monkey." Steve swam to the

pool steps, and the girls followed.

He removed his soaked shirt, then rubbed the towel across his chest and wrapped it around his hips. "Let's eat. I'm starved."

A faint pink streak touched Cassie's cheeks, and she spun away to help the girls dry off. Hadn't she ever seen a guy in a swimsuit before?

She bristled but not his business, and since the chance of future involvement was nil, it didn't matter.

Their families faced one another at the table with Fiona at the end.

Cassie looked around the table. "Who wants to say grace?"

Stella cast adoring eyes at him. "Daddy."

He almost choked on his tea, not having prayed at mealtime since... *Don't think about it.* "Fiona, say grace." Steve bent his head to prevent further discussion. He couldn't bear his daughter's disappointment or Cassie's disapproval.

After the prayer, Fiona's mouth took on an unpleasant twist, and everyone ate in uncomfortable silence. Even the mouthwatering cinnamon cake couldn't reignite their earlier exuberance.

"Can we go back in the pool now, Mama?" Bella, her younger daughter, tugged at Cassie's shirt.

She kissed her daughter's forehead and smoothed her hair. "No, darling. I want you to wait an hour."

"Old wives' tale, you know," Steve said.

Cassie lifted her chin. "Perhaps. But there could be cramping so I'd rather not risk a belly ache, if you don't mind."

One of his shoulders lifted. "Suit yourself." He didn't care for her pursed lips. He had been a collegiate swimmer. He knew what was dangerous and what wasn't. Why couldn't she just believe him? Another reason he didn't want any involvement.

Gabby crossed her arms, and her lips drooped. "Are we going home?"

How would she handle the situation considering how her face tightened?

Cassie glanced at her wristwatch. "Find something to do for an hour, then you can swim for a while." She peered at her daughters and conveyed a silent but firm signal.

Approval lit Fiona's face as she retrieved paper plates and dumped them into a plastic bag.

"We can play board games," Stella said. "Let's go get them."

"Don't disturb Aunt Mia," Steve said.

Cassie cleared the table. "You can play here once we're done." A soft smile covered her lips as she looked at the four girls, and it hit him in the diaphragm.

The girls ambled along to the house with Fiona behind them. He'd had dated here and there, but none of whom he'd ever expose to his daughters. The least he could do was have a casual conversation with her.

"So…what do you do for a living, Cassie?" His thumbs beat a rhythm on the table top. His nerves stretched taut and he forced himself to stop.

"I'm a freelance writer."

His eyebrows rose. "Anything in particular?"

"Blog posts."

"Your own blog?"

She shot him a glance, but then looked over his shoulder. "Heavens no. I don't have time for my own blog. I write for companies who want a professionally written post but don't have the time or personnel to do it."

She seemed as nervous as he was.

"Any particular topic?"

She kept glancing at the door, almost willing the girls to come back. She didn't seem to want to be with him either.

"They assign topics. I research them and write the posts."

It seemed she couldn't look him in the eye. Why was that?

"Anything I would read?"

"I doubt it." Her eyes met his. "Why weren't you paying attention to the girls to—"

The chirping of his phone kept him from an angry retort. He didn't need a woman, much less a woman he barely knew, call him on his shortcomings as a dad.

Grabbing the phone, he rose, and listened for a moment. He turned away from the woman he was sure was watching his every movement. There was nothing he could do. If he didn't sign off on the specifications and get them over to his team today, it could compromise the deadlines. And he had to meet them if he was going to make the Australian deal a reality. If he had done the work he was supposed to do this morning, it would have been done, and he could have spent more time with his girls this afternoon. But because of a long-haired beauty, that didn't happen. And he was angry with himself over it. He snatched his wet shirt and shoes and moved back to the table. "Unfortunately, something has come up and I need to go into my home office to handle it. Mind keeping an eye on the girls? I won't be long." He couldn't keep the terseness from his voice, but waited with a patience he'd cultivated from his business dealings over the years.

Cassie hesitated slightly. "Actually, I do mind, but I'll do it for the girls."

Her hesitation and attitude annoyed him. The request wasn't unreasonable. "Fine. Do it for the girls, then."

He passed the girls on his way into the house. Stella carried two board games.

From the privacy of his home office, he watched Cassie with the kids through the open window. Her childlike enthusiasm charmed him even if her attitude left a lot to be desired. He exhaled. If he crashed the game in a bit, would Cassie retreat and clam up? He shook his head. Forget it. Instead, with a frustrated sigh, he adjusted the plantation shutters so he could hear the girls playing.

She was great with the kids, but wanted to interfere in his life and he couldn't have that. What had happened to her? Glad his focus was on work and not on the lovely Cassie. He gazed out the screens but shook off thoughts of her and reached for a file. His electronics business provided sufficient excitement where no female complications or tantrums existed.

Cassie repositioned the chaise in the shade that left her legs in the sun. Her feet moved in circles as her hand glided a mechanical pencil in rapid fashion across the notebook's pages. She stopped to erase what she wrote, then continued to scribble. What kind of blog post was she writing? Something he'd be interested in?

Irritated at himself, he returned to the task at hand. Engrossed in the specifications and proposal for the upcoming Australia trip, a Beethoven ringtone broke his concentration.

He stared as Cassie scowled and strode to the stone bench beneath the Japanese maple tree near his window. He caught glimpses of her through the leaves.

She almost hissed into the phone. "Now's not the best time, Phil."

A long pause while she listened. "I can't do that. Not possible."

Who was Phil? Too bad he couldn't hear the other side of the conversation.

What did Phil want her to do? Was he one of her clients? Or was she in some kind of trouble? Maybe his sister knew. Nah, couldn't ask her. She'd make a huge deal of it.

Cassie's voice lowered further. "We had a deal. You promised me more time." Another gap. Maybe it was a client. Or maybe she *was* in trouble. His ears tingled. He rarely waffled and he'd been vacillating all day long.

A lengthy silence followed, and then, "Let's shelve this discussion for now. I'll call you next week." Cassie ended the call, and once again settled into the colorful chair. Steve's gaze drifted over her. Despite her short stature, she had fantastic legs.

"Mama, can we swim now?" Gabby begged her mother, who checked the time and nodded. With voices raised in excitement, the girls jumped in.

Cassie rearranged the chaise, opened the notebook, and continued to write.

Steve reviewed the proposal and made notes on PDFs for discussion with his attorney and department heads. He studied a few more files, then closed the laptop.

When he walked outside, Stella and Tina raced from the pool, jumped into his arms, and wet him again.

With reluctance, Cassie's daughters exited and dried off. She whispered near their ears, and they shuffled to him holding hands.

Her daughters bent their heads back. "Thank you for the pool party. For lunch, too." The sadness that clouded their eyes could not have resulted from their pending departure.

"You're welcome, anytime." He smiled, slid his daughters out of his arms and ruffled each of her daughters' heads. They pulled away, and their eyes widened. He drew his fingers back. What caused their distress? Surely not him. Another secret?

Cassie cleared her throat. "Yes. Thank you for lunch and the fun time for the girls today."

"Not a problem." Her cool fragrance, enhanced by the summer's heat, startled his senses.

Stella and Tina waved at their friends until the car pulled out of the driveway.

His stomach's lining crawled. She harbored secrets. His instincts told him she could spell danger for his daughters and sister.

Cassie kissed heads that smelled like strawberry shampoo. Her daughters snuggled in and fell asleep. She slipped downstairs where she could lose herself in her work in quiet abandon.

She moved through the arched doorways with

oversized woodwork, her bare feet silent on the wood-plank floors. The brick Tudor's character had made Cassie fall in love with it on sight. Her daughters called it their *Cinderella house*, and she smiled at the comparison and hoped her daughters could have the fairy tale someday.

Her thoughts strayed to the handsome widower. How could he be thoughtless one moment and wonderful the next? He was an enigma, but she couldn't ponder him or his character traits.

The overstuffed chair in the sunroom drew her, and she curled her legs under her. The industrial-styled table lamp cast a beam out the arched window behind her. She flicked the remote, and the shades lowered to cocoon her in her own little world.

Cassie retrieved her steno pad to work on her project, but her mind drifted to when Steve ruffled her daughters' hair. Did the girls fear men? Or was it just him?

French doors with diamond-shaped leaded glass reflected light like a thousand sparkling rainbows. The extraordinary craftsmanship from an era gone by enchanted her. Her restored grandmother's clock chimed nine o'clock when the doorbell pealed and halted her thoughts.

Her heart thumped like a bass drum. *Lord, let it not be Nico.*

She strode to the front door and looked through the sidelight before she threw it open. Becka Marino, her brother's wife, stood there.

Cassie placed her hand on her chest. "What's happened?"

"Nothing. Robbie's with the kids. I tried to call but

got voicemail."

"I turned off my phone."

"We haven't seen you for some time so I decided to check on you." Becka leaned in and winked. "I wanted adult female companionship and you're it."

Becka's quirky sense of humor and lightness of spirit almost never failed to uplift Cassie, and she needed it this evening. She hugged Becka and was glad to live near family. Her family.

Thank you, Lord, for Becka. You always provide what I need when I need it. I'm always amazed by your loving care.

"Such a tiring day." Cassie led her sister-in-law through the living room and stopped to light fragrant candles. "How's Robbie?"

"You know… He grunts a lot." Becka smoothed her brown shoulder-length hair behind her ears.

"Typical." Cassie sauntered into the kitchen and Becka trailed behind her. She poured tall glasses of iced tea.

Becka's cheerful mood turned serious. "What's going on?" She searched Cassie's face. For what, Cassie hadn't a clue.

They dropped onto the living room's comfy sofa, and she placed their drinks on the table. "I met Mia's brother today."

Becka's eyes widened. "And?"

She sipped the icy coolness of her lemon-flavored tea. "Mia's been after me to meet him, and she's been relentless, pushing photos of him and the girls in my face. Anyway, a stomach bug kept her home, and he brought the kids to the competition." Cassie groaned. "I almost fell on my butt and made a complete fool of myself. My face was paint-chip red."

Becka snickered. "That's one way to make an impression."

"Seriously. It affected me not because I almost fell. I don't... We need stability in our lives." It'd been over a decade since her stomach had twisted in such a way and made her uneasy. Goose bumps traveled down her arms. Must be the air conditioning.

"All *that* at a gym meet?"

"Not exactly. He invited us for lunch and a swim in his pool."

Becka's leaned back and raised her chin. "Curious. If he bothered you, why did you go?"

"How could I refuse when the kids heard the invitation?"

"So what if the kids overheard? You didn't have to accept. Besides, you seemed to have settled in and aren't as jumpy as you were when you first moved here." Leave it to her sister-in-law to be blunt.

"I'm fine. He's an anomaly, you know? One moment he's not paying attention at the meet and then the next he's frolicking in the pool with them like he's their best friend. I don't get it."

Becka sipped her tea. "Well, Robbie doesn't always play with the kids. When he has work, he works and the kids do their own thing."

"I suppose." Nico rarely played with their daughters. "Steve was marvelous with the girls, though." Then shook her head. "But he worked on his laptop and took little interest in their meet."

Becka smirked. "Your mama bear protective streak kicked in, didn't it?"

Cassie tightened her shoulders and breathed in the

candle's vanilla scent. "I have too much at stake. We've settled in with the move here, but the house still needs work plus the kids start school soon. It's been a whirlwind and then there's Nico. He looms in the background like a bad penny."

Becka's head shot up. "Has he been here?"

"Thank goodness, no. He brought the new wife when he collected the kids at the halfway point and complained about driving an hour and a half." She scowled at her drink. "He forgets I drive it too."

"Well, at least he's no longer as demanding as he was when you lived up north. I couldn't get over how he appeared on your doorstep and expected that you cook him a meal or provide a warm bed for the night when you had been divorced for a while." Becka shook her head and grimaced. "It bothered me that he didn't think twice about screaming at you in front of the kids when you said no."

"Let's not talk about him. He's there and I'm here and I'd like to keep it that way."

"What's your plan with Steve?"

"Keep my distance, what else? I don't want a relationship now."

Becka cupped her cheek. "You just met him. There might be more to him than you think. Give him a chance. If for no other reason than your daughters are friends."

"I still don't want a relationship. And you know how I feel about my faith. It's important to me, and I don't know where he stands. Mia brings the girls to church, but I've never seen him there." She knew she was being judgmental, but after all the problems with Nico, handsome men didn't interest her. And she wasn't sure about his faith or his interactions with his daughters. The whole experience with him at the gym and at his home confused her.

"Who says you have to have that kind of relationship? What about having another friend? That would be nice, don't you think?"

"I suppose I could use another friend."

"Good. I've got to get home, but let's pray before I leave." Becka moved closer, and they held hands.

Lord, I pray for my sister, Cassie. Let her walk in your will and do well in your sight. I pray protection around her mind, heart, and soul. May you work everything for her good. Amen.

They hugged, and Becka rose to leave. "Robbie and I want you and the girls to come over for lunch after church tomorrow."

Cassie agreed.

Now if she could keep the tall blond widower with the startling blue eyes in the friend zone, she'd be okay.

Chapter 3

Cassie's mad rush to get everyone ready was over. Dressed in their Sunday best with their hair arranged in tight buns, Gabby and Bella thumbed through their children's Bibles.

Worthy Worship Center was ideal to serve her family and was located a scant ten minutes from their home. Mia and her nieces attended there too. Her thoughts strayed to her daughters' best friends. Would Mia be well enough to attend church, or would Steve take them? She should have offered them a ride yesterday.

The church's lower level housed the children's ministry, where grade schoolers had kids' church and the adults worshipped in the main sanctuary upstairs.

After Cassie escorted her daughters to their classes, Mia glided toward her with coffee in hand and she stifled a yawn. She wore her bohemian-style dress with ease. Amid the waves and hellos, the last few stragglers moved past them.

Tiredness punctuated her friend's vibrant blue eyes. "You seem better."

Mia returned a faint smile. "I am. Sometimes the best thing is to just sleep."

A look of distraction pinched her features, then it cleared, and she changed the subject. "You're stunning as usual this morning. That geometric print dress is amazing on you." She laughed. "And you're almost as tall as I am in those heels."

Cassie was thankful for the smidgeon of confidence her friend gave her this morning and she hoped she wouldn't have blisters by the time church let out.

Mia grabbed her arm and urged her along. "Come on, we'll be late."

They climbed the stairs to the lobby where Cassie stopped short.

Steve looked absurdly handsome as he chatted with one of the church elders. His hair covered his collar, and Cassie detected a hint of his aftershave. She had caught the subtle scent yesterday and it stayed with her even when she laid her head on her pillow last night.

Her middle fluttered, and she fixated on his tieless checked shirt where a tuft of hair peeked through, then shifted her gaze to his brown loafers.

Lord, this is a test, isn't it?

Displeasure formed on his lips as he checked his phone.

Mia tightened her grip on Cassie's arm and muttered, "We'll be late."

When his sister spoke, he shifted his stance. "About time, Mia." His voice was low and his eyebrow rose. "Cassie. You attend here?"

He stole a glance at his sister, who looked the other way. Annoyance etched his features. Why had he come if he didn't want to be here?

"I'm new." She stuttered and wanted to kick herself. Her brief moment of self-assurance faded into a wave of insecurity. A lowly freshman chatting up the senior football player had more sophistication than she did. When would she control this emotional haze she fell into whenever he was around?

He positioned himself between them and offered his forearms to escort them. Not wanting to make a scene, Cassie had no choice but to place her hand in

33

the crook of his arm where it looked dainty as it rested there.

His muscled arm sent a jolt of awareness to her toes. Her heart thumped and made her lightheaded. She worried her leaden feet would miss a step, and she'd trip in the sky-high heels she had insisted on wearing. What was wrong with her?

He stopped and assisted them into the pew. Mia slid in first which forced Cassie to follow. She wanted to crawl over Mia and flee, but the first chords of music resounded.

Since she had become a member, she'd not seen him once. What brought him to church? Not her, she hoped.

"It'll be okay," Mia mouthed in her ear.

Cassie crossed her arms, shook her head, and pressed her lips into a thin smile.

She peeked sideways at him, and his brows furrowed as he glanced first at her then at his sister.

The music ministry leader told everyone to stand as he prayed before they sang.

Cassie strained to hear Steve's voice but not a note escaped his mouth. He stood still as stone and placed his hands on the pew in front of him. He observed but didn't take part.

With worship time over, the pastor encouraged the congregation to greet one another.

She greeted those around her, then hugged Mia. When she turned to him, he touched her fingers and electricity shot up her arm. Was he zinged as well?

To avoid his stare, she sat and pulled out her notebook, and placed the Bible on her lap.

She poised her pen on the page.

He leaned toward her. "Is that the same book you were using yesterday?"

"No," she muttered. Had he watched her while she worked on the project? *Good Lord.* She must take care, or her other writing projects might be exposed, and she couldn't have that. At least not yet.

The pastor's message on forgiveness caused her to squirm. Her thoughts strayed to her ex-husband, Nico. Had she completely forgiven him?

She shook her head and sneaked a glance at Steve. His forehead furrowed as he peered at the floor. Did he need to forgive someone? Who? As far as she knew, he and Mia had a terrific relationship. Still, Cassie would do well to stay out of his life.

When the service ended, several people stopped to talk to Steve. Since he blocked Cassie in, she had to wait and overheard them comment how happy they were he came.

"I have to go." Cassie pressed Mia to exit from the other side.

Mia ignored her when Steve touched her arm. "Would you join us for lunch? Yesterday, Mia couldn't be with us, but today she's better and I'm sure the kids would love more pool time."

"I'm sorry, but I promised my brother and his family we'd lunch with them. We haven't seen them for a while." Why had she justified her actions? Old habits don't just die, they have to be murdered and placed six feet under.

"We won't keep you, then."

She nodded and moved past him.

Bella and Gabby waited in their classroom with Steve's girls, and it warmed Cassie's heart that her daughters had found close friends. More like four Musketeers and always together.

"Can you come and swim at our house?" Stella begged and the other three chimed in.

"Not today. We've been invited to lunch at my brother's house." She raised an eyebrow at her daughters to give them a silent message not to ask again. It pained her heart to deny them time with their friends, but she'd promised Becka, and the girls knew it.

Stella's eyes grew solemn, and she pleaded. "Can't you go there some other time?"

She stooped to the girls' level and cocked her head. "I promised. You don't want me to break my promise, do you?"

Their faces reflected disappointment. Stroking their hair, Cassie gave them a placid smile. "Perhaps another time, hmmm?" Steve and Mia stood in the doorway. Had they heard the exchange?

He placed a palm on each of his daughters' shoulders. "Come on, girls. We have a date for brunch. How about pancakes?" The offer of a restaurant meal eased the sting of her rejection.

She rushed to escape their presence and her jumbled thoughts about a man she barely knew.

Cassie enjoyed the fresh air streaming in the car's windows, but humidity and her queasy stomach when she rejected Steve's offer forced Cassie to turn on the air conditioning.

Becka's two oldest children zoomed to the car and grabbed her girls who raced with them to the fenced-in backyard, a reminder her own yard needed a fence.

She swung out of the car, locked the door, and headed onto the classic colonial's wide porch, and unlatched the door.

"Anybody home?" Silence.

Her sister-in-law stepped out of the kitchen, drying her hands followed by Robbie who lifted Cassie for a gigantic hug. Her cotton Capris and matching camisole allowed for some roughhousing.

He set her on the plank-tiled foyer with a thud. "About time. Haven't seen you for a while. What've you been up to?"

She punched his arm. "The usual. I need a quote for fencing in the backyard."

Becka spoke over her shoulder as she stepped into the kitchen. "He'll work on that later. How was church?"

"Good. Pastor spoke on forgiveness."

He lifted their two-year-old in his arms. "While you two talk church, I'll take the baby outside with the kids."

Becka glanced at her husband through the glass sliding door and gave a brief nod. "Sometimes I wish he'd go to church more. I keep praying for him."

"I pray for him too, Becka. Never give up." Cassie strode around the long kitchen island and hugged her sister-in-law. Her brother had built their dream home with every detail touched by his love for his family.

Becka sliced tomatoes and peppers for the salad. "I love him." Her eyes glazed over. "I dream of us as a church-going family."

"I understand." She continued to set the table as the kids played in the backyard. Robbie tussled with them, buried under a sea of small bodies.

Cassie sniffed the air. Lasagna, maybe? She needed

comfort food after the morning she'd had. Her thoughts strayed to Steve. What had brought him to church? The dishes clanged on the island along with flatware and glasses.

Becka emptied ice into a pitcher and added sweetened tea. "Did you see Mia and the kids?"

"Yes. She looked a little pale." With the table set, she refrained to mention Steve had been there too. "Should I call the kids, including the overgrown one?"

Her sister-in-law chuckled and peered out the window. "He loves to play with them and for that I'm thankful."

"You should be. Another reason I moved to Worthy. The girls needed to experience my family."

Becka nodded and pulled the lasagna out of the oven while Cassie made the dressing for the salad and tossed it. She added rolls to a bread basket and arranged everything on the table.

Grabbing a knife from the drawer, Becka cut the lasagna. "Call them in."

She told the kids to wash their hands while she peered at her brother.

He shot her a look, and Cassie's head shook. "What?"

"Are you happy here?"

With hands on her hips, she blew out her breath. "We've been over this. I am happy and want my kids to have roots besides Nico and his family."

The afternoon breeze ruffled Robbie's long, dark hair. He wasn't as tall as Steve, but he had muscles on muscles. She could count on him if need be.

"I have a few friends who might want to date you."

"Not interested. My kids are what's important. So,

stop with the matchmaking." She drew air quotes around *matchmaking*.

He scrunched his lips and gave a single nod. His care touched her heart, as it always did.

"How's the freelance writing going? Do you have enough money?"

They wandered into the kitchen that smelled of fresh tomato sauce and melted cheese. Rob's stomach growled, and everyone laughed. She ignored the question and sat beside her daughters.

"You didn't answer my question, Cass."

She glanced at the children. "Not now, Rob." His one-track mind had forgotten about the kids. Little ears did not need to hear this conversation.

"Rob, will you say grace?" Becka said.

He nodded and bowed his head. Cassie took her daughters' hands, and Gabby, sitting next to her uncle, reached for his. "Bless us, O Lord and these, thy gifts…"

Spicy tomato sauce tingled in her mouth and the kids ate amid gales of laughter. Dinner at her brother's table gave Cassie a warm sense of family. How different from yesterday when they had chewed their lunch in near-silence.

With the table cleared, Becka promised ice cream later and shooed them outside to play.

Rob picked up the baby who had fallen asleep in the high chair. "I'll take her into the office down the hall. I'll be back later for ice cream."

Becka unloaded and reloaded the dishwasher while Cassie wiped the counters and swept the floor. "Thanks for the comfort food."

Becka clanged silverware into slots in the drawer.

"What was the *not now* about earlier?"

A soft smile appeared on Cassie's face. "Rob's worried about my finances."

"Despite the grunts, he frets over you."

Cassie's mouth twisted into a half-smile. "So sweet, but there's no reason. The writing work allows me to care for my children during the summer and gives me an income. It's a win-win." She grinned at her sister-in-law and pointed her finger. "And I don't need him to fix me up with one of his buddies."

"I told him not to badger you. We had this discussion earlier today," Becka said.

Her brow pinched. "I'm sorry. I don't want to create friction in your household."

"I've been married to him almost sixteen years. I'm used to his moodiness and know when I can and can't push."

Cassie nodded.

A troubled frown gripped Becka's forehead. "Gabby mentioned Steve attended church this morning. That's a step in the right direction. The only time Rob sets foot in church is at Christmas and Easter. Did you talk to him?"

"I sat next to him during the service."

"Next to him? I thought you wanted to keep your distance."

Cassie pursed her lips, poured herself another glass of tea, and sat at the table. "Not my choice. I saw Mia at kid's church and went upstairs with her. And there he was." The sweet liquid slid down her throat. And even more gorgeous than yesterday. But she wouldn't voice it. "He offered his arm to both of us. Mia slipped into the pew first so it left me in the middle."

The spicy scent of his aftershave filtered through her brain. She envisioned the hair on the back of his neck and thought he might need a haircut soon.

The kids clamored for ice cream, but Becka told them to go play. Cassie watched the exchange and knew her sister-in-law would grill her.

Becka touched Cassie's hand. "You must be lonely, but things will work out. And it's a way for you to cultivate that friendship we talked about last night."

"It's a test. Right after our prayer, he shows up?"

Robbie strode in. "After what prayer? And who showed up?"

Becka rolled her eyes. "You're always tardy to the party, Rob."

He retrieved a glass, sat next to Becka, and poured himself a drink.

"Well?" His shoulders hunched in exasperation.

"Girl talk," Becka pointed out, and Rob grunted. She shook her head, and Cassie chuckled.

"Who's the guy? Not an hour ago, you told me you didn't want to date."

"You missed the earlier part of the conversation. That's what we prayed about last night. I'm not ready to date and to keep my distance from a certain guy." Cassie lifted her drink to her lips.

Her brother glanced at his wife, then at Cassie. "You mean to tell me you prayed *not* to date this guy?" He threw his arms in the air. "I can't understand women." Then narrowed his gaze. "Who's the guy, Cass?"

He wouldn't let up. She hoped the kids would come in.

"Steve Nardelli," Becka said.

Cassie glowered at her sister-in-law, who shrugged and smirked.

Rob leaned into the back of the chair, surprise and confusion marred his face. "He's well known around town and a Chamber member. How'd you meet him?"

"You know him?" His wife said.

"Not personally. His electronics business hit the skids when his wife died some years back. Almost went belly up, but he saved it. Word has it, he's partnered with an Australian company. Seems a likeable guy."

Mia hadn't told her his business had been in trouble and Cassie wouldn't dare ask any personal questions otherwise Mia would ramp up her matchmaking. *What else don't I know?* Heck, Rob knew more about him than she did.

"Don't get any ideas, Rob. I'm good friends with his sister, and his daughters are friends with my girls. They go to gymnastics together and will attend the same school in September. Stay out of it."

He held up his hands but she wouldn't back down. She was thankful Becka hadn't mentioned they'd been at Steve's yesterday for lunch and a swim, but that didn't prevent one of her daughters from spilling it.

She eyed the clock. "Let's give the kids their ice cream. I don't want wall climbers tonight."

After the kids finished the cool treat, Rob escorted her to the car. "Come for dinner next Sunday, Cass."

"I have to drive the girls north on Friday to spend time with their father so it'll just be me." She wanted to work on her project, but she wouldn't disappoint her brother.

"All the more reason for you to come," Becka shouted from the porch.

At the car, Robbie hugged her. "Steve's a personable guy. You should consider dating him."

Cassie stiffened. "I'll let you know," she said, over her brother's shoulder.

I just want to enjoy my new life in Worthy and my children. And not be in a dating kind of relationship.

Chapter 4

Steve looked up from his laptop to Mia tapping her foot with her arms crossed. "What?"

"Took you long enough to notice I was here." She raised her chin in defiance. "I need a favor."

He knew that look. Closing the lid, he leaned back in his home office chair. "How much is it going to cost me?" he said with narrowed eyes.

"I don't know. You're the electronics guru."

"You need a new computer or something?" Tapping his finger on the desk, hoping to diffuse her frustration.

She slumped into the chair opposite his desk. "No. It's Cassie."

He shook his head and pursed his lips. "Don't tell me. She needs a date."

Her eyes lit up. "You'll go on a date with her?"

"I will not." He ground his teeth. Why he brought up a date with Cassie, he didn't know. It was just that sort of comment that would send his sister off to la-la land. He needed to keep his mouth shut about Cassie. He didn't know what he thought of her nor did he want to.

His sister laid her hands on the desk, her eyes pleading with him. "Then will you go over to her house and check it for a new security system? There've been three break-ins on her street in the last week and she's nervous about being alone with the kids."

He leaned forward. "Tell her I'll be there in the

morning." Even though he was busy trying to tie up loose ends for the Australian trip, he couldn't possibly let this go. He'd never forgive himself if something happened to them when he had the expertise and the equipment she needed. He grimaced because he didn't want to be around Cassie, but he also didn't want her or her girls in danger. She bothered him and he didn't want to deal with her secrets or the attraction he seemed to have for her.

"I'll tell her." His sister rose with a smile on her face "Thank you. I knew you'd know what to do, and she needs to feel secure."

"Agreed." He pursed his lips and opened his laptop dismissing his sister with a wave.

After Mia's text last night, Cassie's nerves clacked like beads strung together on a necklace. She couldn't even put a pen to paper after the kids went to bed. She'd spent the time cleaning and making sure everything was in its place. It would be the first time Steve would be in her home and she didn't want to examine the reasons she wanted him to think highly of her as the head of the household or as a mother.

The only man who had been in her home was her brother. And that's how she liked it. She'd have to give him a tour of every room and she still couldn't understand why she allowed Mia to get involved in her business. She could have easily asked Robbie to take care of it. But somehow, she wanted to see Steve without the kids around. He seemed wounded or something and she wanted to get to know him better. After all, she promised Becka she'd try to have some sort of friendship with him. But would he be his usual gruff self or would he be different? And Robbie would be upset, but he'd get over it.

She put a pot of coffee on and took out the peach pie she made last night. Why was she trying to impress him? She shook her head. He was off-limits, and she knew it. But it didn't stop her from thinking about him and wanting him as a friend.

The doorbell rang, and she opened the door with a deep breath. Dumbstruck was the only word she could think of to describe her reaction. His jeans fit him like a glove and the gray t-shirt outlined his muscular chest. He looked like a college guy with his ball cap on backward and his smile shook her to her core. She swallowed.

"Come on in." She eyed the case in his hand and frowned. "Don't you have to work?"

"I'll work from my home office after I leave here. Where can I set this while I look around and make notes?"

"In the kitchen."

His delightful aftershave drifted with him into the kitchen and he set his case on the counter. He browsed through the case and pulled out an iPad and tape measure while she stared at his rippling muscles. She clamped her mouth shut otherwise she'd drool.

"Would you like some coffee and a slice of fresh peach pie before you do whatever it is you're going to do?"

He dropped into a chair and he flattened his lips. "Thanks. I missed breakfast this morning."

She hurriedly placed mugs of hot coffee along with sugar and creamer on the table. She plated two slices of pie and set one before him and the other in front of her.

46

He sipped his coffee. His blue eyes bored right into her. "Tell me about the break-ins. I'm surprised because this is a fairly safe area."

Her breath came out in a long wave. "I was quite upset by it."

Clearing his throat, he laid his hand on hers. "Have you spoken to your neighbors?"

Frowning, she shook her head but didn't move her hand from under his. It was comforting in a way she hadn't felt in a long time. Maybe it was the stress of the crime wave on her street. "Just my next-door neighbor who filled me in. I only recently moved in and I don't know the neighbors who were vandalized well enough to ask them about it."

He frowned, but his eyes held a hint of compassion. "It's not something you find in a small town like Worthy."

"That's why I moved here. That and my brother lives here."

He took a hefty bite of pie and swallowed. "Who's your brother? I probably know him."

"Robbie…I mean Rob Marino." She laughed and forked the flaky crust into her mouth. "He hates that I still call him Robbie."

"I've seen him around town. He's in the chamber and does exceptional work. A friend of mine had him do an addition and they couldn't stop talking about it."

Her smile widened. "He'll be happy to hear it."

"Out of curiosity, why didn't you call him about the security system?"

Her fork clattered on the plate. "Because Mia insisted you were the best person to advise me. Isn't it one of the products your company manufactures? Mia said so and I took her word for it." Her hackles rose. Did he think she put Mia up to it?

She could tell he wasn't happy with his sister's interference. "Look, if this isn't something you care to do. I can call Rob to handle it." Her heart sank. She really wanted to get to know Steve on a person-to-person basis and not as two single parents working to raise their daughters.

He bristled and got up. "I promised Mia I'd take care of it. And I will. Can you take me on a tour of your house?"

She nodded as she took him through the living room, to the sunroom where she spent most of her time writing.

He examined the windows and then turned to drag his finger across her old Amish rolltop desk. "Nice piece of furniture."

Her nerves were taut. She hoped he didn't roll the top up.

"It looks like an antique."

"I bought it at a flea market years ago." She held her breath.

He squatted down and stared at drawers, running his finger over the handles and then leaned in close to the side reaching between the desk and the wall. "There's a notebook stuck."

When he got up with her notebook, she snatched it out of his hands. "Thanks for getting it out of there. I didn't know it was down there."

He narrowed his eyes and stiffened. "Is that one of your blog books?"

She hadn't realized her book bible had fallen to the side of the desk and felt heat rising on her chest.

"Yes."

Lifting the roll top desk just a few inches, she shoved the offending notebook under it and slammed the top down then leaned back.

"Why so secretive?"

"I'm not…I don't let anyone read my…posts until I've had a chance to completely edit them." Her breath came out on a whoosh. "Shall we continue our tour?"

He lifted his chin, gave her a curt nod, and motioned to her to lead the way.

She led him back through the kitchen and dining room. He said nothing more as they went into the craft room and finally into the garage. He was stiff and unyielding as he strode from room to room looking at windows, measuring them, and examining the doors. There went any attempt at becoming friends.

They trekked downstairs to the laundry room and playroom then back upstairs to the bedrooms. Still silent, he punched measurements on his iPad. She tried to look over his shoulder, but didn't want to get too close. Irritation came off of him in waves.

He looked out the windows, and she wasn't sure what he was doing so she just waited for him to speak, but he didn't. This wasn't going at all the way she'd hoped. She didn't want this tension between them. Why couldn't they just be friends for the sake of their daughters?

Maybe Steve needed to give Cassie a break. She couldn't be all bad if Rob was her brother. He was a stand-up guy. But he'd give Mia what-for when he saw her later today. Cassie still had her secrets, and he still had his hang-ups.

When they were in the kitchen, he took his iPad and set it on the table and sat down. Her home was comfortable unlike its owner. He liked the house though. It had character.

She wrung her hands. "What's the verdict? You seemed deep in thought while you were going through the house and I didn't want to bug you with questions."

"I was thinking about the best way to proceed." Actually, he didn't want to hear her musical voice. What were she and his sister were playing at? Mia knew better than to involve him in this situation. He could have done this job blindfolded with all four girls screaming and running through the house and for some confounded reason, he wanted to do it himself. But Cassie didn't need to know any of it.

"And?"

"Do you lock the service entrance to your garage?"

"I try to, but if the girls go out, I have to remember to check it all the time."

He leaned back in his chair. "Its location could attract vandals. There's light, but it's on the front of the garage and the light doesn't extend to where the door is. I suggest a motion light above the door and consider replacing the door with a spring hinge that'll automatically close and lock when you go out." He stared at her beautifully arched brows and her long lashes. She had very little makeup on which only added to her beauty. He cleared his throat. "It'll be tough if you forget your keys, but you can leave a key with a friend should that happen. And always keep the door from the house to the garage locked."

"Let me get a pen and paper so I can write things down."

"No need. I'll email you a copy of my notes. Rob can replace the door in a few hours."

Her smile lit the room which already shone with sunlight. "Perfect."

Relief filtered its way through his body at her acceptance of his suggestions.

He straightened his back. He'd never felt the need to protect a woman who wasn't related to him. It felt good. "And you probably should have him replace the basement windows with glass blocks. If someone broke in down there, they could get through and you wouldn't hear them up on the second floor."

Her eyes grew into huge pools of mossy green. "Oh, no!"

The distress on her face killed him. His hand covered hers and he gently rubbed her cold hand. "I'm sorry. I didn't mean to scare you." But when she looked down, he coughed and moved it back to the iPad. "Your brother can arrange for them to be replaced. But have him do it quickly."

"I'll call him as soon as we're through here."

He gave her a single nod. If he hadn't had his dead wife's manipulating ways bubble up to his brain, he could have considered a date maybe. Nah. It wasn't happening. "Moving on. The first floor and basement are where you want to focus your security. I've already walked around the house before I came in. The second floor doesn't seem to need security but the locks on the windows should be checked." Her smile made his throat go dry. "Another job for Rob when he replaces the door and installs the glass blocks."

"Understood."

"The worst room in the house is that sunroom. It has a lot of windows in it with shaded trees right outside."

When her face crumpled, his heart sped up. It bothered him so much he wanted to grab her hands, and put them on his chest to give her comfort. "Doesn't mean we can't fix it for you. It just means you have to agree to have the limbs scaled back. You'll still have your tree and it's a beauty, but having the branches so close to the ground and near the windows could hide vandals quite easily."

"I never thought of the security issue. I liked the privacy they afforded." She looked ready to cry. He felt like a brute, but he had to make her understand the danger.

"The trees are hiding those beautiful windows and the blinds are sufficient for privacy. They'll keep prying eyes out."

She nodded. "The blinds have remotes."

He raised his brow. "That's cool. What company did you use?"

Another of those heartwarming smiles. "American Blind Company. I love those remotes especially when I'm working." He didn't want to be thinking about her smiles or her working in that room without security. She still had secrets, and he didn't want to get involved. But he was already up to his eyeballs. His past and her secrets were a no-go no matter how sweetly she smiled or how caring she was to his girls and hers.

"Back to the plan. We need to put sensors on all the doors and first-floor windows."

They discussed price, and she didn't bat an eye. It was the most expensive unit his company made. From Mia, he knew she was divorced so those writing blog posts must be lucrative. Unless she got a hefty alimony check every month which was probably the case.

"How soon do we have to do this?" she said pulling him out of his musings.

"The sooner the better. My preferred contractor, Eric Winters, specializes in security installations. Let me call him."

He stared at her frightened green eyes while he talked to Eric. Putting his phone on mute, he rubbed her hand. "Don't be afraid. Can you be home this Friday?"

"After I take the girls to the gym. How long will this take?"

"All day Friday and Saturday. I'll come over after Eric's done and teach you how to use it."

He really didn't want to come over here on Saturday, but she kept tugging at him and he wondered just how soft those lips of hers were. He was getting in deeper every time he opened his mouth but for now, shutting it down wasn't an option.

Cassie dropped off the kids at the gym and Mia would pick them up and take them to the house for a swim in the pool so she could supervise the installation on Saturday.

Voices in the hallway drew her from upstairs. Rob stood at the bottom of the steps. He had a hurt look on his face as she came down the stairs. "I have the new door in the truck. Come see it."

That was code that he wanted to talk to her away from all the installation guys. As they stepped near the truck, she noticed another truck. "Is that the glass block guy?"

"Yup."

His annoyed stance rankled, and she wished he'd just say what he wanted to say. "Do I really need to see the door before you install it?"

He gave a drawn-out sigh. "No. Why didn't you call me when there were vandals in the area?"

"Because you would have dropped everything to come over and make sure I was taken care of no matter what you were doing. This is your busy season and your family's finances take priority. But I appreciate you coming out on a Saturday to take care of the door, light and blocks."

He moved to get the door off the truck. "I guess I can't be mad since Nardelli got Eric Winters. He's the best security installation guy in all of Fairfield and Franklin Counties. Can you afford the system they're installing? It's top notch."

"Yes, I can afford it. That's what credit cards are for. Our safety is more important."

"It is. And I see he got you to trim that tree." He hefted the door to the back of the house. "Wouldn't do it for me, but you did it for him."

"Come on, Robbie. Considering the vandalism, his argument made sense." And the way Steve looked her in the eyes with all that compassion and warmth.

"Are you dating him now?"

She could feel the heat rising up her chest and she hoped it stopped before it hit her face. "No. We're just…friends."

He smirked. "Friends, huh?"

She wanted to wipe that grin off his smug face. She should have called her brother and not let Mia steamroll her into it. She didn't want to answer any questions about her involvement with Steve. Not that there was much of that. And for sure she couldn't tell her brother Steve was coming over later to teach her how to use it. "Go on. Just install the door and the light and get out of here."

Humming, he wiggled his lips and got to work. The situation wasn't going as she had imagined, but it was going faster than she anticipated.

Chapter 5

Steve was in a sour mood. He committed to training Cassie but his sister kept giving him the eye with a playful smirk on her lips. That rankled. But thankfully, his daughters hadn't paid him much attention. They were too wound up happily ensconced in his pool with their best friends, Cassie's daughters. He should have been swimming with them, but instead he was on his way over to her house.

When he pulled into her driveway, he saw where the tree had been pruned, glass blocks installed in the basement windows and a new door installed. She hadn't wasted any time getting it done. Or rather having her brother get it done. He wondered if her brother knew about him. He knew. *What an idiot.* If she hadn't told him, he was certain Eric had. The industries overlapped and everyone knew everyone else in the business and this was a small town.

The door opened before he rang the bell or could transform his features into a pleasant semblance of a smile.

Her breath came out in a whoosh. "I heard your SUV pull up and wanted to get your impression on the work that's been done."

He wanted to be frustrated, but how could he be when she'd done everything he'd told her to do and in a short period of time, too. "Glad to see you moved quickly."

"Yeah, Rob and his crew were here this morning. The tree guy came yesterday." She gave a hearty giggle. "Guys were crawling around this house all day long. They kept me busy getting them drinks."

Why did that annoy him? He shouldn't care one way or another if she took care of the guys. But it did.

He stepped through the door and her flowery scent surrounded him. He clenched his jaw. "Ready for your lesson."

She cocked her head. "As ready as I'll ever be."

He glanced at the framed family photos he missed the last time he was here. He recognized the girls, but there were no photos of her in any of the pictures. And no pictures of any guy in any of the photos. Curious. Maybe she was different.

They stood in the kitchen as he opened the manual. She looked as frightened as a rabbit. "Most of this manual is for troubleshooting which I don't think you'll need but if you feel led to read it all, go for it."

She gave him a half grin. "I'll take your word for it."

Whipping out the pen she had hooked in her t-shirt, she marked the tabs he said she'd most likely need. Standing next to her and breathing in her fragrance messed with his concentration. He didn't need these feelings right now and didn't want them at all.

He could hear the gruffness in his voice and wondered if she heard it, too. "They put the command center in that hall closet by the garage, correct?"

"Right." She led him down the hallway to the closet and pulled the coats aside to show him.

No blinking lights glowed on the unit. He frowned and checked all the connections. When the unit lit up, he breathed a sigh of relief. The last thing he needed was to spend more time troubleshooting a defective unit or being in her presence.

Their arms brushed, and he bumped her shoulder while he showed her how to arm and disarm the unit.

Her face took on that same rosy glow from the day they'd spent at his pool. How could she be so calm when he stood next to her?

When he turned to look at her, her face was six inches from his. His eyes met hers and they both stood stunned for what seemed like long minutes, but truthfully was only a matter of a few seconds when she pulled back. His heart hammered in his chest. Her lips looked so soft but they were forbidden. He hadn't felt this way in years. And with her, no less. A woman with secrets. When would he ever learn? He had to get this job done and forget about her.

He cleared his throat. "I guess that's it. Just remember you have fifteen seconds to disarm it once you open the door to the garage, otherwise the police will be on your doorstep."

She gasped. "I didn't realize it was such a short time period."

"That's why they put it in this closet. It'll take you five seconds to disarm it once you cross the door. You want to test it to see if you can do it in fifteen seconds?"

"That would be great."

They tested the alarm several times, and she seemed comfortable with it.

"Is that it? I have to pick up the girls at your place."

"Good time to test it. Why don't you get your suit and we'll order a pizza?" What was wrong with him? Inviting her to swim and to have dinner. Again! Mia would go crazy. He wanted to kick his own butt.

"Maybe some other night." She waved her hand toward the closet. "I'm exhausted with all this.

He left through the garage door and waited for her to

shut the overhead door. He was saddened she refused his offer but realized it was the best thing for him anyway. Drawing a long breath, he went home to relax in his hot tub. Away from unnerving and beautiful   Cassie   Verano.

Chapter 6

Sun-kissed clouds dotted the blue expanse as Cassie, Mia and their girls strolled toward the Doll Museum. They couldn't have picked a better day for it. None of the girls played with dolls any longer, but their curiosity piqued when Cassie described the dolls little girls cherished decades or even a century ago. This outing was a reward for their exceptional performance at the meet three weeks ago.

The girls pirouetted, skipped and danced along the sidewalk as if the smooth red brick surface were a gym floor. She left them to their imaginations and meandered along tree-lined streets to the picturesque picket fence surrounding the massive white colonial housing the collection.

Mia pulled the brochure from her bag. "We going on our own or shall we take the guided tour?"

Cassie rolled her eyes. "Come on. Four gymnasts won't stand still while a guide rattles off details." She leaned close. "We might have been better off taking them to the playground first to burn off excess energy," she whispered.

Chuckling, Mia perused the pamphlet. "You're right about the guide, but they need culture, too."

They approached the entrance to the stately home. The historical significance of the people and their possessions impressed her even though her nostrils twitched at the distinct musty odor.

Gabby wrinkled her nose. "Mama, it smells funny in here." Leave it to her eldest to voice what everyone else was thinking.

"I know it does darling, but we don't want to offend

anyone. This is history, so we need to respect it, okay?" Her tone brooked no argument.

She ambled past doll displays from the late 1800s with real hair, and elaborate costumes with all the accessories used by women of that era.

Bella's hazel eyes widened as she pointed to a beautiful doll. "Mama, did little girls really play with those dolls? They could break."

Gabby crossed her arms. "Maybe her Mama only allowed her to look at it."

"That's why they're still around today. They're over a hundred years old."

The girls examined the rest of the exhibits with deepening awe, sometimes in silence, and occasionally with soft questions.

Mia peeked at her watch. "Guys, we need to move it. I made lunch reservations."

The girls chattered among themselves as everyone left the museum and walked the short distance to the restaurant.

"There's daddy!" Stella and Tina yelled and ran to him.

Cassie resisted the uneasy sensation in her belly. "Why is Steve here?"

Mia shrugged. "No idea. I told him we were going to the Doll Museum. He must have overheard me make lunch reservations."

Steve sauntered over. "I hope you ladies don't mind if I join you. I don't get enough time with my girls." He snatched Tina into his arms and hugged her.

Cassie minded but she wouldn't disappoint his sister or his daughters whose faces shined with excitement.

"I'm sure the reservation can accommodate another

person." Mia hurried inside to handle it.

Cassie, aware they blocked the sidewalk, moved the girls closer to the entrance.

"Mama, look! Aunt Lena." Gabby pointed at a dark-haired woman who strode toward them.

Her former sister-in-law's forceful stare scrutinized Cassie's black slacks, sandals, and V-neck sleeveless top, then glanced at Steve. Cassie interpreted the look as either curious or speculative. The latter more likely.

"Hello girls! I've not seen you in a long time. You have grown like sunflowers."

The girls giggled and returned their aunt's hug.

Lena searched Cassie's face. "How are you? I haven't seen you of late."

"It's been a while," Cassie said.

She turned her attention to Steve and squinted. "And who is this?" Lena, a master at undercurrents, gave her a hard stare. But Cassie kept her mouth shut. Lena hadn't forgiven her for divorcing her brother and most likely never would.

Steve set Tina on the sidewalk and introduced himself. "We're having lunch. Would you care to join us?"

Cassie couldn't open her mouth fast enough to object, and Lena smirked. "No, thanks. I have a meeting and I'm late as it is."

"I'm hungry, Mama." Bella distracted Cassie from the staring match.

"Let's get you food." She forced a smile at Lena. "Say hello to everyone for me."

Her ex-sister-in-law glanced at Steve. "Nice to meet you, enjoy your lunch."

He gave a single nod and Lena rushed away.

The girls ran ahead and opened the door for Mia as she reemerged.

With hands fisted at her side, Cassie forced herself to breathe. "Where were you?"

"Can't a gal go to the restroom?"

Cassie pursed her lips and moved her daughters inside the lobby but also caught Steve signal Mia.

"Where's the table? These little ladies are mighty hungry." Steve ruffled each girl's head, and they giggled back at him.

Dark green carpet muffled their steps as they followed the hostess to their seats while the girls looked around at the other patrons and servers.

Mia slid into the large round booth first with the girls filling in on either side and left Steve and Cassie on the ends to face one another. Why was she so nervous? It's not like she hadn't spent time with Steve or his family. She was being ridiculous. The server smiled and took their drink orders and left the menus for them to peruse.

"What looks good, ladies?" Steve said, glancing at Cassie.

"Burgers," they said in one voice.

He chuckled. "Burgers, it is."

Mia rolled her eyes and laid her menu on the table. "Summer salad for me."

Steve stared at her over his menu. "What about you, Cassie? What'll you have?"

She'd mastered the art of not showing her feelings, but it seemed his blue eyes could see right into her heart and soul. The more she saw of him, the more she liked him but knew their relationship could be nothing more than friendship for a multitude of reasons.

"Summer salad sounds good," she said almost choking on the words.

The server passed glasses of lemonade and iced tea and Steve ordered. "The girls and I will have burgers with fries. And the ladies will have the summer salad. Can you bring the usual condiments including mayo and we'll add what we want?"

"Sure thing," the server said, and left.

While they waited on their food, Stella regaled her father about the dolls they had seen and how old they were. "The old ones smelled, Daddy."

"The Christmas puppets were big!" Tina said.

Steve's eyes widened. "Puppets? I thought this was a doll museum."

"They were marionettes depicting Charles Dickens's Christmas Carol. Someone donated them to the museum." Mia sipped her tea.

He turned his attention to the other two girls. "What did you like?"

"I liked the dolls with the china faces," Gabby said. "The lady there said their hair tells how old the dolls are."

Steve raised his brows. "What lady?"

"The curator," Cassie said.

His grinned. "How about you, Miss Bella?"

"I liked the Alice in Wonderland dolls. Mama read us that story."

His eyes caught hers and his smile caused her breath to catch in her throat.

The girls guzzled their drinks and chattered when the server brought their food.

He directed further questions to each girl as they ate. They remembered minute details about the dolls, which was unexpected. Cassie gaped at the conversation and glanced at Mia who enjoyed the banter.

Engaging with the children increased his attractiveness. Different from how he'd been at the gym, his home, at church, and then at her house. She remembered their staring contest in the closet. What if he had leaned in and kissed her that day? Would she take offense or kiss him back? A rhetorical question. The way she felt that day, she would have returned the kiss.

Wait! No. Why was the restaurant so warm? Was her face giving her away? What if he noticed?

She fork-stabbed her salad, gobbled a crunchy mouthful to distract herself and willed her thoughts away from Steve to a much bigger threat. Lena.

Catching her with Steve could mean trouble. Big trouble. Would Lena tell Nico she and her girls had lunch with a man and his children? What would Nico do?

"Cassie, are you listening?" Steve said.

Six sets of eyes pinned her to her seat.

"Sorry, I zoned out." She gulped the refreshing iced tea as the sudden silence made her squirm. The clinking of cutlery and tinkling of glasses around them grabbed her focus.

"Apparently. I asked which exhibit was your favorite."

She took a deep breath. "I'd say the Portrait Dolls. The elegance and clothing detail were exquisite, and they resembled actual people." She gazed at his bright blue eyes and realized an oasis bloomed in what had been an arid desert only moments ago.

"I'm not into dolls but your visit makes me want to check out the museum if for no other reason than the marionettes would be fun." Steve laughed.

All four girls fidgeted and needed to go to the bathroom.

"Come on. Let's go test the plumbing." Rising, Cassie helped her daughters out of the booth, and Mia followed.

"I'll take them," Mia said. "You're still eating. Besides, I know where it is."

Cassie dropped into the plush seat and peered at her salad. She hadn't eaten even a third of it while everyone else had finished. She wouldn't get out of being alone with Steve.

His gaze locked on hers. "You want to explain what happened outside?"

"Not particularly." She broke eye contact and kept eating. The server came by to ask if they wanted dessert.

"Nothing for me. Could you bring a box for this?"

After the ordeal with Lena, her stomach formed gigantic knots, twisting and turning like an eel. Eating more wasn't possible with Steve peering at her as if he expected she might fall apart and gush the sordid details of her past.

"Cassie, I—"

The girls and Mia returned, and she noticed the boxed-up meal and stared at the Styrofoam container then at Steve who narrowed his gaze, but she remained close-lipped. Must be a twin thing.

Steve smiled, though it got nowhere near his eyes.

"Would you ladies like dessert?"

Nothing like prolonging the agony.

The girls whooped and Cassie shushed them. "We don't want the owners to throw us out before you have dessert, right?" Her sternness quieted them. The server brought a menu. When faced with so many choices, they couldn't decide.

"Why don't you all choose something different and share?" Mia said. Cassie rolled her eyes, and Steve laughed.

"Good because you and I will share, Mia." Steve said.

"What about Cassie?" Mia said. The girls stopped and stared at both parents. Their silence made it worse.

Bella's sad eyes pinned hers. "Mama, I'll share with you."

"The server asked me, darling. Besides, I didn't eat all my lunch, so I'm not allowed to have dessert. You all enjoy." She gave her little one a soft smile and brief caress.

When the girls had filled their bellies with cake, pie, ice cream and pudding, they itched to leave and burn it off, and Steve insisted on paying for lunch. Cassie frowned and wanted to argue, but Mia intervened. "Don't bother, Cassie. He'll never let you pay. So forget it."

Her daughters thanked Steve, but Cassie found it more difficult. She could have paid for her family's lunch. "Thank you, Steve."

"See you later." He waved and headed for the door. Cassie admired his gait and sense of purpose. Somewhere inside, a daffodil flowered and made her shiver.

The sugar rush caused the girls to jump ahead.

Mia leaned in. "I think we should take them to the park before the sugar coma sets in."

Corralling energized little girls proved to be a feat, but she and Mia got them across the street. Hoping to find a shady spot, Cassie longed to let her burdens drift away.

The village green featured an unusual playground. Not sure where to cast their eyes or what to do, the girls appeared stunned, amazement clear on their faces. Patterned after an early American fort, climbing walls, slides and lookouts surrounded other play equipment within the confines of the castle-like structure. Covered seating areas lined the interior where they could monitor the girls' activities.

Cassie lifted her head to smell the fading summer flowers planted nearby. Their petals drooped from the blistering heat.

Mia dug right in. "Tell me what upset you at the restaurant."

She closed her eyes. "My ex-sister-in-law showed up and blindsided me." Opening her eyes, she stared through the trees and beyond the park to scenes from a past life.

"Does she live here?"

"No. She lives north of here in Strickland, the same place as my ex." Cassie rushed on. "She saw me with Steve and the girls." Panic washed through her body.

"So? You're not allowed to have lunch with your daughters and a friend?" Mia's voice rose an octave then she forced herself to whisper. "What are you afraid of, Cassie?"

She shook her head. "I can't explain it. You wouldn't understand." Her soft response barely audible.

Mia's firm fingers wrapped around her arm. "Try me. I won't judge. Promise."

Cassie gripped her pants, and she stared elsewhere to hide her moist eyes. "I married young. My ex and his family controlled our lives. He ran around. He left me long before I divorced him." The painful memories flashed through her mind. "But when I divorced him, they all claimed I was at fault."

"Is that why you moved to Worthy?"

"I wanted to be near my brother and his family and escape the reality of what life had become."

The girls ran to them.

"Mama, we're thirsty," Gabby said.

She brushed damp hair strands from her daughter's brow. "I didn't bring drinks since we had lunch out. We should go. I need to start supper and run a load of laundry."

Bella crawled into her lap. "But, Mama. We're having so much fun."

"I know, darling, but you need clean gym clothes for next week and dinner doesn't make itself even though I sometimes wish it could." Cassie chuckled at Bella's puzzlement.

"Just teasing, munchkin." She ruffled Bella's hair and stood up. "Catch you next week, Mia."

The worry over Lena and her ex was foremost in Cassie's mind as she hurried away.

Chapter 7

If there were repercussions from her lunch with Steve, Cassie needed to know. Dread filled her since she'd spoken to Becka this morning.

The soothing yet somewhat bitter chamomile tea eased the tension in her body. Becka had advised her to move cautiously in her friendship with Steve. They both knew since she divorced Nico, he had and still could cause trouble, if he chose to do so. She agreed in principle, but to deny her daughters? No. Best friends mattered.

Sunshine streamed through the arched windows and made her oasis too warm. She got up and flicked on the overhead fan. Stall tactics. No more procrastination. Mondays were always hectic, but with the girls at gymnastics, she had some time to make a call.

The receptionist answered and put Cassie through to Blake Hardy, her attorney. "What can I do for you, Cassie? Nico still causing you grief?"

She admired his no-nonsense approach with his clients. He had been her rock through her divorce. He was tough and got the best deal for her.

Rustled papers and chair movements reverberated across the line. She envisioned his compassionate eyes but they could turn into steel shards, allowing no one to get the better of him, least of all Nico.

She brought her knees to her chest. "I met a woman who's a nanny for her widowed brother. She and I have become wonderful friends and spend a lot of time together because of the children. They attend gymnastics together and will go to the same school this fall."

"And this is a problem, how?"

"Last Friday we took the kids on a field trip and had lunch. Her brother joined us for lunch. I didn't know he would be there, and neither did my friend. We ran into Lena, Nico's sister." Cassie's words came out in a whoosh. "I'm worried about backlash."

"You had lunch with a guy, his sister and his daughters. Seems innocuous enough."

"My friend Mia was in the restroom. It looked like he and I were together with our kids. Do you think Nico could cause trouble, like maybe try to take away the kids?"

"Cassie, you're being paranoid. Lena was and is a pain, but you have custody because you're a wonderful mother. You didn't move out of state and you take the girls to visit their father when required. Don't worry about it. But above all, don't let Lena or what she will do overrun your thoughts."

"Are you sure? I mean, could he do anything? Anything at all?"

"You've been divorced for almost three years. He's moved on and has a wife. You need to move on, too. Besides, why shouldn't you find companionship? He did. When your daughters grow up, then what? You'll be alone. If this man is someone you're interested in, go for it and don't worry about Nico. He's in the past. Leave him there."

"That's just it. This guy isn't in my life. His daughters are my daughters' friends. That's all. I don't want it to become a problem because of whatever lies Lena

71

might tell her brother."

"Listen to yourself. You're worked up for no reason. No matter what she tells Nico, you have custody. Period. If something were to pop up, which I don't think it will, we'll handle it. Together. Deal?"

"But…"

"Look, I know you had a rough time before, during and after the divorce but you can't live your life worrying about what he'll do. Live each day, enjoy your children and your life with them."

"You're right." She closed her eyes and pinched her nose and breathed in the comforting honeysuckle scent from the vine that grew outside her window. "I need to put it behind me. You know what my life was like. We've been so peaceful these past few months. When she appeared out of the blue, alarm bells went off."

More papers rustled and meant the conversation was over for him.

"I understand," Blake said.

"Thanks for being a sounding board. I'll call if anything crops up."

"You do that. Enjoy those little ones."

When she hung up, Cassie let off a tremendous sigh and prayed for her worried heart and placed the entire situation into the Lord's hands.

She transcribed her notes to the laptop, and as she put the finishing touches on the work she'd already done, her phone rang and she groaned when she saw who it was. *Not done, Phil.*

"I have agency contracts and need to meet with you," he said.

"You know I can't come to New York. My life is

here." Exasperation colored her words.

"Didn't think for a moment you'd come here. You available for a meeting later in the week? I'll catch an early flight, we'll have lunch, discuss the plan and determine where you are on your current project. When's a good day?"

She scrolled through her phone calendar. "How about Thursday around noon?"

"Works for me. Are you at least working on the new project?"

"Of course. Slower than normal, but I should have a first draft by Thursday."

"Great. Could I have a look see?"

"You know first drafts are off limits. Besides, I may not have it done."

"Then, I'll let you get back to work. I'll text you from the airport and we can decide where to meet. If there are changes to the schedule, I'll call you."

She sat back and cracked her knuckles. An annoying habit she hadn't wanted her kids to learn, but in stressful times it came back in full force.

"Yvonne, hold my calls," Steve said.

"Sure thing, boss." Yvonne Baker's brown bob swung as she sauntered to his desk with a fresh cup of coffee. She wore classic slacks with a company polo and sensible flat shoes.

An attractive woman, but he didn't mix personal life with business. Besides, she was an ace assistant, and he didn't want to lose her as an employee.

"Close the door when you leave."

Sipping the aromatic coffee, he picked up the phone

and gazed at his comfortable and efficient private office. His life was on a fast track for success but he needed a guy to talk to and Frank Meadows, his childhood friend and attorney, was it.

He didn't need any entanglements, but a softly rounded woman with captivating green eyes kept him awake at night. How long had it been since he'd lost sleep over a woman? He couldn't even remember.

"Are there issues with the Australian deal?" Frank's voice held a hint of concern.

"Everything is moving along at a good clip for a Monday morning." Steve tensed and tightened the grip on the phone. "The upcoming trip should clinch the deal. The team is working overtime to make it happen."

"You called to talk about something else?"

"Can you get away for lunch and an uninterrupted personal conversation? Business takes precedence and we rarely have time to sit and talk. Wednesday?" He checked his Outlook calendar and pictured the crinkling corners of his friend's eyes with his black hair slicked back.

"I'm in court all day. Thursday would be better, and if we could meet close to my office, that'd be great. How about we meet at a quarter to one and walk over to Café Napolitano's? Anything you want to tell me now?"

"Need to get it straight in my head first. Thursday sounds good." Steve blocked off time on his calendar and hung up.

Should I bare my soul to Frank? He'll tell me to join his men's group and to pray about it. And I haven't been in a men's group for ages. He groaned, but he had it coming. If he were honest, that was the truth.

Chapter 8

Cassie dropped the kids off at Becka's and rushed home to prepare for her meeting with Phil. He got an earlier flight, so he'd meet her downtown at eleven thirty at a restaurant and she agreed even though it was more than a half-hour's drive from her home.

She wanted to look professional and dressed in a black houndstooth dress with a buttonless red blazer. A striking combination. A patent leather belt, shoes, and bag completed the ensemble. With her hair in her go-to French twist, she applied makeup, put on gold hoops and she was ready to go.

Anxious and wary, Cassie's last discussion with Phil culminated in a huge disagreement, where Phil lost his temper and put Cassie almost in tears. They patched things but she harbored some resentment. Worried he would use their meeting as leverage for another agenda, the extra confidence the clothing, hairdo, and makeup provided made her feel better.

A cab rolled up as she strolled to the restaurant and there he was. He paid the cab and met her at the entrance. Her stomach rumbled from the aromas wafting from the restaurant and she couldn't wait to dig into flavorful pasta.

Debonair as always, Phil's stylish European clothing and smooth hairstyle turned heads. "So good to see you, Cassie. Looks like this move agrees with you. You appear relaxed and, as always, beautiful."

Cassie laughed. "Well, aren't you the charmer?"

After they were seated, he fiddled with the folded

napkin. "I've had time to consider the ramifications of releasing you to another agent. Your work ethic is admirable and I never worry about missed deadlines, something newer authors don't get."

"Good." She smirked. "We've had our difficulties but I don't want to re-train another agent. Besides, you stand to lose money."

The restaurant was busy even before noon when the server came to take their orders. Dishes clanged and hushed voices surrounded them. Plants hung from the ceiling and with potted trees strategically arranged, they minimized the cacophony associated with hectic restaurants. Servers buzzed by with delectable smelling dishes on huge trays. She craned her neck, but still couldn't tell what they were.

After they placed their order, Phil focused on business. "I've found several publishing houses willing to take a look at your manuscript."

Cassie leaned in. "You didn't tell them my pen name or what I've written, correct?"

"You were clear on that, but the new direction and using your own name caused me some headaches. But I'll do your new series and genre justice." His penchant for patting himself on the back legendary. Talent didn't matter. Specifically, her talent.

"I sure hope you aren't making a mistake." He pulled out his agency's paperwork for her review. "You made me work this time, Cassie." He fumbled with his tie.

She narrowed her gaze and cocked her head. "You've been coasting for a few years on the huge success of the book series. So, working for your fee isn't much to ask. Tell me about what your thoughts are on the new series."

"I still say you could make so much more if you continued to write the Jade Parker series. People love her and have voiced their dismay that the one coming out after Christmas is the last of the series. You could still write under that pen name. No one would be the wiser."

It was his last-ditch effort to change her mind. She frowned into her drink and her stomach knotted. "*I* would know. Books about Jade are off the table, Phil. Have been for over two years. Didn't I make myself clear the last time we met? I don't want to be associated with that series other than for royalties."

"Can't blame a guy for trying, now can you?"

She rolled her eyes and dipped her fork into the gemelli pasta with tomato cream sauce and although her meal proved fabulous, it made her queasy. Her dress was tight as she thought about the pasta going to her hips and stomach. She cringed and vowed to get more workouts in the coming week.

As they ate, he outlined his ideas on her marketing strategies and which publisher he thought would be the best one to pursue. Since her new series was different than anything she'd written before, she was interested in his ideas.

"We could have had this discussion on the phone but I wanted to see you," he said.

"I know you, Phil. You wanted to gauge my reactions. I've had three days to think about why you were coming in person."

Feigning innocence he spread his hands. "I have other business, you know. I'm killing two birds with one stone. Besides, having lunch with a beautiful woman is always a plus." He gave her a brow wiggle and smirked.

She could feel the heat rising up her chest, but remained silent.

When he paid the check, they left, and stepped onto the not-so-busy sidewalk.

"I'll email the contracts later today. It was great seeing you." He looked into her eyes and pulled her into his arms and hugged her tight. A little too tight for Cassie's liking, but since she only saw him once in a while, she'd let it go.

A muscle quivered in his jaw as if he wanted to say more. No way this was going in a romantic direction. Cassie had never been interested. Even though he cut a suave figure she couldn't see herself with him, ever.

She moved out of his arms, smiled and thanked him for lunch. He kissed her cheek and nuzzled her hair. Cassie stiffened, and he released her.

How different Phil was from Steve and the more she saw Steve the more she liked him. She needed to get to know him more. Was he really a man who could be a friend or something more? She needed to come to terms with her own baggage before going out on a limb with him.

She left Phil standing there and walked to the parking deck.

Steve and Frank exited the building and turned to walk to Café Napolitano three doors down. Steve halted causing the man behind him to plow into him. He stumbled and his face paled. The man behind him cussed and walked around him.

"What the heck?" Frank stopped and grabbed his arm. "Are you all right?"

He clamped his mouth shut, but stared in the direction of the café. Out of the corner of his eye, he noticed Frank scanning the street but hadn't seen Cassie.

When Frank jiggled his arm, Steve's jaw clenched. With covert eyes, he followed the man's progress toward him and when he turned the corner, Steve glared.

"What's wrong with you?" Frank's voice was low, and he looked worried.

"Let's go to lunch. We have to talk." Determined to get off the sidewalk, Steve's gut churned. Who was that guy hugging her? And why leave her and walk away?

Steve's stomach grumbled, half from the shock of seeing her in another man's arms and half from hunger. They placed their pizza orders and sipped sweetened tea.

When the server left, Frank cleared his throat. "You want to explain what happened out there?"

Frank stared at him as if he'd grown another head and Steve suspected he'd lost every one of the marbles rolling around in his brain. "I saw that guy hugging her." He groaned. This was not the way he wanted to start the conversation.

"Wait. You're telling me you stopped in the middle of the sidewalk, almost got pummeled, and acted like a zombie because of a woman?" Frank chuckled. "This should be good."

"Ridiculous." Steve muttered. She twisted him inside out. Not good.

"So, who is she?"

"You remember the woman I sat next to at church a few weeks ago?"

"Cassie, right? Cute little thing with incredible green eyes and a lovely smile." Frank said in a matter-of-fact way.

"You checked out her eyes?" Steve's voice rose.

"She's beautiful. Why wouldn't I check her out? There's not a man in church who hasn't noticed her even if they won't admit to it. And, I think a few guys would like to get to know her, but she's pricklier than a holly bush."

"Who?" He hated the hint of jealousy in his voice.

Frank laughed. "Aha! You are interested. Except, she's not your type, is she?"

"You didn't answer me. Who's interested?" He sounded like an eighth grader.

"Is it important who they are? You've already staked your claim, man. What's important is you're interested. About time, too. If another guy hugged her and caused you to stop in your tracks, I'd say you have it bad. You can't stay single forever, you know. A life of solitude is brutal."

"From a guy who has a wonderful wife and four super kids, you can speak to my life?"

"Look. You had a rough time, but not every woman is like Laura. She wasn't the wife you thought she was. She lied and cheated. You never saw it coming and it did a number on you, but you need to put it in the past." Frank's voice held a hint of exasperation.

"I'm content with my life as it is. This thing with Cassie has me in knots. I don't want to think about her. But I do. A lot." He took a bite of the spicy pizza and swallowed. "I could put her out of my mind if I tried. But there's a problem."

"What's the problem?"

"Her daughters are friends with my daughters and she pops in and out of my life. I can't have any distractions now. I'm not getting enough sleep as it is. It's crazy."

"Whoa. First, are you trying to convince me or yourself? Second, how do you know about this other guy? Have you been spending time with the lovely Cassie and her kids?" His eyes narrowed and his voice wheedled.

"Not trying to convince anyone. I'm trying to give you a picture of what's going on. Yes, I spent time with her. Mia strong-armed me to check out her house for a security system. We aren't dating or anything like that. And I went to lunch with her and the kids and my sister."

"But you *do* want to date her, correct?" Frank lifted his chin and gave him a hard stare.

He pictured Frank standing in front of a judge and grilling him as a defendant. His stomach lurched. His friend always could ferret information. Quite easily, too.

"I don't know what I want. She bothers me and she *is* prickly."

"She bothers you because you're interested. Otherwise she wouldn't bother you at all. And I think this whole conversation is more about you than it is about her. You just don't want to go there." Frank smirked as he chomped his pizza.

Trust Frank to cut to the chase.

"I overheard her talking to a guy named Phil when she was at our house for a pool party. Then she looked stricken when she saw her ex-sister-in-law. She has more baggage than the luggage carousel at

82

JFK International and she's hiding something. Maybe even a whole slew of things. That's what's bothering me most about her. I think that guy may have been that Phil guy. It couldn't have been her ex, because he looked like he wanted more from her or he may have even been someone else. Who knows?"

"You're suspicious. One of two things need to happen. Either you get to know her better and realize she doesn't have the secrets you think she has, or she does. After all, Steve, everyone has secrets, even you. Why would you expect her not to? Bottom line, get to know her better. Get some clear-sightedness. Prayer is the answer."

"I haven't prayed in a long, long time." Steve mumbled and his shoulders drooped. "This situation keeps me awake at night. I keep thinking what an exceptional mother she is to her daughters, and she treats my girls the same way." Steve took a huge breath. "This is so beyond me right now. I needed someone to hear me out and I can't talk to Mia or Fiona. They would jump to the same conclusion as you and then I'd be done for."

"Come to the men's group tonight. If for no other reason than your daughters need you as the head of your family. Continue to take the girls to church. You can't depend on Mia to provide leadership. That's your responsibility." Frank grabbed the check and paid it.

He had been dodging Frank and his well-meaning remarks for years. His friend reached for his arm. "Let's go back to my office and spend a little time in prayer. You need it."

"Old habits are brutal. Unrelenting," Steve muttered.

83

"Don't you have to prepare for court tomorrow?"

"This is much more important," Frank said as they walked back to his firm.

"Are you going tonight?"

"Of course. I go every Thursday. No matter what's going on at work, I won't miss it. Keeps me grounded and focused. I get so much more accomplished. I learned a long time ago when I'm mired in work and skip the study, the work doesn't go well but when I go, the work seems effortless despite me thinking I don't have time for it."

Steve nodded. As Frank shut the door to the office, Steve focused on the comfortable space Frank had created. The smooth leather chairs and classical music made the room cozy. Light poured in from the plate-glass windows. No wonder Frank got a lot of work done here. Pictures of his children and wife adorned the wood bookcases where thick volumes of law books stood at attention.

He didn't understand the gem about the men's group but then, his father died before he was man enough to dig deep into spiritual issues with him. As he sat and waited for Frank to complete his call, he remembered his father, no matter what was going on in the office, always made time for his men's group. He'd do the same. Why did it take so many years for him to figure it out?

As Frank prayed, a sense of peace overwhelmed Steve's heart. A lightness of spirit enveloped him. Steve couldn't remember the last time his spirit was this buoyant. He would go to men's group tonight. It was the first step in finding who he was and who he would   become.

Chapter 9

The next morning Cassie reviewed Phil's emails in the gym's bleachers while the kids practiced. She weighed options as she researched publishing houses and various editors online and ruled out one as unrealistic and left with her with two options. Prayer was the best solution now.

She wouldn't rush, but the deadline loomed. Next week the kids started gym camp, and she'd have more time for prayer and revisions.

Phil's ringtone chirped. Their discussion turned heated, but she made her position clear, then hung up and wilted. Was this the direction she should take?

Her other books required less time to write and edit. The time had come to move on. No longer would she write the spicy mystery novels loved by many. She'd changed and she couldn't do it.

"So, who's Phil?"

Mia's voice startled her as she slid beside Cassie and nudged her leg. She straightened and struggled for an answer.

"A friend."

"That conversation sounded like more than a friendship."

"You were eavesdropping?" She questioned how much Mia overheard and prided herself by being cautious in phone conversations, especially with tiny ears around. Cassie strained to think of a way to change the subject.

"You won't tell me about him, will you?" Mia prodded as she waved to the girls who had applied chalk to their hands before they practiced their bar routine.

"Nothing to tell. He's a friend. End of story."

"All righty then," Mia slapped her thighs. "Steve's in meetings all day tomorrow before he leaves for Australia. Let's get together and have a pool party. Weatherman says it'll be a scorcher. We'll have a cookout with dogs and burgers. What do you say? Just the six of us and we'll have a girl's afternoon." She rubbed her hands together.

"I don't know. Last time we came, it proved awkward."

"He'll be at his downtown office all day. Told me not to expect him till late. Said he had to get his ducks in a row." Mia air quoted *ducks in a row*. "He's a tad OCD when he's got a deal in the works and this one's huge. He's worked late every night this week." She grumbled. "I worry about him."

Mia's forlorn expression caused an ache in Cassie's heart. Mia needed some girl time with her, after all. Cassie gazed at her dear friend and touched her arm. "What worries you?"

"His hours. His health. He doesn't spend enough time with the girls, and he doesn't sleep much."

"You need to talk to him about your concerns. Maybe he'll sleep on the fifteen-hour plane ride."

Mia ignored her. "Are you coming or not?"

"All right. We'll come, but let's not tell them." She motioned to the girls. "Otherwise they'll never sleep tonight."

"Isn't that the truth?" Mia laughed. "Let's make it ten-thirty and bring your suit. The girls can't play with you in the pool if you don't actually get in the pool."

After midnight Steve dragged himself through the back door and into the living room, comforted by the scene before him. Mia rose from her favorite arm chair. "You're home." The room glowed with soft light from the floor lamp. Melodic strains of classical music surrounded them.

"You missed good-night hugs and kisses, and they pouted till they fell asleep," Mia chided as she trudged to the kitchen with the book she'd been reading. "There's a casserole in the fridge."

"I ate earlier." Steve massaged the bridge of his nose. "I'm exhausted and need sleep. Another long day tomorrow."

"You need to slow down. We need you more than the business needs you."

"After this deal closes, I plan to reduce my workload and devote more time to the girls. I've worked toward this moment for years."

"I know it's important you provide for us, but I worry you'll have another goal and then another. Not to mention your health." Mia held up a book up from his library. "You're a big fan of this series, aren't you? Engaging. Do you mind if I borrow it?"

He scanned the title. "I bought a new one yesterday. I plan to read it on the plane. Apparently, there's only one more in the series. Won't be out until after Christmas. Bums me because one of my favorite authors, Veronica Cannon, wrote them."

He yawned and waved his hand. "Go ahead but put it back when you're done. I'm headed upstairs to kiss the girls, take a shower, and fall into bed. I have a long week ahead." He groaned, rolled his shoulders and yawned again. He pushed himself too hard for far too long.

"Will you be able to sleep on the flight? What time do you leave? Will you be in church on Sunday?" She fired questions in staccato fashion, and Steve's head throbbed.

"Hopefully, seven-thirty a.m. and yes, of course." He answered and stepped on the first tread, exhausted and bone weary.

She nodded and left for her apartment over the garage.

"Good morning." Steve yawned and scratched his stomach. "Is there cereal for me?"

Mia retrieved another bowl and spoon and placed the items in his usual spot at the breakfast bar.

The girls ate with quiet intensity and sneaked glimpses of him. He prepared his bowl and tucked into the crunchy cereal. Mia poured herself a bowl and stood near the sink. She eyed him and the girls.

They finished in uneasy silence.

The girls squirmed.

"Are you done?" Mia said.

Her gentle voice irked him. When they nodded, Mia sent them upstairs to straighten their rooms and dress for the day.

Steve sipped his now lukewarm coffee while his sister cleaned the kitchen. He eyed her when she leaned over the center island with her hands firmly planted.

"You want to explain why the girls cautioned me to be quiet when I came in? I haven't seen them act like this since I came to live here. Why?"

Steve cringed at the censure in her voice and pretended to examine his coffee. "They got up at five and I needed sleep," he muttered. "I yelled at them, okay? I told them to go downstairs, watch television, and be quiet."

His sister leaned in further. "They've been happy these past several years. It took forever to get them to smile and act like normal children. You need to fix this and do it now."

"I know I have to apologize but my baby girls don't understand the pressure," he whispered.

She leaned back and crossed her arms over her chest. "They don't need to know your business pressures." He couldn't mistake the anger. She stormed at him with a low-pitched voice. "They need to know you love them. Hug them. Tell them you were a jerk."

Chastised, he put his bowl and spoon in the dishwasher. "I wouldn't tell them about my pressures."

She shrugged and drank her coffee.

Even though he and Mia connected as twins often do, they hadn't been on the same wave length for a long, long time. She had gone her way and he, his.

Steve retrieved documents required for his meeting and his sister's muffled voice drifted into the hallway. He edged closer. Eavesdropping wasn't an activity Steve engaged in, but Mia rarely whispered on the phone. Did she call Fiona to complain about his treatment of his daughters?

When he peeked into the kitchen, his sister had her back to him. Cassie. Mia told her to come at noon and she'd explain later. *Darn.* He hoped Mia would keep silent about family business. Bad enough Cassie popped into his head at the most inopportune times. He listened for a few more minutes until he heard his daughters in the upper hallway.

He eyed his girls at the bottom of the stairs. "Let's go into my office and have a chat." He used his softest voice.

The girls followed him into his home office and climbed onto the plaid loveseat. He perched on the coffee table and studied them.

"I'm sorry I yelled at you." When they stared at the floor and didn't respond, Steve's heart sank as he took their tiny hands in his and kissed them. Peering first at Stella and then Tina, he hoped his stupidity didn't evoke awful memories.

"I was tired and shouldn't have shouted. Will you forgive me?" He looked into eyes so much like his. They were slow to smile.

He grabbed them in his arms and thanked God for his little girls. His heart ached with tenderness for them. "I love you both and would never hurt you."

"We love you too, Daddy," they said as they hugged him as tight as their little arms allowed.

He sniffed their soft hair. "You smell like lemons." They giggled and relaxed in his arms.

"You coming home early tonight?" Their eyes pleaded as they wound their fingers in his hair.

His lips thinned. "I have a lot of work to do today, but I'll do my best. I'm working hard today so I can spend all day tomorrow with you before I fly out." *Lord, I love them so much. Help me be the father they need.*

A knock interrupted their conversation. "Come in," they chorused and laughed.

Mia strode in and placed her hands on her hips. "Did you clean your room? We need to brush and braid your hair. Go grab the brush, comb and bands."

They jumped off the sofa, ran out of the room. In an instant they were back to the noisy children they always were. Mia shook her head.

"Didn't hurt too much, now did it?" she drawled as she sat in their dad's leather office chair and swung the chair back and forth.

No sense in getting into a discussion about his lack of parenting abilities.

"I don't have time now but before I fly out, we need to have a chat about Cassie." His voice was quiet and tense.

She stopped and tapped her foot. "What about?"

He packed files in the bulging bag. "Now's not a good time. The girls will be down in a few minutes."

Mia stood and leaned on the well-worn desk. "You can't drop that bombshell and expect me to let it go."

"She might not be who you think she is."

"What do you mean?"

He raced upstairs to get dressed and passed his daughters on the stairs. "We'll talk about it later."

Chapter 10

Gabby and Bella jumped into the pool while Stella and Tina frolicked under the waterfall. Cassie invested in swimming lessons but never left them alone in the water. She hoped Steve wouldn't appear unexpectedly like he did when they went to the doll museum.

Cassie dropped her bag and towels onto the yellow chaise while Mia reclined on its turquoise twin. "Sorry I'm late. I wanted to make treats. They're on the table."

Mia bookmarked the page and laid the book on the table between them. "What did you make?"

The book was one of hers. Cassie choked and managed a smile. "Chocolate cupcakes with chocolate frosting and sprinkles, what else?"

"I read until late last night and woke up late." Mia yawned. "We had a minor issue with the girls this morning."

Cassie glanced at Mia's nieces. "They seem okay," Cassie sat and whispered, hoping to divert attention from the book. "Want to talk about it?"

"Nah. Let's chat about gym camp and schedules next week."

Her eyes narrowed. "What about them?"

Mia leaned back and closed her eyes. "I've been thinking about getting back into professional photography and next week would be a splendid time to start. I may be late to pick up the girls and I wanted to okay it with you."

"Not a problem. You never told me you were a

professional photographer."

She opened her eyes and shrugged. "I studied photography in college. With the girls in school all day, I want to dust off the equipment and bolster my portfolio."

Mia wasn't her usual gregarious self and seemed distracted.

"Do you want to coordinate daily?"

"Collect them if I'm not there, I'll text you and pick them up at your place."

Cassie searched for clues. "Is something bothering you? You seem a little out of it."

"What? No. I'm fine." Mia smiled as she faced Cassie. "What are your plans for next week?"

"I have a project and other things I've left undone."

"Steve didn't get in till after midnight. He leaves for Australia tomorrow night." She gave a deep sigh. "I wish he didn't have to travel so far, but this business deal is his dream and I think there are some wrinkles, but he won't say and I won't ask."

"Why do you think that?"

She shrugged. "It's just a feeling I have. Something is bothering him. Big time. But I could be all wrong." Mia grabbed the sunscreen and squeezed a blob on her leg, then gave Cassie a sly grin. "Maybe you're on his mind."

Her head snapped. "Me? Why would I be on his mind?"

Mia smoothed the lotion on and laughed. "I don't know. He seems preoccupied. And more so ever since you installed the security system."

Cassie didn't want him fixated on her. She only wanted his friendship, but she knew she'd feel his loss. His family would miss him more. Time to cut the conversation. "I didn't swim the last time and I need to change." Good thing Mia didn't ask about the project. Another slip could prove awkward.

"You can use the changing room." Mia pointed to a door on the other side of the garage.

"That's convenient," Cassie drawled and sniffed the delightful pink and white flowers planted around the backyard.

Cassie wandered out of the bathroom and strolled over and sat. "Aren't you going in the pool?"

Mia shivered. "I don't swim. Besides, I haven't been able to put this book down since I filched it from Steve's collection last night. He has the entire Jade Parker series. I can't wait to read the others. Have you read them?"

Bella begged her to go into the pool and saved Cassie from the question.

"Let me at least remove my cover up." Cassie laughed as Bella tugged on the offensive garment.

Later, Mia grilled hot dogs and hamburgers. "They're almost ready," Mia called out and readied plates for everyone.

They ate, talked and giggled. Afterward, Cassie told the girls to stay out of the pool for an hour. Despite the groans, the girls obeyed and played badminton.

She stored leftovers, then relaxed. Mia, enthralled with the book, zoned out, and Cassie didn't want to disturb her but worried about the book series and how they would affect her friend.

Mia closed the book. "Have you read Veronica Cannon's books?"

Cassie nodded. She never discussed her books with

anyone but her agent and learned to ignore such conversations. "I think they're ready to swim."

Mia cocked her head and smirked. "Ya think so."

Steve and Mia stepped into the sanctuary after they accompanied the girls to kids' church. The church's interior kept its minimalistic décor despite the now padded pews. Nothing elaborate enough to hinder their focus on why they were there.

Mia plopped next to Cassie and Steve trailed in behind her. Mia whispered something to Cassie, and she giggled, a sound that wormed its way into his heart. He must be nuts. She was trouble with a capital T. He shook his head and concentrated on the music.

Cassie sang her heart out and raised her hands in worship. She had secrets. Maybe even one about the man Steve saw kiss her. He shook his head. *I have my own issues, and it's not my place to criticize anyone.*

After the service, he was glad he didn't have to spend time in Cassie's presence. He wanted to spend every second with his daughters before he flew out.

When they returned home, Mia placed Fiona's Sunday casserole in the oven and then set out plates and glasses. "What time is your flight?"

Steve helped with the drinks and the silverware. "My flight changed. It's tomorrow instead, which means I'll be a day late returning." His lips drooped at the sight of his daughters' gloomy faces.

Tina's eyes glittered with tears. "Why do you have to leave, Daddy?"

"Sweetheart, I'll be back before you know it. I timed this trip for next week on purpose. You'll be at camp all day, tired when you get home, and won't miss me at all." He smiled and ruffled their hair, but his heart broke. This is what he longed for. This made all the work he'd done in the past six years tolerable.

"But Daddy, we'll miss you," Stella added to her sister's pleas.

Steve sat and pulled both girls into his arms and breathed in the floral scent of their shampoo. He hugged them tight and glanced at his sister over their shoulders. Mia's eyes filled with tears and turned to retrieve napkins. Good thing, or he'd have wept, too.

He pulled them away from him so he could memorize their faces. "Don't you want me to buy you something nice from Australia?"

They jerked simultaneously. "What will you bring us?"

"Let's see. What would you like? A koala bear?" His voice serious.

"You can't bring us a bear, Daddy. They won't let an animal on the plane," Stella said with superiority.

"True. How about a stuffed koala bear?" Steve yanked Tina's pony tail and smiled.

"I want a surprise," Stella said.

Tina raised her hand. "Me too!"

With a covert motion, Mia wiped her eyes. "Why don't you go upstairs and play till lunch is ready?" The girls ran out, excited for their surprise gifts.

Mia pulled the salad fixings from the fridge and chopped vegetables and gazed at her brother. "You ready to talk about what's bothering you?"

He rubbed his neck, ambled to the kitchen window, and surveyed the backyard. "Not especially."

She stopped chopping and pointed the knife at her brother. "No way. You opened Pandora's box, now spill."

His breath whooshed out as he faced his sister, crossed his arms and blurted, "I saw Cassie with a random guy when I went to lunch with Frank."

She was the first close friend Mia had since she returned home and he hated to spoil their relationship, but Cassie interacted with his daughters and Mia needed to be aware.

"So? She could have had a business meeting. Why are you so quick to judge? She's not Laura, Steve. Maybe it had to do with her writing. She said she'd work on a project next week."

He gathered the flatware, set the table. "More like monkey business. He hugged her in the middle of the sidewalk and seemed enthralled. She's an adverse influence on the girls." Why was he jealous? Just like Laura, she had too many secrets for his liking. "Something's definitely off, Mia. She was dressed to the nines and quick to walk away." He wouldn't tell her she snatched her writing notebook out of his hand and shoved it in her desk when he was at her house. Mia's curiosity would be out of control and that could spell more trouble.

"When did you become so puritanical and suspicious? What does any of this have to do with the kids? She's wonderful with her girls...and yours." Mia shrugged and chopped more vegetables. "Did she see you?"

He leaned against the kitchen island and grabbed a red pepper that tasted sweet but became bitter in his stomach. "No. She walked the other way." The situation twisted his gut.

Mia glared, then smirked. "You're jealous."

"Are you nuts? Why would I be jealous?"

"Because she bothers you more than any other

woman since Laura."

He balked. His sister, without knowing it, said the same thing as his best friend. *Am I jealous?* He didn't know but he wanted to be sure of her. "I'd like to know what she's hiding."

She placed all the chopped vegetables in the enormous salad bowl, then stilled. "Secrets? We all have them, Steve. You're not exempt."

"This conversation is over. I have a few things to get ready for the trip. Fiona will be here next week, right?"

Mia placed salad on the table. "Why wouldn't she be?"

He nodded and left the room.

Chapter 11

Cassie's daughters, exhausted from the long hours, almost fell asleep at the dinner table during gym camp week. Thank goodness it was Friday and they could sleep in tomorrow.

She saw Mia only when she dropped off or picked up the girls, and she appeared preoccupied. Maybe it was the photography.

Cassie performed a final out-loud read through of her latest novel and pushed the proverbial send button. Phil would have to handle it from here. She wouldn't stress over whether or not a new publisher would be found. That was his job. Today was all hers. She drank refreshing iced tea, read for pleasure and wished she'd caught Mia this morning.

She would have enjoyed sharing Mia's delight in photography. But she'd already brought her nieces to the gym and left. Mia explained she shut her phone off when on a shoot. And Cassie hadn't bothered to text her and gave her professional courtesy for her work. Despite Mia's week-long preoccupation, she was on time to retrieve the girls.

Amazed at what she accomplished when she had no children underfoot, Cassie handled pesky household tasks she shelved since their move. Praying always helped.

Perhaps with camp over they could have one last swim before the season turned cold and Steve returned. Cassie smiled to herself. She'd ask Mia tonight.

The road detour made the congested rush hour traffic unbearable. Cassie would be late. She peered through the windshield while traffic sat at a standstill. The dismal gray skies from the afternoon's sporadic thunderstorms put her in a less than stellar mood.

She bit her lip and drummed her nails on the steering wheel. The dashboard clock mocked her and her stomach churned. *I will be so late...*

Miss Beverly, the gym's owner, ruled the gym with an iron fist in a velvet glove.

When classes were over, she took tardy parents to task. Being called into Miss Beverly's tiny gym office was akin to being called to the principal's office, except Cassie wasn't a teenager. Not what she wanted to sit through.

She glanced at the clock again and grimaced. She'd be thirty minutes late. She only hoped that Mia forgot to turn her phone on, and she was already at the gym. It would save her from a reprimand. But Mia hadn't responded to Cassie's frantic texts while she sat in gridlock.

As she drove through the light industrial complex that housed the gym center, Cassie squirmed. She glared at the lone car in the parking lot. Miss Beverly's. Cassie groaned. There was nothing she could do now. Late was late.

Rain pounded on the windshield. Slamming the car in park, she reached around the back seat in search of an umbrella, but found none. Instead, she scrambled out of the car. The driving deluge of rain and wind stung her face and prickled her skin. She locked the car with the remote as she ran into the building. The rain water hit her tongue in icy fury. Her t-shirt and hair were drenched as she entered the front door.

Miss Beverly met her in the reception area with a grim face. Cassie pursed her lips with wariness and slowed her steps while she wrung water from her long ponytail. Goosebumps blossomed on both arms when she hit the cranked-up air conditioning in the lobby.

Her eyes begged the coach to understand. "I'm so sorry I'm late. There was an accident, and I had to take a detour."

"Cassie, I'm not worried because you're late." Miss Beverly's voice had a gruff edge. She went behind the reception desk and opened the floor-to-ceiling cupboard and handed Cassie a fluffy towel.

The woman was all business and didn't suffer fools, so her demeanor confused Cassie.

She shaped her students into fruitful individuals by inspiring confidence and competitiveness, yet always instilled kindness. Miss Beverly cared. A delicate balancing act, for sure. Judging by how the children in her care loved her, she succeeded.

"Let's talk in my office."

Cassie nodded and followed the coach and dragged her feet.

Her daughters and Mia's nieces practiced on the gym equipment. Mia retrieved her nieces all week long and Cassie had no reason to think there was anything wrong.

But uneasiness permeated Cassie's spirit, and she sensed something else was going on here besides her being late. Even with Miss Beverly's penchant for punctuality, Cassie's delayed arrival was not the only thing on Miss Beverly's mind. There seemed to be a hint of worry in her gray eyes.

Miss Beverly's office was small with framed pictures of the various teams on the wall behind the no-nonsense desk. The two metal visitor's chairs lacked comfort so visitors wouldn't linger.

The door shut with a distinct thud and the coach placed both hands on the desk and leaned forward. Cassie studied her face for clues.

She exhaled. "I tried to reach you and Mia several times."

Cassie cringed and stammered. "My phone's battery died texting Mia, and I didn't have a car charger. My apologies for being late."

Miss Beverly waved her arm at Cassie. "I tried Mia's cell phone. It went straight to voicemail. This is very unlike her. She's almost never late and is quick to respond to my voicemails. I tried her at home, but voicemail was full."

Cassie shifted in her seat. "Mia said she'd shut her phone off when she was taking photos which is why you couldn't reach her. But Fiona, their housekeeper, is usually at their home to prepare dinner during the week."

"I tried their father, but it was after five and there was no answer. Stella and Tina told me he's in Australia…" Miss Beverly's voice trailed off for a minute. "Unfortunately, a prior commitment keeps me from taking them, otherwise I would." Miss Beverly's distress radiated from her frame. "I can't stay much longer. Do you think you could take the girls?"

"Of course. Mia and I agreed if she was late this week, I would take them home and she would retrieve them at my place." Cassie's gut told her something

102

was amiss, but she wouldn't voice her suspicions.

Through the horizontal blinds in the office window, she stole a glance at the girls practicing.

Miss Beverly breathed a sigh of relief, "I hoped you'd take the girls. I'm sure you'll reach Mia later and get this situation sorted."

Cassie wouldn't relay her fears to Stella and Tina. Her daughters would keep them distracted while Cassie tried to reach Mia.

"Let's try Mia one more time before you leave." The coach dialed the number. Cassie glanced at the girls while they waited for Mia to answer, but it went to voicemail.

In the gym, Stella shouted and ran to them. "Where's Aunt Mia?"

"Your aunt is a little late so you and Tina are coming home with us. Miss Beverly has to close the gym. Is that okay?" Cassie smiled. Despite her tense posture, the woman's face gave nothing away because she hadn't wanted to upset the girls.

"How's Aunt Mia going to know where we are?" Tina's eyes wavered from Cassie to the coach and back again.

"We agreed that I'd take you to my house if she were late. Get your bags and let's go." Cassie prodded them along.

The girls, rambunctious as ever, skipped and did cartwheels over the floor mats to grab their bags stowed under the bleachers, and returned somewhat breathless, but excited for more play time. Chalk and sweat permeated the air.

They waited under a dreary sky for Cassie to unlock the car. One last look around the parking lot. Where was Mia?

An insistent buzzing pierced Cassie's sleep-addled brain. After the grueling week of work-related tasks, exhaustion took its toll. She opened one eye and groaned. The moon peeked through the curtained window and cast filmy shadows along the wall.

She reached across the nightstand and grabbed the phone just as it went silent. She turned on her back, closed her eyes and placed the offensive phone on her chest.

The vibrations started again, and Cassie lifted the phone. Three a.m.! Who in the world would call at this hour? She sat straight up. Mia! She didn't recognize the number but answered the phone, full of hope.

"Cassie. Finally." Steve's words rushed out. "Where's Mia? I've been trying to reach her." His voice rose. "Cassie. Are you there?"

"Yes, I'm here, and half asleep."

"Sorry. Forgot about the time difference." Steve muttered. "But I didn't know what to do. No one answers at home and Mia's voicemail is full. Something is wrong."

Her stomach clenched. Difficult as it was, she had to tell him the truth.

"Fiona's sister fell and broke her hip and she went to help. That's probably why you couldn't reach her. Mia worked on her photography all week while the kids were at camp. At the end of camp on Friday, Mia never arrived."

"What do you mean she didn't arrive? Where the heck is she?" The frustration in his voice spoke volumes.

"I got to the gym late, and the girls were still there. I brought them home with me. We stopped to check your house and her apartment, but her car wasn't in the garage. To keep their minds off Mia, I took them for burgers. Your offices were already closed by the time I got to the gym. And I didn't have a number for you." Cassie rushed on. "She's missing, Steve."

"Did you at least call the police?" Steve bit out.

"Of course, I called the police." She huffed. "The kids were scared after I got them home. You were in Australia, and their aunt was missing. They needed a calm adult. How else was I supposed to handle the situation?"

His voice cracked, and he exhaled. "You're right. The girls are okay, yes?"

Cassie squeezed the phone. "Camp wore them out, but excitement for a sleepover caused them to not fret. And it didn't take long for all four of them to fall asleep."

"Did Mia say where she would take photos?

"Mia didn't say, and honestly, I didn't think to ask. Why would I?"

"She's an adult so no, you shouldn't have had to ask. But I'm worried about her." The telltale catch in his voice vibrated through the phone line. "This isn't like her. What did the police say?"

"I thought a person had to be missing for twenty-four hours, but that's not the case. I called Worthy Police Department and filed the report over the phone."

"But I didn't have Mia's details and told them what I knew. I was in bed when I remembered we took photos and I had one on my phone. I'll take it over to the police in the morning.

"You won't take the girls to the police, will you?"

"No. My sister-in-law will stay with the girls while I go. I don't want to upset them anymore than they already are. I'm worried. With the massive flooding reports in the outlying areas from yesterday's tremendous storm, the weathermen expect three more to hit over the weekend and into next week that will dump even more rain."

"My scheduled flight is for Tuesday, but this changes everything. I'll take the next flight out. Could you care for the girls till I get home? I'll figure things out when I get there."

"The police will find her. They have to." Cassie insisted. "I fell asleep praying for her. Could we pray for her now?"

His voice was gruff. "Just continue to pray. You need sleep."

Cassie's shoulders slumped. He didn't want to pray. Or maybe he didn't feel comfortable praying out loud or with someone who was a virtual stranger?

"I'm truly sorry I'm not there to handle this situation, Cassie."

"Not your fault, Steve. I'd call all my brother's friends if he were missing.

"Get some sleep. I'll call you when I land."

They hung up after Cassie gave him the police department's number. She placed the phone on the nightstand. She could care for the girls until the police found Mia, but dealing with Steve without Mia as a buffer gave her the jitters. Hopefully, she would turn up soon, but until she did, Cassie could be his friend.

Chapter 12

Pizzas bubbled in the oven. The aroma of fresh dough and red sauce permeated the first floor. For weeks her daughters clamored for pizza. But on a steamy August day? The constant air conditioning hum waged war with the heat of the oven.

The doorbell pealed, startling Cassie, and she skimmed across the cool wood floor through the darkened foyer. She pushed her glasses up her nose and threw open the thick oak door. Steve! She gaped before she caught herself and clamped her mouth shut.

He could be a GQ magazine cover with his finger hooked on the jacket over his shoulder. His hair fell over his forehead as if he had been running his fingers through it. Blonds weren't her type, but the more she saw him, the more he wormed his way beneath her skin.

"We thought you'd be here tomorrow."

Steve frowned as he surveyed her. Her cheeks flamed as she remembered her daisy-duke shorts and the hot pink unicorn t-shirt that'd shrunk from too many wash cycles.

"I caught an earlier flight. Where're the girls?"

His soft voice could tame a savage beast, and it reached her weary soul. What was this wild attraction? Thoughts of him swirled around in her brain since she met him.

"They're in the basement. I made pizza because the girls expected to stay the night," Cassie's eyebrows furrowed. "I went to the police station on Saturday, but they couldn't tell me anything."

He stepped into the foyer, and his presence closed in on her. "I spoke to them on the phone before I left Australia and gave them Mia's car details, but I wanted to come straight here to make sure the girls were okay." Craggy worry lines etched his forehead, mouth, and eyes.

"They're fine. They relaxed when they heard you were on your way," she smiled and led him into the kitchen. His stomach grumbled, and she stifled a grin. Steve leaned against the breakfast bar and lifted his head. "Smells good in here."

"Let me call the girls." Her skin tingled as she yanked open the basement door. "Come upstairs, girls. I have a surprise for you."

Feet rumbled up the stairs with Gabby leading the pack. She stopped short of plowing into Cassie. They peered around the basement door. Stella and Tina raced to their father and hugged him tight as he crouched and wrapped muscular forearms around them. They adorned his cheeks with kisses and demanded his attention.

Gabby and Bella stood rooted to the spot. Was that jealousy she spotted on her daughters' faces? Her heart ached for them. She understood their father's lack of affection hurt them, but she'd never witnessed it on their faces. Or had she been so consumed with the move and her own misery that it blinded her?

He winked at his daughters. "That's what I call a welcome. Maybe I ought to leave more often."

"We don't want you to leave ever again. Aunt Mia took us to the gym and never came to get us," Tina said.

Steve hugged his daughters and glanced at her and her girls.

Tears gathered in Stella's eyes, and she wrapped her arms around his waist. She nuzzled his chest and Tina mirrored her. "Where is Aunt Mia, Daddy?"

His voice hitched. "I don't know, honey. The police are looking for her and we have to let them do their job."

Gabby interrupted the family moment. "And pray."

Both he and his daughters looked surprised.

"We continue to pray for Mia's safe return," Cassie said. "Why don't you girls wash your hands. The pizza's ready and we can pray for her before we eat."

While the girls left to wash their hands, she removed three pizzas from the double ovens.

"Are you feeding an army?" he said.

She chuckled. "If I'm messing the kitchen, I make enough to freeze."

With expert movements, she cut the pizzas while she talked.

He surveyed the room. "Can I help?"

With the pizza wheel in mid-air, Cassie stopped as she followed his gaze to the granite countertops covered with pans of dough and pizza toppings. She hadn't expected his offer of help. "Everything's under control."

The girls skipped into the kitchen and fell into their seats.

"Stella. Your turn to say grace," Cassie said.

She nodded and bowed her head while Steve glanced at each girl.

Stella thanked God for bringing their father home safe. She asked God to help the police find Aunt Mia and thanked Him for the wonderful pizza that smelled so good. Cassie held back a grin at the sweet prayer. At the Amen, little voices demanded pizza with their favorite toppings.

Busy eating, the girls seemed oblivious to the tension in the room. Their missing aunt was foremost in her mind with a dash of her handsome brother thrown in for good measure. She motioned to Steve for his plate. "Which do you want?"

He examined the different pizzas. "One of each."

Cassie's eyebrows rose, but she placed three slices on his plate. He took the plate, sniffed it and set it on the table. Cassie grimaced. Typical male.

Her chest tightened, and she exhaled and placed her heel on the chair's seat, letting her knee touch the table. She served herself and ate, focusing on the flavorful pizza.

Stella broke the uneasy silence. "Isn't this the best pizza in the world, Dad?"

"It's fantastic, and she even makes my favorite." He grinned.

Cassie raised her head. "Which one?"

"Sausage and mushroom." He took another bite and made smacking noises which caused the girls to giggle.

Bella's eyes shot wide and glanced from Steve to her and back again. "That's Mama's favorite too."

He stared into her eyes. "Well, that's—"

"Daddy, can we stay for s'mores later?" Stella said.

"Sure, honey."

They avoided a discussion about Mia and her whereabouts for the sake of their girls and focused on his trip to Australia and their activities.

"Why don't you girls go downstairs and play for a while. I need to clean up the kitchen before we have s'mores. Take your plates to the sink and you can go," Cassie said.

She shut the basement door, but sensed Steve following her movements and made her uncomfortable as she cleared the table.

Cassie grabbed a box of storage bags. "I need to prepare to freeze the bread. If you'll excuse me."

He trailed her down the hall. "Can I help?

"Sure." She moved to sit on a bar stool and motioned for him to sit across from her.

When was the last time Steve had fresh, homemade bread? Fiona made wonderful meals, but he never remembered her making bread. The aroma intoxicated him.

She lifted the tea towels to expose perfect rolls. Pulling on plastic gloves, she handed him a set and placed four rolls into each plastic bag and stacked them in another basket.

He copied her movements. "This is a ton of bread. Is your freezer big enough?"

"I have an upright in the garage. I'll send bread and pizza home with you."

"That's kind of you."

Cassie stopped to stare at him. "Mia's disappearance so worried me I forgot to check in with Fiona." Her worried eyes looked enormous in her face. His gaze captured every long lash brushing her cheeks through her glasses' lenses. Her eyes reminded him of the green waters of Lake Tahoe's Emerald Bay.

"Fiona was beside herself and wanted to return, but I

told her you stepped in. She'll bring her sister home in two weeks and wants me to call her when I have news."

He struggled with asking Cassie to help with the kids because he still had reservations, but now, he had no choice. He needed his daughter's lives to return to a pseudo-normal so he could focus on finding Mia.

She had proved trustworthy. Yet, she hid something. He guessed she had an unpleasant marriage, but her daughters were well-behaved, kind, and loving. It was something else. Something to do with her writing? He didn't like secrets. Since his dead wife kept so many of them, he couldn't trust his own judgment.

Swallowing, he rubbed his chin with his forearm. "I know this is asking a lot, but could I hire you to care for the girls till Mia's found?" His brow furrowed, but he pushed through and pleaded. "If Fiona didn't have her sister to care for, I'd ask her. And I don't want to waste time to hire someone. Besides, the girls are used to you." Everything came at him at once. It reminded him of when... No, don't go there. That was then, this is now.

Cassie bit her lip, but her expression remained a mystery. *Please say yes.* He hoped other obligations wouldn't prevent her from helping him. His heart hammered as he waited.

"What do you mean by 'care for them'?"

"I haven't paid attention to Mia's schedule, I'm sad to say. I don't know what she does and Fiona's tied-up so..." His voice trailed. He despised admitting his shortcomings. He choked. How would he cope if Mia was...?

He stared out the window when the truth punched

him in the gut like a boxing champion. He'd depended on Mia's sweet nature and hadn't involved himself as he should have in the girls' lives since her return. With contracts almost signed, he vowed to spend more time with his girls and give Mia a break. He had to focus on finding her.

Why hadn't his twin-sense kicked in? It was as if she ceased to exist. Experience told him something was wrong before Cassie called him. At first, the deal made him jumpy, but now he recognized it was more than business jitters. His sister called to him.

"Taking them to classes and preparing meals is not a problem, but it might be easiest if they stayed here," Cassie said.

"I prefer they sleep at home and I can fix them breakfast and an occasional dinner, but getting them to classes and picking them up would be impossible with my work."

"Understood. It's doable, and if you'll be too late, they can have a sleepover. We can text when issues arise."

He gave her a single nod. "I've got to hire a private investigator to find Mia." He hoped he didn't portray how on edge he was.

Cassie cocked her head. "Mia seemed to always know when something was bothering you. Do you have those same kinds of feelings?"

His head shot up. "Sometimes. In Australia, I knew something was amiss, but assumed it was business related. My skin still prickled after my business concluded because I sensed her pain." He paused and gulped. "Then nothing at all."

"You don't think..." Cassie's voice broke and her

eyes filled with tears.

He lowered his eyes and whispered, "I…don't know."
She placed her fingers on his forearm. Her warm touch comforted him.

"We're going to get through this. I pray every chance I get and I'll put her on the prayer list at church."

He flinched, and her hand dropped. "I want to protect the girls from anyone who may say something that could hurt them, but I also know the more people who know she's missing there might be a chance someone will have seen her."

She let out a lengthy breath. "The kids may initiate a conversation because everyone loves Mia. Most people will help to look for her. The problem is, we don't have the slightest idea where to look." She shook her head. "And we could use every prayer we can get. The more specific, the better."

"You have a point about the kids. We'll just have to be prepared to answer questions and protect them as best we can."

"Agreed."

He hung his head. "Finding Mia and protecting the girls are my top priority. She has been like a mother to them since she returned home."

"Understood."

He toted the basket through the hallway just as Cassie's phone rang. "I'll get this, you answer the phone"

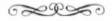

Cassie's stomach dropped. A phone conversation with Nico while Steve was nearby? Nothing she could do.

Nico came straight to the point. He wanted her to

drive the girls to Strickland on Friday because he couldn't make it to their usual meeting place.

She worked to keep her voice calm. "We've had this discussion before. I'm not driving to Strickland only to turn around and come home. That's a three-hour trip. One way."

He ignored her response and told her to spend the weekend with one of her friends.

"No. I hadn't planned to visit anyone and I'm not missing church. End of discussion." She gritted louder than she planned and wouldn't allow Nico to dictate to her. Those days were over.

Her ex-husband's anger vibrated through the phone.

She didn't feel virtuous right now, but refused to feel guilty. If she gave in, even once, he'd cajole her into driving all the time.

Her daughters needed to spend time with their father, but not at Cassie's expense. "Then you forgo a visit with the girls till the baby is born. Our agreement states we meet halfway. You'll see the girls when you're able to make the drive." Cassie's stomach performed the back handsprings her girls did at the gym. When would the insecurity end? His calls roiled her stomach.

He screamed a vulgarity loud enough to make her pull the phone away from her ear, then he hung up. That familiar dejected feeling made her shoulders slump, and her head lolled as the hand that held the phone   dropped   to   her   side.

Chapter 13

Guilt plagued Steve because he added to her responsibility when she had her own troubles. What had he been thinking? The steel in her voice during the phone call unnerved him.

Footsteps rumbled on the stairs and moved her into action. She replaced the phone on the charger and shoved her hands into soapy water when the girls charged into the kitchen.

Gabby's hands flew to her hips. "You're not done cleaning, yet?"

He stepped in, leaned on the door frame and raised an eyebrow at Gabby.

"You know, you could always lend a hand." Cassie put her hands on her hips, and mimicked Gabby, then waited. He barely kept the smirk off his face.

Gabby backed up.

"We don't like to do dishes. We have to clean all the time," Bella said.

Bella's sister clamped a hand over her mouth and gave her a warning glance. "Hush up." She nodded and went silent.

Cassie narrowed her eyes. "What clean up?" She walked around the island drying her hands and crouched to Bella's level. She looked everywhere except at her mother. Stella and Tina took in the exchange.

"You have a big mouth," Gabby sneered and crossed her arms.

"Quiet, Gabby." Cassie snapped.

Had she forgotten he and his girls were there? He

stepped closer. Should he be listening? What the heck, he was curious.

"It's… nothing, Mama," Bella said.

She took her daughter's chin in hand and lifted it so she could look into Bella's eyes. Her face was less than six inches away. "It's something, and you're going to tell me." Her quiet forcefulness would have felled a grown man, much less a tiny girl.

Bella teared up. "I'm not supposed to tell." She turned to her sister. "I'm sorry, Gabby."

Cassie zeroed in on Gabby. "You're in on this too? I want the whole story. And since Bella started it, Gabby, you can finish it." Steve watched as she took each child's hand and walked them into the family room without a backward glance.

Her body stiffened, and he longed to comfort her, but kept silent. His girls shuffled to his side and wrapped their arms around him. He hoped this display wouldn't spark memories of their mother. They stood in the kitchen and were silent.

Cassie settled herself on the coffee table. "Out with it, or there will be consequences." Gabby looked away.

"I'm losing patience."

"Will we still be able to have s'mores?" Gabby begged.

"If you're truthful, yes. If not, you two will go to your rooms while we enjoy s'mores."

Gabby gave an exaggerated sigh. "Oh, all right. Every time we go see Daddy, Charlotte makes us do dishes and clean."

"What?" Shock reverberated with one word.

Gabby shifted her eyes to the floor. Both girls' faces appeared miserable because it looked like they didn't want to hurt their mother.

"How long, Gabby? And exactly what have you been cleaning?"

Gabby squirmed on the chair and pulled her lips into her teeth.

Cassie's shoulders stiffened. Although angry, she kept her voice calm. Her children used as maids repulsed her. And he didn't blame her.

"Since they got married. We do dishes, dust, sweep, scrub the floor, run the vacuum and clean the baseboards," Gabby whispered.

"We cleaned out the car once," Bella said.

"You're not helping." Gabby's voice was an angry whisper.

"Enough." Cassie held up her hand, her body tense. The fear in her daughters' eyes nearly killed her and she took a deep breath. "You're not in trouble. Go downstairs till I call you. It's not dark enough yet to make s'mores."

Gabby and Bella jumped up and scampered downstairs with Stella and Tina right behind them.

When the thumping feet faded, Cassie braced her elbows on her knees and covered her face. He sat at the end of the sofa and when she looked up, there were tears in her eyes and a hint of surprise which she masked in seconds.

Cassie rubbed her eyes and hurried into the kitchen. He followed and leaned on the island.

"I'm sorry you witnessed that." She apologized and took the other pizzas from the oven. She let them cool while she stored the rest of the toppings and prepared a cloth grocery bag with pizza and bread. She placed the bag on a clean section of countertop and attacked the various dishes left in the sink.

He couldn't think of anything to say, so he grabbed a cloth and dried the dishes as she rinsed and put them on the drain rack.

"I've been so consumed with our move I failed to notice they were a little different every time they came home. I thought their tiredness was because they played hard and never guessed child labor was involved. Of all the…" She slammed and banged pots as she scrubbed.

"It might not be as bad as you think."

Cassie stopped the frantic washing and stared at him through narrowed eyes. Her lips formed a disapproving line, and she blew out a breath.

"Really?" She drawled, and he squirmed. Had she taken lessons from Fiona?

She folded the dish towel and drained the sink. "Could you prepare the fire pit for the s'mores while I get the ingredients? Firewood is next to the deck. Don't make it too big or it'll never die down and we don't want the kids hurt."

"Sure thing." He pursed his lips and stepped through the glass sliding door to the slate patio where the fire pit occupied the center. Like he would allow the kids to get hurt on his watch. Cassie was a control freak, no two ways about it.

Did he do the right thing by asking her to help with the girls? But what choice did he have? He lit the fire and peered deep into the flames. Exhaustion made his shoulders slump.

How did he get to this point? Spending time with a woman who had a boatload of secrets sucked him back into a similar vortex of lies and secrets from all

119

those years ago. He wouldn't, couldn't go down that road again.

Forget about her and think about Mia. Where could she be?

Steve shook his head to remove the cobwebs as the fire spurted angry ember flashes and wafted a burning wood scent to his nostrils. He gazed at the sweet set up around him and thought he might like to have the same thing in his yard. Thinking about the fire was better than thinking about Mia missing or the woman inside.

The sliding glass door whooshed and caught his attention. Cassie had a loaded tray of marshmallows, chocolate squares, graham crackers and long metal forks with cork handles.

He took the tray and set it on a teak bench that wrapped around the fire pit.

"Let me get milk and plastic cups and call the kids." Her anger had cooled. She didn't seem to hold a grudge. Good to know.

He jabbed marshmallows on the long prongs as the kids bounded toward him with enthusiasm. Cassie trailed behind them.

"Slow down. We don't want you to get burned," Steve said.

The sticky treat melted in his mouth and the kids ate more than their fair share. He hoped the vast amounts of sugar they swallowed would dissipate before they got home. The trampoline called to them as Cassie grabbed the leftovers and disappeared into the kitchen.

While he was glad the girls weren't fretting over their aunt, he couldn't stop the pain that invaded him.

Where was his sister?

He meandered over to watch the girls do gymnastic tricks. He grinned as each one explained a different trick and was fascinated at how they could get their little bodies to contort.

Cassie strode out and also watched for a few minutes.

With a smile on his face so his girls wouldn't worry, he half-turned to Cassie. "Thanks for helping us take our minds off Mia with the pizza and s'mores. I really appreciate it."

Her lips turned up and she glanced at the girls jumping. "I'm really worried about Mia and your girls. I've tried to keep them busy so they couldn't think about it."

"Still, you took care of them as if they were your own. I'm grateful."

She nodded. "Wind it down, ladies."

Steve chuckled as all four girls had pitiful looks on their faces. "Come on, you've been playing all day. Baths are in order." He'd text Cassie when he went to the Police Station. Would there be any news?

Chapter 14

Ten days. Mia had been missing for ten days and he struggled with her disappearance. She was his twin. He would know if she were dead, wouldn't he? Or had he grown so far away from his twin that their unusual ability to sense things was dormant or worse, gone? No, it couldn't be true.

The gloom from the kitchen window reflected his mood. He nursed a fragrant cup of coffee and hoped the aroma would help him come to terms with his twin's loss, or at least…what? Maybe coffee would keep him awake after the many sleepless nights.

"Cassie's here to pick up the girls." Fiona called from upstairs.

The doorbell pealed several times before Steve made the connection between Fiona's shout and the doorbell.

Stella stood in the doorway with her head cocked and hand on her hip, Tina right beside her looking from him to her sister and back again. "Dad, aren't you going to answer the door?"

He ran his hand through his hair before he stepped to the front door. "Yeah, sure."

"I'm a little early." Cassie smiled at Stella and Tina. "Why don't you get in the car and I'll be there in a minute." Steve bent and gave each girl a tight hug and forced a slight smile for them as they ran to the car.

"I wanted to catch you before you left."

The smile left his face. "I'm working from home today."

"Well, then, I'll drop off the kids and come back."

Steve nodded and stared past Cassie to watch the kids as they strapped themselves into the car. "That'd be fine."

"Half an hour." She nodded to Fiona as she left. Steve shut and locked the door as Cassie's car rumbled in the distance.

He trailed Fiona past the laundry room and the water's sound soothed his mind. Steve took up his position at the kitchen window and stared at the dreariness and rain while he sipped coffee.

"Since Cassie's coming back, I'll put another pot on and slice the chocolate cake I made yesterday," Fiona said.

Steve sat at the table and exhaled a lengthy breath. "Where is she, Fiona? I've spent long nights awake trying to figure it out. The investigator said there've been no credit card transactions and her car hasn't been found." He folded his napkin and played with his spoon. "The police said..." He stopped and swallowed. "The longer she goes missing with no clues, the more likely she's dead."

"Dinnae be thinking that way," Fiona snapped, her accent came out thick and fast. "We're praying for her safe return. God is with her."

"How are you so sure? I feel nothing." His voice broke. "I should know where she is. She's my twin. What if Cassie knows more than she's saying?"

"You dinnae believe that nonsense, do you?" She censured his train of thought.

"She was the last person to see her."

Fiona's ire blossomed. "So?"

His fingers clutched his cup. "She has secrets."

"Everyone has secrets. You included." His frown

123

mirrored Fiona's as she sat across from him and placed her hand on his.

"Just because Cassie has secrets doesn't mean she's guilty of wrongdoing. Have you forgotten Mia's penchant for going her own way?"

When he objected, Fiona raised her hand. "I haven't forgotten the pain she put you through when you needed her. But she went away a girl and came back a changed woman. Have you considered that perhaps her past came back to haunt her?"

She patted his hand and got up. "I need to take my sister to physical therapy. I'll return later this afternoon to prepare dinner." She stopped mid-stride and pointed a bony finger at him. "Put your faith in God and not in the enemy chirping in your ear."

Steve nodded absently. Making herself scarce when Cassie returned wouldn't help him, but she had her own responsibilities and he was grateful for her support.

He struggled with Cassie as his children's caregiver. Was Fiona right? Was he blaming her unjustly? Her concern seemed genuine and always asked if the police turned up any leads. Or was it because she tried to hide her own involvement? Had she orchestrated Mia's disappearance? He didn't care for his suspicions, but they kept popping up.

Frank would be a good sounding board because Fiona only confused him. On more than one occasion he arrived and found Cassie writing in that blasted notebook, then she closed it and dumped it into her bag. Too quick, it seemed. Were her blog posts that confidential? Or was she writing something else? Like a journal. He didn't have the courage to ask.

Was it about Mia? Or was it something else?

He needed to think. His entire life threatened to come apart at the seams. It was happening all over again. His daughters, his sister missing, his business, and now Cassie. It was too much, but he was grateful for the stand-up guys in his men's group who prayed over him and with him. It gave him a peace. The church prayed for Mia's safe return and she needed every prayer. They all did.

He dreaded the meeting with Cassie, but at the doorbell's jingle, he moved one foot in front of the other as the hallway clock ticked a comforting rhythm.

Worry tinged her eyes, and he motioned her to come in.

He led her to the kitchen and grabbed a mug. "Fiona made fresh coffee and sliced some chocolate cake." The familiar zing raced up his spine as he brushed his fingers against hers. He didn't want to have feelings for Cassie. Not when there were so many unanswered questions.

He sipped his now lukewarm coffee. "What was it you wanted to talk about?" He lifted the cake to his mouth, and the chocolate's richness on his tongue energized him.

"Two things, actually. First, anything new on the investigation?"

Her face expressed sorrow, and she reached across the table to touch his hand, but he pulled away and she snatched her hand back. The hurt on her face squeezed his heart, but he ignored it. Despite her being so good with his daughters, he lacked trust. Nothing mattered when his sister's life was at stake.

"I spoke to the police." He weighed each word. "The longer she goes missing, the less likely she'll be alive when they find her." He stared into his cup and relived memories of his twin.

She exploded. "I don't believe she's dead. Not for a moment. There has to be another explanation."

"Yeah, and what would that be? You were the last person to see her. Shed some light in that direction, would you?"

"Are you suggesting I had something to do with her disappearance?" Unbelief skimmed her face. Her pain was clear, but he couldn't help it. Was she capable of hurting his sister?

"I told the police same as I told you," she choked out. "Mia went to take pictures. She didn't say where and I didn't ask. Did you think if you ask the same questions my story would be different? It never will change because the truth never does. Have I done anything while caring for your children to give you reason to distrust me?"

He chose his words carefully. "With the children, no. But I wonder about your secrets." Maybe he should contact her ex-husband or her brother. No, he couldn't afford to make her so angry she'd stop caring for his kids.

She narrowed her eyes and blustered, "Why do you think I have secrets? Even if I had secrets, they wouldn't have anything to do with Mia."

He had nothing to lose at this point. "Then tell me who the guy was whose arms you were in a few weeks ago."

"Arms? A few weeks ago?"

Her dumbfounded look angered him.

"Oh, come on, Cassie." His lips twisted. "I met a friend at Café Napolitano's a few weeks ago. You were decked out and hugged some guy in the street outside the restaurant. Are you having an affair with him?"

Cassie's eyebrows lifted, her face turned red, and her hand shook as she pointed to him. "You think I'm having an affair? When would I have time between caring for my two daughters and yours?"

He drew back. He'd never seen her so angry or so shaken.

"You're being rather defensive for someone who isn't guilty." He shrugged and stared at her. "I guess you don't want the girls to know, right?"

She threw her hands in the air. "Of all the pig-headed, crazy accusations," then stilled. "He's a business colleague."

His mouth formed a straight line. "Business colleague? You mean monkey business."

"Are you serious? I've done nothing wrong and have had your daughters' best interest at heart because I care about them. Maybe you didn't notice, but they miss Mia."

"I know they miss her."

"For reasons of your own, you've never liked me and now you accuse me." Her eyes glistened with tears. "Your accusations are groundless."

He was hurtful, and he knew it, but he had to know the truth. And he had to find his missing sister.

"If you feel that way, perhaps you had better find yourself another caregiver."

His teeth clenched. "I. Want. The. Truth."

"You've already decided, Steve." A sadness filled her

voice. "You put two and two together and came up with five. I'm not having an affair, nor have I had anything to do with Mia's disappearance. If you don't believe me, then that's on you and I can't do anything about it."

"What about that guy?"

"None of your business."

"If you weren't caring for my daughters, it wouldn't be my business. But since you are, I think I have a right to know." He waited for her to respond, but his patience waned.

His daughters would suffer if she were to end their arrangement and Fiona still took care of her sister. They've already had one blow by losing Mia, then to lose Cassie? No. He couldn't do it. Did he actually think she had anything to do with his sister's disappearance or was it his hypersensitivity to secrets and lies that caused him to lash out? Was he jealous? Jealous? He hadn't known her that long. He couldn't possibly be jealous. No, it was his worry over his sister's disappearance that caused him to say things he'd never otherwise say. He was falling apart at the seams. And he couldn't seem to stop himself.

"My personal life is off limits for discussion. It has nothing to do with Mia vanishing and that's what's important. We have to be strong for the girls."

Her composure told him she was still angry. He remembered the conversation with her ex-husband and how she hadn't enjoyed being put on the spot. Perhaps that's where the anger originated.

He had to reel it in for the sake of his daughters and his sanity and his shoulders slumped. "I'll try. Mia vanishing has tied me up in knots and I took it out on

128

you. I'm sorry."

Her hands snaked across the table and gave him a hearty squeeze. It went straight to his heart. He cleared his throat and stared at her green eyes. "You said 'two'. What's the second thing?"

Her sigh signaled her relief as the conversation headed in a different direction. "The girls are beside themselves that Mia isn't around for school shopping. I could help with that, if you like, but I won't do it on my own."

The subject took him off guard, especially since she had been rubbing his hands the entire time, and he blinked. "School shopping?"

"Back-to-school shopping. I'm guessing Mia shopped alone."

She spoke to him as if he were a child, and he rankled at her tone. "I gave her my credit card, and she bought whatever they needed."

"Well, I'm happy to help because I have to shop for my girls but I won't take your credit card. Come with us. If not, I'll give you a list and you can go on your own." She made demands on him for school shopping? Mia never did that. To be fair, he hadn't given Mia a choice. For the past four years, his business consumed him. But now the girls were older and needed to see him as a father who took an interest.

"I'll check my schedule and text you."

She nodded and got up. "Don't make it too long or they'll not have what they need."

"School doesn't start for a few weeks. Does it need to be done soon?"

"The sooner, the better. I have a system so it

shouldn't be too painful for you." She said over her shoulder as she walked toward the front door. She opened it and turned to him. "I had nothing to do with Mia's disappearance. I'm praying for her safe return and will continue to do so till she's found." With that, she walked to her car, never once looking back.

He slumped against the door. His mind swirled with thoughts of his missing sister, his daughters and their needs and finally to the woman whose sincerity caused him to question everything he knew about her. When had she invaded his heart?

Chapter 15

Steve watched her drive off and then took coffee and cake to his home office. Calling Frank was the first thing on his list, but he got voicemail and asked Frank to call him back as soon as possible.

His assistant dumped more reports to his email inbox and he plowed through emails and phone calls, but he wouldn't tackle reports until he wrapped his mind around Cassie. He stood by his window and recalled Cassie on the phone as she sat under the tree outside his window. And when Cassie snatched her notebook from him. He recalled the tension in her face as she grabbed it. He shook his head. Secrets. What were they? His sleepless nights made his thoughts jumbled and incoherent.

When Steve's phone buzzed, he picked it up. It was Frank. Maybe he could slide in a question or two about school shopping.

"Everything's going according to plan with the Australian deal, Steve. Quit worrying about it," Frank said.

"Glad to hear it."

They discussed deadlines, dates and correspondence that needed Frank's attention.

"Frank, I have a question for you. It's about Mia, Cassie, and school shopping."

"Whoa! One topic at a time. Easiest one first, school shopping."

Glad for the reprieve to get his thoughts in order, Steve said, "Do you take your children school shopping? Since I've been working to keep the business going, I just never had the time or the inclination to go shopping with them." He swallowed and wished he had.

"Sometimes. Depends on my schedule. My wife likes to include me and I could do without it, but I understand why she'd want me there. Another person to bounce ideas off of and those put-your-foot-down moments. So yes, I go most of the time. It's that time, isn't it? Does Fiona want you to take the girls school shopping? I assume Mia shopped before and you never have." Steve cringed. He had half as many kids and had never gone. *What kind of father am I?*

"Not Fiona, Cassie."

Frank chuckled. "Do tell."

"She won't use my credit card and told me we could do it together. I don't think she's wrong, but Mia's disappearance and Cassie's secrets have me tied up in knots."

"As in your interest has grown? Or something else?"

Steve squeezed the bridge of his nose and sighed. "Both. All of the above? Cassie was the last person to see Mia before she disappeared. She has secrets, so I confronted her. She lost it, Frank."

"It could be you're just overwhelmed with Mia's disappearance, but what'd you expect? You confronted a woman who has been nothing but kind to you and your daughters. She cares for them at no cost to you and at every cost to her. A woman who has shown your daughters more compassion and love than Laura ever did. What were you thinking?"

"I know it sounds somewhat petty, but I want to know what she's hiding."

"Your past has reared up to bite you in the butt, Steve. Put that nightmare behind you. And concentrate on finding Mia."

Steve paced between the window and his desk. "Doesn't matter. She wouldn't admit to anything and gave me the same story she told the police."

"You already played your hand. Now she thinks you hold her responsible even if you really don't."

"That's not the worst of it." Steve slumped back into his chair. "I let it all hang out and asked her about the guy who hugged her in the street the day we went to lunch. She balked. Said he was a business colleague. What kind of business colleague, she wouldn't say. How can it be anything other than monkey business? I know she writes articles for blogs. She writes in those notebooks all the time and puts them away whenever I show up. And she hasn't said what kind of articles or blog posts she writes."

"Listen to yourself, Steve. Your paranoia about Laura colors your relationship with Cassie. Are you truly worried about the children and Mia? Or are you searching for excuses not to be interested?"

Put like that, he sounded like a love-sick puppy. "I don't know."

"You need to think about how your attitude affects Cassie's relationship with your girls. This whole situation requires thought and prayer. Unfortunately, I have an appointment in five minutes but we can talk about it tonight at the men's group. Deal?"

"Yes, of course. I'll see you tonight."

He hoped he could get past his insecurities and move forward, but Mia is still missing with Cassie's potential involvement and her secrets kept him off kilter.

Cassie couldn't stop the four squealing little girls who ran past Fiona as she opened the door. They were halfway up the stairs when she reprimanded them to slow down.

"Find something to play with for a while, I need to speak to Fiona," Cassie said.

Fiona moved toward the kitchen. "I think you need a cup a tea."

"I'd love one. Steve's not working from home today, is he?"

"No, he isnae. Did you need to speak to him, lassie?

"No. I wanted to talk to you. He texted me a few days ago and said he'd be available to go school shopping on Saturday. Thank goodness."

Fiona prepared fine bone china cups for them. "I'm glad."

Tea was just what she needed. Cassie arranged herself and inhaled the distinctly English brew and savored its rich taste. She needed a short rest with the four whirlwinds excited about going back to school. "I wanted to talk to you about Mia and school shopping."

Fiona's blue eyes twinkled. "Goodness. Those are two opposite subjects."

"Has there been any news at all? I hesitate to ask because Steve thinks I had something to do with her disappearance." Cassie stared into her cup and frowned.

"Pish posh. I know you dinnae have anything to do with her disappearance." Fiona scolded. "And so does Steve." Fiona hesitated. "Past hurts are rising up and he cannae come in out of the rain," she whispered.

"What do you mean by that?"

Fiona stared out the window. "Tisnae my story to tell, Cassie. I've said too much already. No news about Mia. Discouraging for Steve, but I know in my heart she's out there. My bones told me from the beginning she'll be back." She nodded and poured herself another cup of tea. "Now, the school shopping?"

"I'm scrambling to put my list together not only for my girls, but his girls, too."

Fiona raised incredulous eyes in Cassie's direction. "List? You make a list for school shopping?"

"Sure." Cassie arose and placed the exquisite cup in the sink and turned to Fiona with confused eyes. "Doesn't everyone?"

Fiona raised her brows. "Mia never did. She'd spend days shopping with the girls till they were in tears and she became upset."

"Well, I have a system and it's worked for me since the girls started school. I worry Stella and Tina will not be as receptive to my methods."

"Ach. You worry too much, lassie." Fiona grinned. "As long as Gabby and Bella are with them, they'll be fine.

"I hope so." Cassie said as she climbed the stairs to work her system.

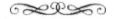

Steve's mind couldn't grasp that there'd been no movement on his sister's investigation so when Cassie's ring tone sounded, he cringed.

"Do you have a minute to talk?" Her voice sounded far off.

135

He pinched the bridge of his nose. "Is this about school shopping?" He knew the words came out with a bit of irritation, but he couldn't help it. He didn't need a call from her today.

"No. You sound busy. Maybe this isn't a good time."

"I'm not busy. Just tell me."

"All four girls have been invited to a sleepover. I've not given my girls permission because I wanted to talk to you first."

"You don't need to talk to me before you give your daughters your permission." She could hear the confusion in his voice.

"No, I don't. But you're forgetting the girls are really close. If I give my permission and you say no to your daughters, it will cause hard feelings."

He got up and paced, picking up pictures of his daughters on the bookcases that lined one side of his downtown office. "So you want permission for my girls. What is this sleepover? The girls have never asked to do this."

She let out a pent-up sigh. "Yeah, it's new for my girls, too. A girl from the gym is having a birthday party sleepover." She paused. "They need a break from thinking about Mia being missing." She rushed on. "And I know the mother. She's cautious and there are two older sisters who would help with the group."

He blew out a breath. "You're right. They do need a break. I've been so worried about Mia and I know they sense it. But I don't want to make them any more afraid than what they are. Nor do I want to keep them from having fun."

"Understood."

When they had discussed the ins-and-outs of a first-time sleepover, she breathed a sigh of relief when he gave his permission. He'd tell his girls tonight. When the date rolled around, he'd take them there and Cassie would pick them up the next morning. The girls would be so excited to attend. His daughters were growing up, and he hadn't spent enough time with them. That all would change as soon as Mia was found, and they were back together and he didn't have to interact with Cassie as much as he did now.

He didn't want to be alone this evening. With the Australian deal completed, he had more time on his hands and the girls were always a welcome relief from thinking about his missing sister. More calls and pleas to the private investigator and the detective, but it was like she vanished from the face of the earth. Where was she?

Cassie had texted him with the sleepover address. He wondered if he would see her. He cringed. Even her face would be a welcome distraction. Glancing in his rearview mirror he spotted Cassie's car easing up right behind him.

He groaned as he heard his daughters bouncing in the back seat, a plethora of just-purchased sleeping bags and duffels wedged between them.

"Look, it's Mrs. V. right behind us," Tina screamed.

The back-passenger door flew open and their paraphernalia sailed onto the grass with the girls scrambling out after it.

He made his way around the SUV and met Cassie in front of her car. He scratched his head and took in the mountain of stuff in the grass. "It looks like these kids are staying for two weeks rather than one night."

"They're girls. Get used to it. It'll only get worse."

At his heartfelt groan, she giggled. It tickled his ears and made its way down his stomach reminding him he hadn't eaten since early this morning. It betrayed him with a huge rumble.

She grinned. "Sounds like someone is hungry."

"Starving. Let's get the girls inside and go get some dinner." He hadn't expected that to come out of his mouth. They hadn't shared dinner since the night he returned from Australia, even though between her and Fiona, he and his girls were well fed.

"If you want to," he added at her startled expression.

She eyed him cautiously. "Sure. I was just going to heat up leftovers if you care to join me."

"That'd be great. Your leftovers are better than restaurant food."

"I don't know about that. But thanks anyway. Just follow me home." She gave him a shy smile.

They accompanied the girls to the door, and they rushed inside to whoops and hollers. The woman waved and closed the door. What had he gotten himself into?

He parked his SUV and followed her into the house. She turned off the alarm and strode to the kitchen.

"How's the security system working out for you?"

She pulled covered containers out of the fridge. "It took a bit getting used to it, although I don't want to think about what would happen if it went off in the middle of the night."

"Just grab the girls, lock yourself in the master bathroom and call 911. They'll keep you on the phone until the cops get here to check out the house." He leaned on the counter. "Anything I can do to help?"

"Grab the dishes in the cupboard and the flatware in that drawer," she said, pointing to a cabinet and the drawer below it. Convenient.

They moved around the kitchen and bumped into each other twice making his heart race. Her face was flushed, and he hadn't wanted to examine why he agreed to having dinner with her. Maybe he wanted to see if she'd share her secrets or tell him something more about the last time she saw Mia, and then he stilled. What if Mia told her she wanted to disappear? No. Cassie wouldn't make him worry for nothing.

As they sat for their meal, he said grace and they tucked into the delicious meatloaf, mashed potatoes, and peas. Comfort food. He could get used to this.

What was he saying? When Mia returned everything would go back to normal. *But do you want normal?*

Her fork was halfway to her mouth. "Did the investigator find anything? What about the detective?"

He leaned back. "I spoke to both of them this morning. Nothing from either of them." He shook his head and placed his hands on the table. "It's like she disappeared off the face of the earth. Body snatched." An ache grew in his heart.

She moved her hands to his and squeezed. "We can't lose hope. She means too much to too many people."

Her touch gave him strength, and he didn't want her to let him go. "How do you maintain such optimism?"

"We have to or we'll fall apart. And we can't do that…not for us, and not for the girls."

They made small talk about the girls and the challenges they would face in the years to come.

She placed the last dish in the dishwasher and turned to stare at him.

He swallowed. "I don't really want to go home yet."

"Then don't. You want another glass of tea?"

"Sure."

He prowled around the kitchen, checking out her small appliances and decorations, then stared at the twilight through the glass sliding door when she handed him the drink.

"Shall we go into the living room? Would you like to watch a movie or something?"

The frown he had turned into a small smile. "I don't know the last time I watched a movie that wasn't a kid's cartoon."

She grinned, then laughed. "I know the feeling. And it's no fun watching a comedy when you're the only person laughing."

"That's true."

He sat on the sofa in the middle and she had no choice but to sit next to him. She curled her feet under her and grabbed the remote. They settled for an action flick neither of them had seen.

When the movie got tense, Cassie turned her head into his shoulder and he wrapped his arm around her keeping her in place. It was comforting to share this movie with her. The bubble they were in would soon burst, but for now he wanted to savor every moment.

When the credits rolled, he turned to look at her. Her eyes turned that mossy green, and he knew he'd kiss her. It was inevitable. If he was honest with himself, he had wanted to kiss her from that first day in the gym watching her stiff back and pony tail bob as she climbed the steps ahead of him. It was the secrets that scared him and still did. But right now, this moment, he needed the kiss regardless of her past.

Leaning in, he touched her lips with his. They were as soft as he'd thought they'd be. He cupped her silky face. She drew a breath in and he deepened the kiss. He didn't want to think, he only wanted to feel. Feel alive and free. But he wasn't free. Thoughts of Mia chastising him pulled at him and his past kept him from having a relationship. And her secrets confused and bothered him.

He pulled back and sank into the sofa, his breathing harsh. His stomach tightened. He'd never felt this way, not even with Laura. Or maybe he had, but he'd forgotten.

Pulling his gaze to her, he witnessed the mask that came down over her features.

"I think you'd better leave."

He closed his eyes and rubbed his forehead. "You're right." He got up and looked everywhere, but at her. "Thank you for dinner."

"You're welcome." She rose from the sofa and led him to the door.

He turned and gazed into her startled eyes. "For the record. I'm not sorry I kissed you."

Jumping into his SUV, he remembered the things about her that scared him. Would he ever get past his own brokenness or past her secrets?

Cassie had no reason to be nervous, but that kiss they shared the other night shook her to her core. All she wanted was to be his friend and support system until Mia was found. His mixed signals troubled her. Troubled her deeply. She'd seen him watch and analyze her, trying to figure her out. Would she have to

141

divulge her secret? Or was it because he still blamed her for Mia's disappearance?

Cassie checked her watch and paced the hallway. He'd be here soon, and she had to push these thoughts to the back of her mind.

I need to understand what's going on between us and I'm lost. He's a fine man and I like him, but I'm worried about everything. Mia. The girls. Let the police find my friend safe.

Steve's daughters had closets and drawers filled with clothing they had to purge. Her daughters, not so much.

She scrolled through each child's list and calculated the time each stop would take. With four girls, could they get through the entire process in a day and with no meltdowns?

The doorbell interrupted her thoughts. Gabby and Bella raced up the stairs from the basement and put their shoes on. Cassie threw open the door. Stella and Tina ran in while Steve frowned at their exuberance. The girls hopped up and down, excited about their shopping extravaganza. Cassie eyed the girls and then glanced at Steve.

"Gabby, Steve needs a drink. Why don't you take the girls out to the trampoline for a while?"

Her daughter eyed Steve and nodded. The other girls traipsed behind her to the back door. At the sliding door's whoosh, Cassie heaved a sigh of relief and glanced at Steve. His face mirrored his confusion.

"Come on in, I'll make you a cup of coffee and tell you what I'm thinking."

Apprehensive, he nodded and followed her into the bright kitchen. At least it was a nice day. He crossed his arms. "Why are you letting them play when we

142

have to shop?

Cassie laughed. "Didn't you see them jumping around? I want them to get some exuberance out before we head to the stores so they'll be manageable, that's all."

He leaned on the island counter and sipped his coffee. "That makes sense, and I needed the caffeine. Thank you."

She smiled. He'd need extra fortification to deal with five females.

"Yesterday I went through Stella and Tina's clothes and determined what they'd outgrown and their replacements and made a list. I'd already done the same thing for my girls the day before. Stella and Tina had clothing they hadn't worn in a few years. No offense, but I don't think their closets and drawers were ever purged."

"No offense taken." He grimaced. "Mia didn't hoard, but she may not have wanted them to grow up any time soon."

She touched his hand and sneaked a glance at the girls outside on the trampoline. Knowing full well, she and Mia had talked at length about not wanting the girls to grow up too fast. "I want your permission to donate those clothes and make it a teachable moment for all four girls."

"Sure."

Had he even paid attention to anything she said? He'd ask questions soon enough.

"I promise I'll make this as painless for everyone as I can because I hate to shop," she said.

He blinked and held the cup in mid-air. She smirked. He hadn't expected that.

143

She smiled. "My method for school shopping is straightforward and takes me about three hours. But there are four girls, so it might take longer.

"I'm all for that," he said. "But they go to private school and wear uniforms. Why do they need school clothes?"

"For weekend activities. And they need shoes, socks, underwear, coats, scarves and gloves. Basically, a new wardrobe since they grow out of clothes so quickly. I had the girls try on everything they owned and liked. What didn't fit, or they didn't like, we put in bags. There are six big bags.

His eyebrows rose. "That must have exhausted you."

"It wasn't so bad. I do this twice a year for my girls so it's a snap, but since your girls had never gone through the process, I used different techniques to move them along. My girls helped." She grinned and shrugged. "Doing it this way saves so much time you have an exact list and you buy only what is needed."

A thoughtful expression covered his face. "Makes sense. Mia was forever asking for the credit card to take them shopping. I think Mia enjoyed shopping more than they did." He frowned, and Cassie was quick to change the subject.

"Kids don't want to be cooped up in stores all day. My girls tolerate shopping expeditions because it's just twice a year with an occasional shopping trip if there's a special event."

"I'm with them on that."

"I have an itinerary of the stores we'll hit, and I thought if we could get it done before one, we could take them to lunch. Your thoughts?" She crossed her fingers and hoped he could stand it.

144

"When we return, we can purchase the uniforms online. That way, the kids can play."

"I'm exhausted thinking about it."

A panicked look passed over his face. "While the girls are outside, I need your help with something else that came up last night and I'm at a loss."

"What is it?" Her heart dropped, and she grabbed his hand and he let her. Was it something to do with finding Mia? She didn't want to bring it up again because it upset him, and the last thing she wanted to do was spoil today's outing.

"It's Stella." They both looked outside at the girls jumping on the trampoline.

"Is she sick?"

He pulled his hand away and pinched the bridge of his nose. "No. I don't know." He heaved a long sigh. "She came to me last night and asked me if I thought her legs were fat. It was so unexpected I didn't know what to say. I'm sure I looked like a fish out of water flopping around on the shore.

She giggled. "I'm sure you were."

He raised his chin and glared. "You think this is funny?"

Swallowing another snicker, she pulled her lips in. "No. Your reaction caught me by surprise." She took a deep breath. "Body shaming even at this young age is serious. It could lead to health issues. What did you say to her?"

His face tightened. "I was curt and asked why she would even think such a thing. She burst into tears, ran into her bedroom and wouldn't talk to me. I was lost and called Fiona, but she told me to talk to you. What kind of health issues?"

She stared out the glass sliding door. "If Stella is asking this question, chances are another girl made fun of her. Girls can become anorexic or bulimic. Both can have dire health consequences. We need to nip this in the bud for all four girls. We'll talk to them together. You need to be a part of what bothers them."

"What will you say? And can you get her to talk to me again?" His pleading tone and emotional stance touched her heart.

"I don't know what I'll say yet, but I'm sure she'll talk to you again."

He grabbed her and gave her a quick hug. "It's such a relief to have someone who knows what this is all about."

His warm chest felt so good for that quick second until he rinsed his cup and placed it in the sink, then waved to the kids outside. "How long are you going to let them play?"

"I think they've played enough. We'll talk about it in the car."

"Let's take my car, it's roomier."

The girls buckled into their seats.

Cassie spoke in low tones to the girls about body shaming. They didn't speak at first, but she got them to admit that they'd seen girls teasing other girls on television and worried about their own bodies. She was able to get them to understand they were quite normal. They took her word for it. And promised they'd speak to her if anything ever happened to them like that.

"First stop. Jack & Jill children's boutique," Cassie said. "Do you want me to plug it into the GPS?"

He waved to go ahead and then glanced at the display.

"Aren't we headed to the Clearview mall?"

She shook her head and punched in the address.

Steve still wasn't sure of this whole school shopping expedition. Even if they didn't go to the mall, it looked like other people had the same idea. "Is it always like this right before school starts?"

"Yep. Which is why I plan it out. Normally, I'd have had the school shopping done two weeks ago, but…" her voice trailed.

The traffic got to him and he didn't look forward to running around tons of stores with four little girls and one pain-in-the-neck female. He still didn't know her secrets or if she knew where Mia had gone. And she still hadn't told him about the hugger guy. Every time his mind went back to that day on the street, his stomach churned. And yet, sleepless nights had taken its toll and wearied him.

"How many stores are on your list?"

"Three, maybe four. It depends if we can find the bulk of what we need here."

Cassie seemed to be a master of organization. She looked at her phone and told the sales clerk the girls' needs. She delegated the younger girls to the clerk while she shopped with the older girls.

Another clerk came over and told him there were some chairs near the fitting room if he cared to sit. He was totally out of his element and uncomfortable, but he'd suck it up for his daughters. He'd never shopped for them. Not even when his wife was alive. He was too busy trying to save the company.

She put the older girls in one changing room and the younger ones in another. Both sets of girls had mounds of clothing. He shook his head.

She caught him. "What?"

"Do they need all those clothes?"

"Not at all. We need to see what fits. I want the clothing a tad bigger so they'll be able to wear them longer."

He nodded.

The clerk brought him a bottle of water. "Your wife knows what she's doing."

"She's not my wife." He didn't want anyone to get the wrong idea about their relationship. "She's a…friend." Had Cassie heard the conversation?

"Well, no matter. Working with a mother like her is a pleasure. She knows exactly what she wants," the clerk said.

Each of the girls modeled three outfits. Cassie must have instructed the girls to save time. He didn't trust her with his heart, but he couldn't fault her on how she cared for his daughters.

His heart? He sat up straight and stiffened his shoulders. How long had it been since he considered his heart? Somehow, she wormed her way in. It wasn't through his stomach, it was how she cared for his daughters.

But what about the woman herself? What about all the secrets? He couldn't reconcile his heart and his mind about Cassie and yet, if he weren't careful, he'd lose his heart to her.

I can't deal with this right now. I need peace.

He needed divine help with Cassie and glared when she came out of the dressing room with four little girls loaded down with clothes. At all their happy smiles, his heart all but melted.

"I think we're done here." She sighed.

"I would think so," he murmured as he helped to relieve them of some of their burden, dropping articles of clothing as he approached the counter.

"Daddy, you're dropping all the clothes." Stella sighed and crossed her arms.

Cassie smirked and raised a brow. "Looks like you left a trail of clothing from the fitting room to here."

He turned and followed her gaze and felt his face heat. He dumped the load he had on the counter and backtracked to pick up all the items on the floor.

When he returned to the counter, Cassie pointed at his feet and chuckled. "Don't forget the underwear and socks at your feet."

"This is going to be a long day," he muttered.

Chapter 16

Cassie suggested lunch for their four cranky little girls. Over lunch, she recommended they tackle the uniform purchases online at her house. After they dragged their bags upstairs, the girls trailed to basement.

"Now they'll play?" Steve shook his head. "Where do they get their energy?"

She grinned. "They'll watch a video and fall asleep," she whispered. "Shopping is hard work, you know?"

"I'll say." He helped Cassie prepare cools drink for them and took them to the family room and set them on coasters while she gathered dinner from the freezer.

She sat in the rocker while her laptop booted up and he leaned back on the sofa.

Gazing at the dozing man on the sofa, she felt an odd contentment settle over her. Steve hadn't lost his temper when the girls complained or chattered non-stop. He indulged them in a way Nico never had. Steve came to her rescue when she needed a security system. He listened and spent time with both of their daughters while Nico threw money at her girls. In his eyes, they needed nothing more. Had Gabby and Bella noticed the difference? She hoped not.

Steve cared about God, and family plus he was attractive, personable, and successful. What wasn't to like? She'd misjudged him. Nico would have never endured a back-to-school shopping trip without losing his mind. This man's gentle snores reminded her they weren't a happy, blended family. Not by a long shot.

He hadn't trusted her, and she understood his skepticism. She decided Mia's disappearance had definitely taken its toll on him. And something Fiona said about his past niggled, but what did that have to do with her?

No matter. Cassie needed to regain his trust if she ever had it at all. And if she revealed her secret life? What if he wouldn't allow the kids to be friends anymore? She shuddered and hoped it wouldn't damage the girls' relationship, even if it meant she'd have no further contact with him.

Her heart ached to think of him not in her life. When had he invaded her heart? Until she had a conversation with him and Mia was found, dreaming about them together was a pipedream.

She placed the laptop on the coffee table and sat next to him. His aftershave wafted around her head and went straight into her belly. She nudged his arm.

He choked, blinked, and yawned. "Oh, sorry. I can't believe I nodded off like that." His voice's velvety sound gave her goosebumps. "I haven't been sleeping well." His mouth clamped shut and she feared Mia's disappearance had taken a much bigger toll than she could comprehend even given that his sister was her best friend.

"Well, you've had a busy day and we're not done yet." Her half grin, meant to comfort, hadn't.

Grabbing the laptop, she logged into the school's uniform site. While he snoozed, she placed her daughters' uniform order. They'd be shipped and arrive before school started.

"I already entered what your girls need, and it's in the shopping cart. All you have to do is approve the purchase and enter your card information."

"That's it?" He seemed awestruck as she approached shopping with methodical ease.

As he entered his credit card information, the doorbell rang. His eyes narrowed, and he seemed puzzled.

Moving to the foyer, her heart sank as she looked through the sidelight. No mistaking the figure standing there. Nico.

Cassie took a deep breath to calm her nerves, pasted a neutral expression on her face, and opened the door.

"How long was it going to take to open the door, Cass?"

Anxiety built in her chest. "I was busy."

"Whose car is that?" He pointed to Steve's shiny SUV. She'd almost forgotten about Steve and the girls being there.

Protect me and my girls. But most of all, protect Steve and his girls. They don't deserve this.

Despite her prayer, anger welled inside. How dare he question guests in her home? She was done with fear and she wouldn't allow it in her life anymore.

"A friend and none of your business. Why are you here?"

"Because I haven't seen my daughters for a long time."

"Charlotte must have had her baby, then."

He crossed his arms and leaned back on his heels. "I called, but you didn't answer."

"We were school shopping."

"Aren't you going to invite me in?" His pushiness made her nervous.

"No. I don't want you in my home." His jaw clenched. And his hands made fists. Cassie took a half step back. Could she shut the door in his face and have time to call the police before he banged on the door and brought the girls running?

"What?" He sneered. "I want to see my daughters and I want to see them, right now." He glanced over her shoulder. Steve's aftershave hit her nose before she felt his presence. Her domestic issues were hers, and hers alone.

Steve wrapped his arm around her waist. "Is there a problem?" His voice sounded far away, but exuded strength, and she swayed toward him. Half with relief and half with dread.

"None of your business. Who are you anyway?" Nico gritted. His face altered to that awful shade of rust red right before he lost it.

"I'm a friend of the family and you're upsetting Cassie. She doesn't want you here and I believe she doesn't want you to distress the children. I suggest you leave before I call the police." He sounded calm, but the tension in his body signaled he was fighting mad. He dug out his phone and dialed nine-one-...

Nico backed up. "This isn't over, Cassie. You'll be sorry you ever started this. And you, friend of the family, stay out of my way or you'll be sorry too."

Steve steered her into the house and shut the door. She slumped against the wall until he guided her back to the family room, sat her on the sofa and wrapped his arms around her.

When her breathing became normal, tears threatened. "Why...Why would you get yourself and your family involved in my problems? Nico is vindictive. He'll make our lives miserable." The tears slid down her cheeks, and he wiped them with his thumbs.

"I couldn't let him treat you that way. Seems he wants it all," he whispered.

"What do you mean?" Cassie hiccupped.

"He's got his new wife and family but he still wants to control you and the girls' lives." His blue eyes, so compassionate, drew her. In that moment, she realized she could tell him the truth and her fears disappeared. "It's not right, Cassie. Even someone as far removed as I am can see that. I heard how he yelled the night I came back from Australia."

"You heard that?"

"How could I not? He was loud and intimidating. I couldn't say anything then because I didn't know you well enough, and then you shut me down at the restaurant, so I let it go." He shrugged and watched her. "Do you want to talk about it?"

"Yes and no." His confused look made her smile. "Yes, but I want to check on the girls first."

"Good idea. I'll come with you." The basement was in semi-darkness with the video playing. All four girls were cuddled together and slept under soft afghans. Cassie thanked God they hadn't come upstairs.

Steve motioned to Cassie to follow him upstairs. "You were right."

"It happens every year. They're tired from the preparations for school shopping and the actual day wears on them to sleepiness. I'm certain it's the same for your girls."

He dipped his head, sat on the sofa and patted the seat next to him. "You ready?"

She squirmed and stared at the floor. "What do you

want to know?" Her soft response surprised him. Would she tell him only what she wanted him to know? On second thought, she'd tell him it wasn't his business.

"Tell me about Nico and your marriage. I promise I won't judge." He bent toward her and surveyed the golden flecks in her large green eyes and saw her lips were a natural pink without cosmetics. He wanted to touch them, kiss them, remembering how soft they were.

Her tear-filled eyes threatened to overflow again. "The girls will awaken soon and there's no time."

"Give me the condensed version, then."

She groaned and breathed. "Nico was a larger-than-life guy. He was in his junior year at college, and I was a young freshman. He had great plans and wanted me to be in his future. I was awestruck a junior took an interest in me."

"Why? You're beautiful. No reason to think otherwise."

"No. He was interested because my Dad took an interest in him and Nico found it easy to manipulate me. I followed him everywhere like a lost puppy dog. Did whatever he wanted. His friends became my friends, and my friends were dropped like the proverbial hot potato. I quit school, eloped, and thought we were happy."

Their situations were similar which comforted him because he could tell her about his marriage and believed she'd understand, but he still didn't know if she were involved in Mia's disappearance. One secret at a time.

"Once the ring was on my finger, he dictated what I

could and couldn't do. After the third year of the frightful merry-go-round, I realized I had to plan in case the situation got worse. And it did. His business had been all-consuming, and he spent almost no time with me or the girls. One night, by accident, I discovered he was cheating, and it shattered me."

He understood the devastation and dejection. It pressed in until your lungs compressed, and you gasped for air.

He placed his hand on hers and rubbed tiny circles with his thumb. "I married my college sweetheart right after we graduated. I know this may sound awful, but she wasn't the best mother or wife. But then, I wasn't the best husband either."

Both were lost in their own thoughts.

She drew a long breath. "I begged him to stop, but he claimed it was his life and I'd have to live with it," she said.

He couldn't imagine anyone hurting her and his heart squeezed, but he had to keep the wall intact until he found Mia.

Nico was a poor excuse for a man. But he had done the same thing with his daughters and grimaced. He learned though, but it didn't appear Nico learned the lesson. Nor was he likely to.

"The abuse was unbearable," she murmured and shivered. "I stopped begging him to get counseling. When things didn't go his way, and he got enraged, I learned to keep my mouth shut and let him do as he pleased. He took Charlotte to business events and when strangers approached me about her, it humiliated me."

"People are thoughtless. That isn't likely to change.

That's when you left him?"

"I thought to stay with him for the girls' sake, but that was a joke." She stared into the fireplace. Lost in memories, Steve acknowledged the resolve on her face. "I had to bide my time and live with it till I was ready to leave him."

"I finally had the courage to serve him with divorce papers. He threatened to kill me, and I got a restraining order. He couldn't see the kids for almost a year. Although he lost, he and his family continued their efforts to control me, and that's when I moved near my family and started a new life here." She looked up, a sadness in her eyes. "Now you're smack dab in the middle of an ugly divorce and I can't even guess what he'll do."

"What could he do? You're overreacting." He stared at her and willed his strength into her.

"That's where you're wrong. He'll do anything to get his way." She got up and paced. "I need to call my lawyer. When Nico's sister saw us, I knew she'd stir the pot." She heaved a deep breath and slumped into a chair.

"What did you mean when you said you had to plan? What did you do?"

"I planned to tell you after dinner tonight." She paused. "You're staying for dinner?"

"Sure."

She wrung her hands and fidgeted and her eyes begged him to understand. "When I realized I made a mistake marrying Nico, I hadn't gotten my degree, so I enrolled in correspondence courses to learn how to write. I had so much time on my hands at night, so it worked for me. I figured if I could learn how to write

157

and do it well, I could support myself and the girls."

"Why the big secret? You found a productive career writing blog posts to support your family and still have time for them."

A sigh of relief whooshed out. "Not just blog posts. The guy you saw hugging me is Phil Donaldson, my literary agent, and there's nothing between us. Never was and never will be. He's the only person who believed in me and has been my agent for years."

"I hadn't expected that," he murmured. "I wondered about the blog posts, but you're obviously a successful novelist otherwise you wouldn't have been able to afford this house and send the kids to private school. Besides blog posts, what do you write? Would I have read your work?"

"I write under two pen names and I don't do interviews or anything like that." She laughed. "Kind of like Elvis without the publicity."

"Really? Now I'm thoroughly curious. Maybe someday you'll trust me enough to tell me. I hear little feet tromping on the stairs." He winked and grinned. She revealed her secret, and his angst about Phil dissolved. Now if he could only broach her about Mia's disappearance. The timing was wrong, and after the day they'd had...No. He needed to strategize.

Chapter 17

Gabby and Bella came home subdued from their father's home that weekend. Cassie wanted to ask them, but let it slide. There'd be time later in the week when they settled into their back-to-school routine.

Had Steve known his girls invited them over for an end-of-summer picnic? She texted him with the excuse of asking what to bring and when to be there. His response satisfied her.

Gabby and Bella were thrilled to have more pool time at Steve's. The day dawned bright and clear with glimpses of a prolonged summer. Perfect for a pool party. The weatherman forecasted temperatures in the mid-80s. A more than welcome relief from the massive rain and thunderstorms that slammed them since Mia disappeared.

Labor Day. The last day of summer before school started, and the kids would celebrate in style. She'd missed him. They hadn't had more than a passing hello in the past week. Her girls whined all morning that preparations took forever. Cassie finally enlisted their help with swim gear, lawn games and extra clothes while she handled the food. Cassie chuckled and directed them to unload the trunk.

"Can we go swimming after we're done?" Gabby hopped from foot to foot. Cassie grinned at her excess energy.

"We'll see. Still a little early, yet. Perhaps you could play some lawn games we brought. How about croquet?"

When they arrived, she noticed Steve had hosed the flagstone and wiped the patio table. He waved and called his daughters, who raced to the car. Cassie set up the game and let them play as she organized the gear and food.

Steve peeked into various containers Cassie brought. "Do these need refrigeration?"

"The fruit salad. Where's Fiona?"

"She headed out a half hour ago, but she left what we needed for the grill and it's ready to go. Still a little early for lunch, though."

Cassie fingered her ponytail. "Can we rest for a few minutes while the kids play?"

He nodded and marched into the house with the container. She watched his smooth gait, appreciated the way his calves tightened as he hopped up the steps and the way his shoulders bunched under his t-shirt as he grabbed the door handle.

She sunk into a lounge chair and watched the girls play. The game would not be over soon, so she relaxed and put her feet up. After running around the house this morning, she welcomed the respite.

Steve brought a pitcher of lemonade, poured her a drink and she took a sip of the tart refreshment.

He groaned as he sat down, and Cassie watched him out of the corner of her eye.

"Tough morning?" A half grin formed on her lips.

"Between fielding questions from the girls and Fiona, then cleaning the pool area, I could use a few minutes rest."

"Maybe this wasn't the best idea," Cassie murmured.

He flashed her a grin as he eyed her over the top of his sunglasses. "Not on your life. I didn't do all this work not to enjoy it. Stella and Tina have been looking forward to it. And besides, they have to have a last bash of summer, right?"

They sat in companionable silence, and his presence comforted her. Cheers from the girls broke their peace.

Cassie squirmed. "Any news on Mia?"

"No." His voice sounded hard and unyielding. Cassie determined not to pursue it further.

"Are you ever going to tell me what actually happened and where she is?"

Cassie's mouth dropped open and her head whipped around. "You still think I am involved?" Shrillness touched the edges of her voice.

Steve shrugged but wouldn't look at her. "Been thinking about it for a while. Maybe you weren't responsible, but maybe she's hiding out. And maybe you know where but aren't saying. Or maybe she was tired, wanted to get away from her responsibilities and be free. And maybe it was convenient for her to leave and allow you to take over."

His plausible explanation infuriated her.

"You can't possibly mean that," she snapped with a fierce whisper. How could he believe something so heinous? "Not for a moment would Mia shirk her responsibilities. I never once heard her even allude to such a thing. Sure, she wanted a break now and then and we provided that for one another. She loves those girls like they were her own. You should be ashamed! If I had any inkling, I would've told you when she disappeared. Do you think I'd let you or Fiona worry and not say anything? Don't you think I've been worried, too?

She took a deep breath, slumped into the chaise, and whispered, "It's been fifteen days and I've been thinking, how's she surviving without money?"

Steve's head jerked and surprise widened his eyes as they stared at one another. He apparently hadn't thought of that.

Tina ran toward her Dad. "Can we go swimming now, Dad?" She jumped on his chest and hugged him as he groaned. "Bella and me won, Dad."

"Bella and I won, Tina. Bella and I."

"No, Dad, it was Bella and me, not you and Bella!" Tina corrected.

Cassie bit her lip and looked away. Despite her anger, she stifled a grin at the conversation. The other girls traipsed over. Bella had a wide smile while Stella and Gabby scowled and crossed their arms.

"Go get your suits on and we'll go in the pool." He gave her a thoughtful stare. "You can use the half bath off the kitchen to change."

"No need. I'm not swimming today." With the conversation going the way it had, there was no way she'd swim with him.

Steve blinked, and a bland expression crossed his face.

The girls ran out and cannon-balled into the pool. Steve dove into the fray after removing his t-shirt and sandals. She watched him play with the girls, water falling into his eyes.

She shouldn't be thinking about him now. Not after the realization he still blamed her for Mia's disappearance. It had to be his grief over his sister's disappearance that was causing him to be so irrational. And it made sense that it would, but she had to rein in her own feelings so they all could get through this tragedy until Mia came home. She reached in her bag, pulled out her notebook and wrote.

Whenever she glanced at the kids, she caught him staring. Sometimes his eyes were troubled, and sometimes they narrowed. She could almost see the gears grinding in his head.

Aside from the strained conversation during the yummy lunch, it was a so-so day. What would it have been like without Mia's disappearance hanging over their heads? Would their relationship be different? Would they be closer? Could they ever be close?

Not until they found Mia. And what if she were dead? She shivered. What then? Her heart plummeted. Strengthened by her determination, she vowed they'd shoulder the burden of loss together and be there for the girls.

With the day's activities behind them, they would sleep well tonight. Cassie helped Stella and Tina dress for bed. She'd brought her daughters' pajamas should they fall asleep on the way home, making it easier for her to put them to bed.

"Why don't they just sleep here?" Steve said, careful not to let the girls hear.

If he hoped to get on her good side, it wasn't happening. Only when he quit accusing her of duplicitousness, would she have a good side?

"Because we need to get into a school routine and that won't happen if they sleep here. Besides, they're excited about tomorrow. If they stayed, chances of them sleeping would be nil and they'd be tired tomorrow. Not going to happen."

Steve shrugged and hugged his daughters while her daughters changed into their pajamas. He escorted them to her car and helped Cassie load her stuff into the trunk.

"I'll be here at seven thirty to pick up the girls. They already laid their clothes out, just make sure they wash up and have breakfast. I'll bring their lunches with me." Cassie said, her voice curt and unfriendly.

He leaned on the car's back-quarter panel. "About this afternoon…"

Cassie held her hand up. "Don't. Your mind is made up, but I won't let those girls suffer because you're bull-headed and lack trust."

He moved off the car and rubbed his neck. She hoped she'd made an impression, but doubted it. She pulled out of the driveway without a backward glance and prayed.

Gabby and Bella fell asleep on the top of the covers and Cassie smoothed their hair and tucked them in, leaving night lights on to illuminate the hallway.

Tired after a pleasant, but hurtful day, Cassie unloaded the car, did laundry and made her grocery and to do list for the week. She showered, brushed her teeth and tumbled into bed.

She awoke with a start and sat straight up. Was it real? Or was it her overactive imagination brought on by yesterday's argument with Steve?

Her heart pounded, and she took deep breaths to calm herself.

She had to tell him. Or did she? Would the dream just underscore what he'd been saying all along? Shaking her head, she swung her legs to the floor. It didn't happen often, but she'd learned to focus on the specifics. Recording the details might be critical.

Padding barefoot through the darkened hallway and down the stairs, she flipped the kitchen light switch and squinted as she dug around in her purse for the notebook, then sat at the counter and wrote the tiniest details.

A few pages later, she put the pen down. With elbows on the counter, she cupped her face and stretched her neck. Her eyelids drooped, and she yawned. The adrenaline from the dream vanished, and she squinted at the clock. Three a.m. She'd be exhausted for the first day of school.

She'd had night visions like this before. She got up and extended her arms above her head, stretched and didn't bother with the notebook. Back in bed, she turned on her side and willed herself to sleep.

Chapter 18

Cassie gritted her teeth and prepared breakfast. Her daughters' endless chatter frayed her last nerve. A consequence of not enough sleep and excess worry. If the girls noticed her distress, they hadn't commented on it.

She organized school bags, stowed her notebook in her purse and took a moment to text Becka. They'd meet at their favorite coffee shop in an hour.

Cassie rubbed her temples as the girls barreled down the stairs and sat on the last step to put on their shoes. She prodded them into the car and drove to Steve's.

Stella and Tina waited on the front step. Steve kissed and hugged each girl and whispered to them.

Incredible in his charcoal gray suit and navy-blue tie, Cassie remembered his touch on her waist. She basked in that one touch. What in the world was wrong with her? She needed to forget about him as a man and think of him only as Stella and Tina's Dad. He waited for the girls to buckle themselves in before he went in the house without so much as a wave. Her daughters hadn't seemed to notice, but she had. And it hurt.

The first day chaos took longer than usual. Parents forgot how to drop off their children. Cassie drummed her fingers on the steering wheel and waited.

After the girls trotted into school, she inched her car into traffic. Cassie arrived first. She bought coffee, slid into a cozy booth and scanned through her notes. She let the aroma of hazelnut waft over her and glanced out the window.

"What are you writing?" Becka said as she peered at the notebook. "Have another blog post deadline?"

Cassie jerked her head and dropped her pen.

"Becka! You scared me."

Her sister-in-law shrugged and took a seat across from her. She straightened her pony tail and leaned closer to Cassie. "You were so enthralled in what's in that notebook you didn't see me come in or get my coffee. What's going on?"

"Sorry." Cassie closed the notebook with a snap. She sipped her coffee and avoided Becka's gaze. "I had a dream last night."

"Did you eat something that didn't agree with you? Wait. You had a dream about Steve?"

"Not exactly." Cassie rolled her eyes and bit into the crunchy pecan roll.

"Do the police have any leads?"

"You know you ask too many questions," Cassie murmured and steered the conversation away from Steve.

"Questions you're avoiding. Out with it."

"The police have no leads. And the dream wasn't about Steve. It was about finding Mia. I think I know what happened to her."

Becka's eyes widened, and she leaned in. "And?"

"I need someone else's perspective," Cassie said.

"Why? Go tell Steve your dream and see if you can find her. You don't need a perspective and don't question it. Your dreams have come true."

"Not that simple." Cassie's breath whooshed out.

"Why not?"

"Because Steve believes I had something to do with

167

Mia's disappearance. He thinks I know more than I'm saying. That she disappeared purposely, and I had a hand in it. Now I do know...at least I think I do...but I didn't when he accused me yesterday."

"Yesterday?" Becka's lips flattened. "Already I don't like where this is going."

"It's not what you think. He's been accusing me off and on all along. If I go to him with this now, he'll figure I knew all along and lied to him. I need to convince him I don't control my dreams, but when they occur, I have to pay attention."

"Tell him. If there's a remote chance of finding her, you must do it regardless if it'll damage your relationship with him." Becka held her hand up and shook her head. "Don't bother telling me you don't have a relationship because it's written all over your face."

"A relationship forged on necessity. He needed someone to care for his kids. That's all it is, Becka. I'm the nanny, nothing more and nothing less."

"Tell that to the judge."

"You're not helping. I need a strategy to deliver the news."

"We need to pray about it."

"You're right," Cassie whispered. If she said nothing, she'd feel guilty until she unburdened herself and it would alienate Steve further. If she told him now, it would sever their relationship, but at least her conscience would be clear. A no-win situation. Didn't matter what she did, there'd be consequences. God was greater and bigger than any circumstance. She'd listen to Him.

So they prayed. Fiercely and fervently for a way for

Cassie to reveal the dream without damaging their relationship and open a path to find Mia. They prayed for her safety and a softened heart for Steve.

It was all they *could* do.

Cassie threw the cup in the trash, and her voice quavered. "I need to spend some time alone."

Becka hugged her. "Text me if there's anything I can do."

The ominous gray clouds mirrored Cassie's soul, and a breeze stirred her hair. She shivered despite her long-sleeved sweater and sat on the well-worn bench.

Reading through various psalms, she focused on Psalm 25. 'The troubles of my heart are enlarged: bring me out of my distresses,' spoke to her heart. She lost track of time as the wind blew dead leaves and swirled them around her feet.

She tapped in a text to arrange a meeting with Steve, but waffled on sending it. Instead, she got up, and went directly to his office.

The office itself had a subdued air with a muted color palette and soft lighting. Never having been at his office, it intimidated her. She took the elevator to the top floor and asked to see Steve.

"There's a Cassie Verano here to see Mr. Nardelli." The receptionist nodded, put the phone down, and escorted her to Steve's office.

His inner sanctum mesmerized and fascinated her. It was so like Steve. Low-key, but impressive. Cassie glanced at the executive assistant nameplate on the desk.

The assistant eyeballed her. Should Cassie have waited until tonight to tell Steve? No. She had to talk to him now. Her navy slacks and soft violet sweater hugged her body. She held her head up. She couldn't lose her courage now, and she stiffened her back.

"I'll see if Steve can see you," the assistant said.

Cassie nodded and sank into the chair while the assistant checked in with Steve. She looked around the office as Steve strode forward, concern etched his face.

"Are the girls okay?"

"The girls are fine." She glanced at the assistant. "Could we speak in private?"

"Sure." He led her to his private office and shut the door. "Have a seat."

"I'd rather stand."

His eyebrows drew together, and he leaned against the desk. Steve crossed his arms and waited.

His silence only made what she had to say harder. "This is difficult." She paused. "I had a dream last night. About Mia." Her voice wobbled.

He straightened and narrowed his eyes. "What kind of dream?" Already the conversation was not going as she had hoped.

"I wrote it down." She opened her bag, pulled out her notebook and turned to the pages where her dream had been re-written while she waited for Becka.

"Regardless of what you think of me, I couldn't keep this dream to myself. It would've been wrong."

"Why don't you sit and tell me?"

She sat on the buttery soft leather sofa's edge, leaned forward, and clutched the notebook. The phone's jarring ring left knots in her stomach. He told his assistant to hold his calls and dropped into a matching club chair and placed his forearms on his knees.

She must be a sight. Smoothing her wind-blown hair

behind her ears, she took a deep breath.

"It seemed so real, so vibrant. I was there and experienced it all. Difficult to explain."

He squinted and couldn't seem to grasp her words.

"She was on a road I'd never driven before, out in the country maybe…going up hills…around bends. Are there any places like that around here?"

"Maybe."

Cassie closed her eyes. "She braked…maybe to avoid something in the road but…but the car skidded and lost control. The pavement was wet. She tried to stop." Cassie shook.

"I felt her fear…heard her heart thumping…saw her scream." Cassie blinked and shuddered. "Her car is in a shallow ravine."

Steve jumped up and paced. "You're just realizing this now? It's been weeks. She could be dead by now. The car could have blown up!"

"I don't control my dreams, Steve." Cassie breathed, tears welling in her eyes. "Mia is not dead. She's out there and I have to find her." She stood up and stomped toward the door.

He jumped up, grabbed her arm tight. "Just where do you think you're going? Where is she, Cassie?"

"Let go of me! Do you think if I knew where she was, I wouldn't have gone after her that first day? Do you think I'd have waited this long?" Her voice cracked. "I need to look for her."

Steve blocked her from the door. "We're going together. I'm not letting you out of my sight.

Steve's SUV climbed higher on the narrow road. It seemed they had been on the road for hours. The overcast skies kept their mood somber. They stopped for snacks but didn't waste time stopping for lunch.

His anger seemed to dissipate as they drove to all the places he could remember from his childhood. With his hands tightened around the wheel, he glanced at Cassie now and again. He gauged her reaction to the passing scenery.

She strained forward and stared at passing trees and peered into gullies. They proceeded around a tight bend on the mountain road, and she gasped. Her eyes widened, and she grabbed the dashboard. Her lip trembled. Steve pulled the car to the shoulder, slammed it in park and leaned toward her.

"Is this it?" His voice a quiet rasp.

The scent of her peach hand cream filled his nostrils and overwhelmed him. Now was not the time.

"I'm so scared." Her voice soft and her eyes brimmed with tears.

He observed her shiver even though fall temperatures hadn't dipped much. Her clenched hands rested in her lap. He folded his hands over hers and massaged them, then moved to her sweater clad arms and rubbed them to give her warmth.

"Let's get out," he whispered.

He unlocked the doors and made his way around to her side. She stood on the running board facing him. He reached for her hands and massaged them with his thumbs.

"We're going to find her. It'll be okay." His eyes bored into hers, and he moved in closer.

Her eyes closed, and she swayed toward him.

"It has to be." He whispered and wrapped his arms around her, holding her close. Was he trying to convince her or himself? He needed her strength and warmth right now.

His smooth cheek rubbed against hers. He heard her sigh. This was what was missing from his life. He drew her closer. His hands stroked her back. When he pulled away slightly and gazed at her lips, she bit her bottom lip and he groaned. He stared deep into her eyes, to her very soul. He wanted more, much more, but couldn't right now. They had to find his sister.

He drew her back into his arms and held her tight against his chest. The wind picked up, and her hair flew around his head. The crisp fall air mixed with her scent filled his nostrils.

"We have to go," she whispered in his ear.

He nodded, broke away and helped her from the SUV.

Chapter 19

Cassie stepped off the running board and released Steve's hand. She closed her eyes and remembered every dream detail. Opening her eyes, she breathed deep and twisted in a circle one step at a time, scrutinizing the landscape for topography features.

Conscious that Steve squinted to scan the surrounding area, he cupped his hands to his mouth and shouted Mia's name, but the wind only whistled through the trees. Steve's shoulders drooped, and he stopped. The corners of his mouth turned down.

The road ahead bent in an almost ninety-degree turn. She strode past the bend and stopped. No guard rails and flattened trees evidenced something had occurred here. Was it the storm or was it Mia's car? Steve jogged down the rocky and grass-covered embankment.

"Steve, wait." Cassie scampered to catch up, thankful she wore hiking boots. He slipped, and she grabbed his arm. They stumbled together down the difficult incline, but caught themselves.

"Your shoes are no match for this terrain. Take it slow," she said. "The last thing we need is for both of us to topple and get hurt."

"We need to find her," he said through gritted teeth. Did he believe her now? But did he believe her innocence? Time would tell.

Holding his hand tight and stepping forward through smashed saplings and tall weeds, they followed the destruction's path. Then Cassie spotted the car. She let his hand go and sprinted the rest of the way. She heard Steve as he slipped and slid behind her in the wet grass.

The car sat angled and submerged in a swollen creek. Cassie tiptoed to the water's edge and surveyed the car's shattered windshield. The water lapped near the driver's door handle. From her vantage point, there was no sign of Mia. Had she drowned? If she did, wouldn't she have been visible? Had she abandoned the car? Had someone picked her up? Where was she?

She glanced at Steve, whose expression mirrored hers. One of grief and pain.

Cassie tried to get as near to the car as possible, but Steve grabbed her.

"You'll fall in."

She gave a single nod and surveyed the creek's placid water flowing around the car. She shielded her eyes and scanned the creek's both sides. Steve pulled out his phone. "No signal. We have to call the police."

"Do you think she made it out before the car sank?" Cassie choked.

He jerked his head and frowned. His face grim. "Let's go." He led her in silence until they stopped near the SUV. "Still no signal. We have to go down the hill to make the call."

Steve took the mountain curves faster than he'd intended and skidded on wet leaves. She gasped, and he spared her a brief glance. White knuckles grasped the overhead door handle, and she strained against the seat but hadn't uttered a word.

What was it with her? Steve's anger returned full force. Why hadn't she had the dream the day Mia vanished? His sister might have been saved. He shook his head. What was the matter with him? His sister couldn't be dead. He would have known it, felt it in his soul.

When they arrived at the bottom of the hill, the phone had gained four bars. He dialed Detective Dean Landers's cell.

"We found Mia's car. She wasn't in it." He glanced at Cassie. "Can you meet me at Hardyville Road and route thirty-three?" He paused. "I know it's out of your jurisdiction. But it's your case. Can't you work with the locals?" Another pause and then, "How quickly can you get here? It'll be dark soon, and we need a tow truck. The car is partially submerged in an overflowing creek. It's a long story."

He pinched the bridge of his nose and heaved an elongated sigh.

She dug in her purse and pulled out the phone. "I need to text Becka. How long will it be before the police get here?"

"Totally forgot about the girls." His hand rubbed the back of his neck.

"I texted Becka earlier to pick them up at school and take them to her house if she didn't hear from me. We'll pick them up later. When do you think it'll be?"

"No idea." He grated, annoyed she'd even ask. Didn't she want to find Mia? Was his sister lying in the creek somewhere? Why hadn't he scanned the creek for her? Instead, he had flown into action, rushing down the hill to call the police. Maybe subconsciously he feared she was dead and couldn't face it. Now restlessness overtook him to continue the

176

search.

He punched on the hazards and jumped out to escape the tension.

Cassie pinned him with her stare. "Where're you going?"

"To get a flashlight." He watched her slump in the seat and slammed the door. He couldn't deal with her, couldn't even look at her. Fresh air might help his anger and frustration. He breathed deep and slapped the flashlight in his palm while he paced. How long would it be until the police showed up?

He eyed the skies that turned a dusty rose. The wind picked up and brought a chill that surrounded his heart.

Was she part of it? He wanted her out of his vehicle, but he couldn't leave her stranded. He would see this through. Steve flinched. What had he done? Had he invited his sister's murderer to care for his children? He'd hire someone from church to help him. He should have done so when he returned from Australia. What was wrong with him? How could he have hugged and kissed the woman who might have had a hand in his sister's accident and potential death?

Steve trotted over to the local police's vehicle when the tow truck pulled up. He explained the situation to both men. The tow driver declared a bigger truck with a longer tow line would be needed. Steve refused to wait for another truck. He'd wait at the site.

He climbed into the SUV and started the engine.

"Now what?" Cassie said.

"We go back." Steve bit out.

The local police followed him, and when they reached the bend, he pulled over and parked. She

177

moved to get out. "Stay here."

"No." And she jumped out and slammed the door.

The officer nodded to her and followed Steve down the embankment and through the trees. He twisted to see Cassie had followed them and grimaced.

When they got to the car, the officer looked from Steve to Cassie and back again.

Cassie stood in stony silence. Good. Otherwise he'd have chewed her head off. She crossed her arms and remained quiet.

The officer examined the area and surveyed the water's edge, then inspected the car.

"There doesn't appear to be any personal possessions in the car. The creek is swollen to ten times the normal size. If there hadn't been any rain, only the front tires would have been in the water, if that. Are you sure she didn't take off somewhere?" The officer said.

Steve gave Cassie a black look. "She'd have come home. Been almost a month. If she's dead, I want to bury her. I don't want her out here any longer than what she's been."

"She's not dead." Anger throbbed in her voice. "You're her brother. Her twin. Where's your faith?"

"How do you know she's not dead, Miss?" The officer's penetrating gaze held hers.

"I know in my spirit," Cassie said without shame or fear.

The officer rolled his eyes and glanced at Steve. "You need to be prepared for the worst-case scenario. When we find her, you may not want to see the body."

"No," Cassie screamed. "She's not dead."

"Aside from your spirit, how do you know? Are you involved somehow?" Steve's voice just loud enough for the officer to hear.

The officer whipped around and eyed Cassie. "Are you involved, Miss?"

"Other than having dreamed about what happened to her, no, I'm not involved." She crossed her arms.

The officer scrutinized her first then him. "Why don't you tell me the entire story?"

"I think I want to speak to my lawyer first," she said, and Steve's eyes grew black.

Worthy police detective, Dean Landers, tramped to them. "She'll need one." The tow truck driver followed close behind.

"We need to get this car to Worthy. It's part of a missing persons investigation," the detective said.

The other officer gave Dean his contact information, asked to be kept in the loop, and left.

"I'll need you at the station for an interview, Cassie," Detective Landers said.

"Not tonight. I have two small children, but I'll be happy to come in tomorrow after I've spoken to my attorney." The belligerence on her face wasn't lost on Steve.

"I'll guarantee she makes that appointment, Dean. Can we get the car out and see what's in it?" He said, his voice low.

Steve noted she fumed, but it didn't matter. He'd make sure she appeared for that interview.

The tow driver returned dressed in hip waders attached the tow line to the car's undercarriage.

Cassie shivered and turned away from Steve, but he didn't let her out of his sight.

"We'll need divers in the creek. It won't be till morning though, and we have to mark the area," Dean said. Steve gave a nod and turned angry eyes at Cassie.

As the towline pulled, the car groaned under the strain. Inch by inch the car rolled out. Water sloshed around the sides until it reached dry ground and exposed broken headlights and a crumpled hood.

Cassie stepped closer to the car, but Detective Landers held her back. "This may be a crime scene, you can't touch it."

"What does it matter? My prints are all over it. I've ridden with Mia quite a few times. Besides, I wouldn't touch it." Cassie clamped her mouth shut.

Steve stole a glance at the detective. He appeared to be making a mental note of Cassie's comment. He came by her side and looked in. No Mia. No purse or camera. Nothing. Her possessions could have washed away.

Oh God. Please bring her back alive and well. I can't take another accident.

Steve pointed to the interior. "The keys are in the ignition. Can we look in the trunk before it's hauled away?"

Detective Landers pulled a set of crime scene gloves from his pocket and opened the door. Water splashed out, and he jumped back. He removed the key from the ignition.

They waited by the trunk while the detective unlocked and opened it. Steve moved to grab the purse and camera, but the detective stopped him with a hand on his chest. "Everything in the trunk is part of the investigation. We'll process her car and belongings. Then, as soon as we figure out what happened and find your sister, we'll return her car and belongings. I know this is difficult, but we must follow protocol."

He pulled out his phone and took photos of the car and trunk.

"We can't allow you to photograph the car or its contents, Steve. This is an ongoing investigation."

"But I need to have a record of it since you're impounding everything." He wasn't above begging and didn't care if Cassie saw his vulnerability where his sister was concerned. "Please."

"It's not something we normally allow, but since you recovered the car, I'll let it slide just this once. I have your number, Steve, and I'll be in touch. In the meantime, we'll put divers in the water." A sad look crossed the detective's face.

"What are the chances she'll be found alive?" Steve said, his face downcast. He chanced a look at Cassie, and she frowned. Just the right amount of chagrin.

"I don't want to give you false hope but in situations like these, with the time that's passed, the flooding waters, and the car in the water, chances are slim." Detective Landers slammed the trunk lid and signaled the driver to haul the car to the police impound.

The detective sprayed the ground, the slope, and marked the highway. He looked all around. "It looks like faint skid marks, but I won't know for sure till the tow truck is out of the way."

"We'll wait," Steve said with crossed arms. Cassie stood at his side, silent and watchful.

The driver took ten minutes to get the car positioned on the truck and left. Detective Landers studied the roadway and pointed to the skid marks. He grabbed a tape and measured the marks.

"It looks as if she was going at a reasonable rate of speed…but it looks like she braked and flew over the edge. She must have panicked and hit the gas because she went quite a distance before coming to a stop," Detective Landers said, and turned to Cassie. "I want you at the station at ten a.m. tomorrow."

Steve eyed Cassie as she nodded and got in the SUV. He climbed in after her.

"What's Becka's address?" Steve said.

"One-zero-three Tilby Lane."

Steve punched in the address. The drive to Becka's passed in stilted silence.

Chapter 20

When they arrived at Becka's, it was the girls' bedtime. Cassie knocked on the door, and Becka answered. "Do you want some dinner?"

"No thank you, we have to leave. The girls have school in the morning." Steve's voice was quiet and forceful.

Becka's eyebrows rose. "Let's get the girls ready."

Cassie nodded.

"I'll wait in the car." Steve turned and stepped into the night.

"Is he always like that?" Becka whispered, when the door closed.

"How would you feel if your sister went missing, and you just found her car under water?" Cassie said.

"I have no family except you and Rob," Becka chided. "What happened?"

"Sorry. My muscles are on fire, and we need to get the kids home. I'll call you after they're in bed."

Cassie bundled the girls into the car, where the four girls promptly fell asleep. She smiled and caught Steve's gaze, which was even worse than when she shared the dream.

None of this is my fault, Lord. Please help him forgive me and help me be understanding.

Steve pulled into the firm's parking lot and helped her unbuckle the girls and helped her move the girls from his car to hers.

"I don't want our girls upset," he said before he shut the door. "I'll be at your home at nine forty-five after you drop off the girls. We're going to the police together."

Cassie didn't answer. Without so much as an 'I'll see you in the morning', he got in his SUV and left.

She called her attorney and explained the situation. He promised to bring his colleague who had more experience in criminal law. They'd fly from Strickland early in the morning and she promised to be at the airport in plenty of time for the meeting. Then she called Becka. While he was a family law attorney, she trusted him to act in her best interest.

She fell into bed and slept through her alarm, barely making it in time to take the girls to school. Cassie almost called him to take his girls himself, but didn't.

Racing to the airport, she arrived when Blake texted that he and his colleague, Attorney Trey Witfield, waited outside in arrivals. They jumped in the car and he made the introductions. "Do we have time for coffee?"

Cassie glanced at the digital clock. "Barely."

"Then let's stop so we can go over it again. Last night you weren't making sense," Blake said.

"Sorry. I was tired."

She told them the story and left out nothing except Steve's warm hug. His brows furrowed while Attorney Witfield listened intently as she spoke and sipped her coffee.

"A dream, Cassie? That could be damaging," Trey said.

"I had nothing to do with her disappearance. I sometimes have dreams that come true. Ask Becka.

She'll tell you."

"Your sister-in-law is not a good character witness because she's related. I hope you have other friends you could call on if the need arises," Blake said.

Cassie's heart plummeted. "Do you think it will?"

"Not sure. I'm not a criminal lawyer, I'm here to attend this briefing with Trey and protect your interests."

"They could just want to rule you out as a suspect. We won't know till we meet them," Trey said.

"My prints are all over Mia's car and she's still missing."

"Why wouldn't your prints be there? You're friends, right? Where were you when she'd gone missing? Tell me you weren't home alone," Trey said.

Cassie nodded, and tears pooled in her eyes.

"I took the girls to the gym that day and missed seeing Mia. I thought we'd have a picnic at her place the next day and would ask her that night, but she never showed."

Cassie got a text. "It's Steve."

"Don't respond," Blake said.

"I have to. I care for his daughters and he told me he'd be at my house this morning and we'd go together to the meeting."

"Tell him you'll be at the police station in ten minutes and shut off your phone," Trey said.

The air was muggy and it looked like rain. Again. Steve stormed over to Cassie just as they got out of the car at the police station. "What is wrong with you? I told you I'd pick you up. I knocked on your door for ten minutes."

Blake stepped in and put out his hand. "I'm Blake

Hardy and this is Trey Witfield, Cassie's attorneys."

Steve ignored the proffered hand and turned on Cassie. "You wasted no time getting your attorneys involved." His voice was ugly and accusatory.

"She'll answer the police's questions and then, we can have a conversation," Blake said.

Steve sneered. "If she's not guilty, she doesn't need an attorney, much less two."

Cassie shivered, but ignored him, and they marched into the nondescript building. Other than the small marquee, the only indication it was a police facility were the police vehicles outside.

Detective Dean Landers greeted them and introduced himself to Cassie's attorneys.

"Follow me," the detective said.

Steve trailed behind them, and her skin tingled at his closeness. What was the matter with her? She could be in trouble. And she's thinking about the hunky man who strode behind them? Stop it. *Stop it, now.* She had to focus on Mia. The narrow and dim halls closed in around her.

The detective opened a door and showed them in. "Steve, return to the lobby and take a seat. This shouldn't take long. I'll take your statement afterward." The detective shut the door in Steve's face.

Cassie sat ramrod straight in her chair and looked at the two-way mirror on the wall, wondering who was watching. *Help me say the right words at the right time and prove my innocence.*

"Do you have any objections if I record the interview?" The detective peeked at her negative nod and then at her attorney.

After asking her to state her contact information for the record, he began his interview.

"Tell me what happened in the past forty-eight hours."

"Steve's daughters had invited us to their house for a Labor Day picnic. Steve accused me of having a hand in Mia's disappearance."

"How so?"

"He thought I helped her escape," she said with air quotes around escape.

"Why would she need to escape?"

"Because he thought Mia was tired of being their caregiver. She wasn't, you know. She and I traded off caring for the girls so we both could have time for ourselves. Tough enough being a single mom or a single aunt, but she loved those girls and nothing would have kept her from them."

"So, he thinks she took off, and you helped her. Correct?"

"Yes, but it couldn't be further from the truth."

"Tell me about the dream."

She trembled, but Blake's hand squeezed her forearm in a gentle acknowledgement that he was there for her, and Trey gave her a single nod.

"I don't dream often but when I do, I pay attention because the dreams are usually premonitions. I awoke at two a.m. and wrote the details, then went back to bed because it was the first day of school."

"Do you have water?" Trey said.

"Sure thing." The detective grabbed the phone and asked someone to bring in three bottles of water. "Continue, Cassie."

"I took Steve's girls to school at seven-fifteen. Then I

met my sister-in-law for coffee so we could discuss the dream. We agreed Steve should know."

"Understood."

"I left the coffee shop after our discussion around nine and told Becka I needed time alone. So I went to our children's favorite park. I sat, read my Bible, and prayed. Then I drove to Steve's firm to tell him."

"What was his reaction?"

"Anger. He wanted to know why I hadn't dreamed about it earlier. I just thought...they're twins you know?" As if that would explain her thought process. Trey wasn't looking convinced either.

"They're twins?"

"Yes. Steve is older by a minute or two."

"Okay. Continue."

She peeked at the detective to gauge his reaction and then glanced at her attorney. "I explained I don't control my dreams, and I wanted to look for her even though I hadn't the slightest idea where to find the location I saw in my dream."

"You would search for this place without knowing where it was?"

"Yes."

"Why?"

"Because Mia's my friend and I wanted to find her."

"Continue."

"He said I wasn't going alone, and we'd search together. We drove around and discussed where it could be. There was a place his parents took them when they were little. He hadn't thought about it before, but my description brought back memories."

"Was it the same place?"

"No. We drove around till I saw a road, and my gut

churned. So, we took it. But he'd never been on that road. He seemed to think it wasn't there when he was a kid. I figured she may have researched a perimeter to determine how far she could go without being late for the kids, but the location was further afield."

"When I saw the landscape, I realized we were in the right place. We got out of the car and I did a three-hundred-sixty degree turn to observe all the topography. In the meantime, he yelled her name."

"I jogged to the bend in the road and that's when I saw the trees and trampled grasses."

Cassie stopped and sipped her water.

"We followed the path and found the car in the creek. I looked up and down the creek searching for her."

Cassie shivered at the memory.

"Why?"

"Because I couldn't see her in the car and I had to know if she was lying somewhere or worse under water. I prayed that wasn't the case, but my gut tells me she's alive."

"I wanted to get closer to the car, but Steve stopped me. He didn't want me to fall in. Then when the officer came, he questioned me about my involvement and that's when I said I wanted my attorney."

"This is all innocuous, detective," Trey said. "My client has taken over caring for Steve's children till Mia returns. Why would she do that if she were involved? She wouldn't. She'd want to get as far away from the situation as possible."

"I didn't know you continued to care for his daughters after he returned from Australia, Cassie," the detective said.

"Yes. The girls had been with me for a few days and they were already traumatized, having been left at the gym with no one to pick them up, and their father so far away. Besides, Steve asked me to." Cassie shrugged.

"Can you make copies of your phone bill since the disappearance with all the phone numbers you called and received? Highlight the calls to and from Mia," the detective said.

"Are you issuing a warrant for the phone bill?" Trey said.

"I believe Cassie would want cooperate in any way she can, so a warrant would be unnecessary. But I'll have one prepared," Detective Landry said.

"I'll cooperate and give you the phone bills."

"You said your fingerprints are on the car?"

"Yes. Occasionally we carpooled. Her prints are on my car, too."

"Is the interview over?" Blake said.

The detective pulled out a business card and handed it to her. "Pretty much. I'd like to see your notes on the dream, though. If you could copy them and email them that would be great."

"It's in my shorthand, but I'll transcribe them."

"Copy us on them, Cassie," Trey said.

"You're free to go, but don't leave the area," the detective said.

She nodded, and they left the room. They passed Steve who was deep in a phone conversation, but glared when they strode past.

Chapter 21

When Frank entered the police station, Steve shook his hand and stared at his grim face. He'd advised Steve to wait for him since he'd already been interviewed, but now that the car had been found, the detective would want to talk to him again. They followed him through the narrow corridor and stepped into a windowless room. The door shut with a thunk, and Steve's heart dropped.

What if they charged him in connection with his sister's disappearance? Why hadn't he called Frank before going off with Cassie to look for Mia? What an idiot! He lost good judgment when Cassie was around, and his brain went on hiatus.

"You and your sister are twins, correct," the detective said. Why was he asking this? He knew this from when Mia first went missing.

"That's right. Does it matter?"

"Probably not. Is Cassie still caring for your daughters?"

"As of today, she'll no longer be caring for them. I'll be handling their care till Mia is found."

"What if she isn't found?"

"Then I'll hire someone. But I won't do that till I find my sister." His breath whooshed out. "Dead or alive."

Detective Landers squinted and Frank squeezed Steve's forearm to keep him in check.

"That's an odd thing to say. You've been optimistic about this entire investigation. Why are you doubting she's alive, now? Is it because I said the chances are slim or because the car was found in water?"

He looked away. "A little of both, I guess."

"You both have lawyered up."

"Can you blame them?" Frank said. "They found Mia's car under peculiar circumstances so it makes sense you're going to question the validity of their statements."

Detective Landers nodded. "We looked through the trunk. The camera had animals, birds and landscape photos. They appeared to have been taken in other locations. Being a digital camera, we can get locations from the photos and piece together a timeline. There were some family shots too, but they appear to be older. She had shoes, a sweater and other items you might find in a trunk."

Steve felt violated for Mia. "Was there anything in her purse that might tell us anything? Why do you think the purse was in the trunk?"

"We haven't examined everything in the purse so I can't say. But I'd guess if she was taking pictures she didn't want to haul around a purse or leave it on the front seat."

"Makes sense," Steve said, and Frank nodded.

Frank pulled out a business card. "Call us if something comes up. We know you can't release her personal effects or the car until the case is closed."

Dean gave a slight nod and opened a manila folder. "I wanted to brief you on the divers. They were there at dawn and dragged the creek but found nothing. My guess is she didn't drown, but we believe she's injured from the broken glass. There was blood but we can't confirm because the rain deteriorated it. We're still looking for blood samples in other parts of the car."

His heart plummeted. His sister was injured. "Have

you checked the hospitals?"

"They'd been put on notice to call if she showed up when she went missing. We checked other hospitals near where the car was found. No one of her description had been admitted since she disappeared. They all have the photos you gave us."

"What about hospitals further afield?" Frank said.

"We checked hospitals in a fifty-mile radius. We could check a hundred-mile radius but I don't think she would have gotten that far given she had been injured."

"The way the window is smashed, we think her injuries, whatever they were, may have been from a combination of the glass and possibly the air bag but we can't be sure. If that's the case, there would have been…never mind. She may also have injured her arms or legs from the glass."

Steve froze. He couldn't think or talk. All he could think of was that his sister was injured or dead.

"What about Cassie?" Frank said.

"She's answered all our questions. I don't know about the dream she had, but we've had instances where there've been good leads from people with premonitions. I don't discount them, but I'm careful, you understand."

"Can you give her a polygraph test?" Steve said.

Frank looked at him as if he'd lost his mind.

"For what purpose, Steve? Frank, you look like you don't think that's wise, why?" The detective said. "It's not something we normally do in this type of case."

"Steve is thin-skinned where Cassie is concerned. I know Cassie. She goes to our church and is involved in the children's ministry. I'd be shocked if she's involved in Mia's disappearance other than her dream," Frank said.

Steve glared at his friend. "I'm not thin-skinned. I'm cautious. She has secrets."

"You told me yourself, she told you her secret," Frank said.

The detective straightened. "Secrets?"

"Unrelated to Mia or her disappearance," Steve said. "But I still don't know if she's involved."

"So she said." The detective took his folder and got up.

"Wait. She said she was involved in Mia's disappearance?" Steve said.

"No. She said *you* thought she was involved." The detective moved toward the door.

"Steve, you're being paranoid again. I don't believe for a moment Cassie had anything to do with Mia's disappearance. Let's go to lunch and talk about this," Frank said.

"Excellent idea," the detective said. "I'll call you when we have a lead."

Steve gave a single nod.

Over pizza, Frank railed at Steve. "You know in your heart Cassie had nothing to do with Mia's disappearance. You need to stop comparing every woman to Laura."

"I can't help it."

"You have to forgive Laura, Steve. You can't move forward in your life till you do."

The restaurant's sounds reverberated in his brain. The garlicky sauce almost turned his stomach. He couldn't eat or think. He wanted to go home and drown his sorrows, but that would do no good. Not for Mia, his daughters, or himself.

"How do you propose I forgive my dead wife, Frank?"

"I have some ideas but right now is not the time. We need to find Mia first. I forgot to ask the detective a question. Could you get him on the phone?"

"Sure." Steve dialed the number and got the detective. "Steve and I were stunned, and I totally forgot to ask you if the vicinity where Mia was found was being canvassed." Frank nodded and hung up the phone.

He shoveled more pizza in his mouth, chewed and swallowed. "You need to go home and rest. Don't go back to work, and come to men's group tonight."

After dropping off Blake and Trey, Cassie got a text from Steve telling her he would take and pick up the girls from school and their activities from now on.

Huge wracking sobs made her face red and her body quiver. She blew it. What else could she have done? Cassie couldn't even work, not that she had anything to do, but she could have planned her next book.

What about the girls? Would he deny the girls their friendship because of her? Gut-wrenching groans came from the pit of her stomach and unleashed another torrent of tears.

She let calls go to voicemail, and didn't look at the phone until Becka texted and she realized school would be over soon. The last thing she wanted was for them to see her red face. They hadn't seen her with puffy eyes or a red face since they moved and laying this on them was not an option.

Trudging to the kitchen, she poured ice and water in a bowl and flattened cold compresses on her cheeks and eyes. Sunglasses would help.

She texted Becka she wasn't up to a conversation and would call her later that evening.

The phone rang again. She didn't recognize the number and let it go to voicemail. It was local. When she listened to the voicemail, it was Detective Landers. Why would he want her to come in and take a polygraph after all?

She called Blake. "That detective wants me to go in for a lie detector test. Why do you think they changed their mind?"

"Just a formality. He already has you on tape. Give me his number. I'll have Trey call him."

She gave him the number and hung up. When he called back, Blake told her to call the detective and schedule it. He would not be there to hold her hand.

The tears continued to fall, and she had to get a hold of herself.

Her daughters waited with Steve's girls and their teachers when Cassie arrived to pick them up. Thankfully, makeup and a stern self-talk made her ready to face Steve. Kids ran to their parents' cars amid laughter and exuberance for the school day to be over.

The girls would have been excited to visit for a few hours until Steve picked them up, but tonight would be different.

She took the teacher aside and informed her Steve would pick up his children and she'd have to break it to her children and his. She was certain he would not have the finesse to deal with such a task.

Her sadness changed into anger for their children.

How dare he take away this wonderful friendship for his daughters and hers?

Forgive me, Lord. And help me forgive him. I don't want this. I'm innocent of all wrongdoing. Expose the truth, Lord.

Cassie squatted before his girls. "I have a wonderful surprise for you." The girls grinned ear to ear. "Your daddy will pick you up from school today."

The smiles turned to frowns, and Stella crossed her arms. "Why? We want to go to your house. We always go to your house after school and gymnastics classes. You said we could stay with you till Daddy picked us up." Cassie recognized the mutinous stances. Not only from his children, but hers, too.

Who would watch them while Steve was at men's group? Probably Fiona.

"Well, I'm sorry sweetheart but your daddy texted and said he'd be here to pick you up. Tell you what. I'll wait here with you just to make sure he comes for you, okay?"

"That won't be necessary. I'm here," Steve said.

He seemed as miserable as she was. If the look he gave her was one of misery and not something else.

"Daddy, we want to go over Mrs. V's house to play. That's what's supposed to happen." Stella said.

"Not today, Stella."

"But Daddy…"

"I said. Not. Today. Now get in the car." He nodded to her, hustled the girls into the SUV, got in, and drove away.

"Mama, why couldn't they come and play with us. Doesn't Mr. Steve like us anymore?" Bella said.

"Oh honey, I don't think that's the case at all. I think

Steve may have made plans for his daughters that didn't include us. They are a separate family, you know."

"But I want them to be our family. Why can't they be our family? Why can't you marry him like Charlotte married Daddy? Then they could be our sisters," Bella said.

Cassie nearly choked. Whatever gave them the idea Steve could be anything more than their friends' father?

Gabby stood silent as a sentry and watched Steve drive away with their friends. She looked pitiful staring after them.

"Tell you what. Since you haven't any homework, why don't we get a hamburger and French fries?"

Normally a trip to the local burger joint elicited whoops and hollers, but today they merely shuffled to the car and sat in unnerving silence.

Cassie tried to make light of it. "We'll go home and you can change into your play clothes and we'll go to the park."

"It won't be much fun without Stella and Tina," Gabby said.

This would be more difficult than she imagined and was her fault for not promoting other friendships for her children. She never guessed this would happen and it broke her heart to see her daughters unhappy.

The two miserable little girls moped at the park, but then settled in to watch a television program. When they had gone to bed, Cassie called Becka and told her everything.

How this would turn out, she had no idea.

Steve called Fiona to look after the girls while he went to men's group. She frequently offered to give Cassie a break, but he refused, given her care for her sister.

The girls were gloomy, and no amount of extra ice cream could make them happy. They had been looking forward to spending a few hours at Cassie's before they came home. He hadn't realized just how close the girls had become and he'd screwed it up again.

The men of the church would give him what-for. It seemed he couldn't do a thing right in his personal life. Thank goodness his business life thrived. But at what cost? His sister was still missing, and now his daughters were still and silent. His heart ached for them, his sister and himself.

Men's group went better than he had expected. The men comforted him and even Frank didn't bring up the Cassie debacle, but he was certain it wouldn't be forgotten. Frank bided his time. Its ugly head would rear up when least expected.

When he walked into his home that night the house was quiet. Fiona sat in Mia's favorite chair.

"We need to talk, laddie," Fiona said.

"Not now, Fiona." He walked into the kitchen and took out lunchmeat and cheese and made himself a sandwich. She followed him.

"Now, laddie." Fiona's tone brooked no argument.

If he didn't want to talk about something he shouldn't have to, even if the person asking had known him all his life. Had even changed his diapers. He cringed. No getting around it.

He sat and ate without responding and hoped she would give up and go home. Wishful thinking.

"The girls tell me you picked them up today. You told

them you'll be taking them and picking them up every day from school and at the gym. They didn't cry, but they were the saddest I've seen them since Laura was alive."

He said nothing. He couldn't. How could he justify what he'd done? It was in their best interest to stay as far away from Cassie and her girls. Oh, they'd see their friends at school and at the gym, but that's as far as it would go. They'd have to cultivate other friendships, that's all.

"That's right," he said.

"Why? Because Mia's car was found? Or is it because you want to distance yourself from Cassie because she means something to you?"

Steve glared. "I think she had more to do with Mia's disappearance than she's saying."

Fiona harrumphed and got up. "I see the way it is."

"Yeah. And what's that?" He needed to hear it. What was wrong with him? Was he a masochist?

"You're looking for ways to distance yourself and you've latched on to this idea of Cassie being involved to do it. Not going to work, you know." The disgust clear on her face.

"Why is that?" He stuffed his mouth with more sandwich to keep himself from talking further. Definitely a masochist.

"Because Mia will turn up, then you'll have no more excuses, laddie." With that, she got up. "I'll be here tomorrow at three thirty to watch the girls while you work."

Chapter 22

Lack of sleep took a toll on Cassie. She was short-tempered with the girls, but she made the trek to drop them at the pre-arranged meeting point on time.

Her mule-faced daughters begged her not to take them, but Nico had a right to see them. Too many other things vied for her attention and tackling the child labor issue proved harder to deal with than she'd imagined. Her missing friend weighed heavily on her mind.

She desired nothing more than to crawl into bed and stay there, but Fiona called as she pulled into the garage.

"Lassie, I wanted to invite you for tea and a slice of cinnamon cake."

A tiny, sad smile crossed her face. "That's a lovely offer, but I don't think it's wise."

"I understand and I dinnae hold you responsible for anything. I'm praying for you...and for Steve.

Cassie liked Fiona, but she could barely talk.

"Stella and Tina mope around the house and Steve cannae get them to smile no matter what he does. Even promises of trips to the zoo and museum dinnae help."

Cassie rested her head against the steering wheel. "I'm sorry to hear that."

"The more they asked him for playtime with Gabby and Bella, the angrier he became till they stopped asking. They creep around the house like monks in a monastery. It's frightful."

"His decision. We have to respect his wishes."

"I thought if you spoke to him, he might have a change of heart."

"I've seen him several times at school. He won't look in my direction, much less have a conversation. We have to let it go."

"Well, then. I'll let you get on with your day." Fiona's voice sounded hurt.

She wanted to call Dean Landers, but she didn't dare. Not knowing what happened to Mia was killing her. Probably killing Fiona, too. She didn't want to bring it up just to add oil to the already blazing fire of loss. It broke Cassie's heart. All of them suffered. Why couldn't he act like an adult and let the kids play?

Monday dawned bright and clear with no hint of rain. The weather change called for heavier sweaters and warm socks. She sniffed wood smoke in the air as she made her way to the police department.

In the station, she stopped dead. A week had gone by and both sets of girls grieved their severed playtime, but Steve appeared to not have a care in the world. Unbelievable.

Cassie would not let him get to her so she breezed by him and requested Detective Landers.

The officer motioned toward a chair, and she dropped into the uncomfortable wooden seat.

She stared straight ahead but could see Steve out of the corner of her eye and braced as he sauntered over. He stood in front of her but she focused on his shoes. Cassie didn't lift her gaze, otherwise she'd cry again. Fretting over him had to stop.

"What are you doing here, Cassie?"

"I'm here to see Detective Landers," she said, without

looking at him.

"Why?"

She'd be darned if she would tell him anything. If he wanted to know, he'd have to ask the detective. "Why not?"

Detective Landers stepped into view. "You're both here."

The comment startled Cassie, and Steve frowned. "What does that mean?"

"I'll take every time-saver I can get," Detective Landers said. "Cassie, come with me. Steve, wait in the lobby, I'll be right with you."

"But…" Steve said.

"I'll be right back." The authoritative tone of the detective's voice came through loud and clear.

"Fine," Steve huffed.

Cassie swallowed her chuckle. He didn't like being thwarted. Too bad.

Detective Landers brought her into a room with a polygraph specialist and explained what they'd do. Cassie nodded.

The detective grinned. "Did I detect a smirk when I told Steve to wait?"

"Maybe," she said, reluctant to show an expression on her face.

He laughed. "I'll be back in thirty minutes."

Steve paced the lobby. What was she doing here? Why did the detective seem happy both of them were here? He didn't think it had anything to do with killing the proverbial two birds with one stone explanation. He'd get answers. And soon.

Detective Landers caught up with him. "Pacing, Steve? You're strung tighter than a snare drum."

"You wanted to see me?"

"We finished processing Mia's car. We found traces of uncompromised blood and verified it against her recent blood test. Definitely your sister's.

"You think she's dead?"

"I just don't know, Steve. I'm sorry. No leads, and the creek has almost returned to normal. We sent volunteers to look for her, but no one spotted her. It's a remote area. I can't even guess where she could be now or how far she could have gone after the accident. Whether she was picked up or what. We'll keep looking."

Steve's shoulders slumped. He tried not to think about his missing sister. He couldn't. The pain was too great. Instead focusing on the girls and their needs and leaving business decisions to his team. Lack of sleep since Mia's car had been found caused Fiona's concern for his well-being to move up a notch and he couldn't stand it.

At his nod, Dean continued. "We can't release the car or her personal possessions but we did make copies of the photos on her camera. It's the best I can do until the case is closed, one way or another. Come with me."

The detective led him to a nondescript corner office barely big enough to house them both. The station's sounds muffled once the door closed.

"Why is Cassie here?" He grasped at anything to keep himself from thinking about Mia, his girls or Fiona.

"I wondered when you'd get around to asking again. All we have is a car crash scene. No body and it doesn't look like foul play."

The blow came like a hammer. Another fiery coal on

his head. "A polygraph? You said it was unnecessary."

"The situation is so out of the ordinary that we decided since she offered, we're taking her up on it."

Steve sank in the chair and rubbed the bridge of his nose. "When will you know the results?"

"Later."

"When?"

"I'm not at liberty to say."

"Why?"

"Because it's part of the investigation. If something arises, I'll let you know."

"Fine."

Apologizing to Cassie was at the bottom of his agenda. Now this. Talking to her now about the girls would do no good. Where was his sister? He needed to know she was okay.

Detective Landers rifled through his desk and produced a large manila envelope. Steve's heart pounded. He gulped and touched the packet with Mia's photos.

The detective grabbed his arm before he could rip it open. "Take it home. It might be easier if you look at them there."

Steve squeezed the envelope to his chest. "I'm really worried about Mia. Did the divers find anything? What about the canvassing? I haven't slept and can't think straight, but I want every detail. Even if it seems insignificant."

"The divers haven't found anything. That's a good thing. We're still stumped as to where she is. But don't count on any of the polygraph results until after the case is closed."

He left the building, and his spirits sank. He wished he could share his pain with Cassie. He bumbled things in a big way. Now, when she probably needed support and a friend, he'd caused her and himself untold grief. Her attorney hadn't even stood with her. He shook his head. Fiona would not be happy, and the kids were beyond distressed. Way worse than when Laura was alive.

I've been such a jerk and I need to forgive Cassie. How can I get things back to the way they were before I went down this path? I'm desperate.

The drive to school took longer, and Steve worried about Cassie and her girls. He should text her but he guessed she wouldn't respond. The few words spoken at the police station only made him angrier. Not at her but at himself for having been such a heel. His worry for Mia made him appear a crazy man.

He didn't know how he would climb out of this sleek-walled pit, but he needed to reconcile his sister's disappearance with Cassie's involvement, which still rankled.

The terrible fog caused him to arrive late for work.

His assistant set a cup of coffee on his desk and cradled a mug in her hands. "Did you hear about the massive pileup on route two-seventy this morning?"

"No. Not any of our people, I hope." He grabbed his cup, sipped and cast a worried glance at his assistant.

"I've asked department heads to check on everyone who hasn't shown up for work. I think two people died plus several injured folks sent to various hospitals."

"Let's pray no one from our firm was involved."

"I'll let you know."

The phone rang later in the morning.

"Steve, it's Detective Landers."

He gulped, and his stomach tightened.

"We think Mia has been admitted to Columbus General as a Jane Doe. We sent pictures around to the hospitals when we found her car, but it may or may not be her. Until you see her, we won't know for sure."

"I'm on my way."

He hung up and grabbed his jacket, then stopped and punched in a number. "Fiona. They think Mia has been admitted to Columbus General as a Jane Doe. I'm leaving right now. Could you pick up the girls?"

"Aye."

"I'll call you as soon as I can."

"Cancel all my appointments for the rest of the week," Steve said as he raced out of his downtown office.

The trip to the medical center took longer than he expected. He should call Cassie. But what would he say? Hey, I was a jerk and Mia's been found? No, he couldn't. Too much time had passed to repair that rift. Maybe Fiona could call her instead. He was such a coward. Instead, he called Frank on the hands-free. He had to call someone, or he'd burst.

"They think they found Mia. She's at Columbus General."

"Are you on your way?" Frank said.

"Ten minutes out. She's listed as a Jane Doe so it might not even be her."

"They probably listed her as a Jane Doe because she didn't have ID, and they'll need positive identification by a family member. Why else would

207

Detective Landers call? He wouldn't want to give you false hope."

He expelled a long breath. "Dean said she's stable and in intensive care. He's meeting me there."

"I'm headed out, too."

Steve met Frank in the parking deck and they rushed through the hospital doors. The antiseptic smell nearly made Steve gag. He stopped dead, and sweat dripped down his back. The last time he was in a hospital… *No, don't think about that.*

Frank grabbed his arm and tugged. "I'm here. Be strong."

Detective Landers stepped forward and flashed his badge at a security officer. "This way." He pressed the button for the elevator.

Steve choked out the words. "Why is she unconscious?"

"The woman admitted has pneumonia, Steve. The hospital called when she was life-flighted with others from the pile-up and we got here as soon as we could. She has other injuries, but they've indicated someone attended her. I have men questioning the staff to find out what happened."

"Is she going to die?" he whispered. He grasped the lifeline that it was her and not some no-named woman who just happened to be admitted.

"Ask the doctors, Steve. They won't tell us much and I couldn't see her. Confidentiality laws and all that. I'm not even certain it's her. The hospital said so, but…"

When they exited the elevator, Doctor Garrett introduced himself and escorted Steve to the woman's room.

Steve ran to her side, peered into her face, and gave the other men a brisk nod. He swallowed, then composed himself. "What's her condition?"

"She has pneumonia and was barely conscious when she came in. We're pumping her with antibiotics and monitoring her progress. She's had various cuts and bruises consistent with an auto accident. And she looks like the photo that had been sent to us. But without a positive identification from a family member, we kept her as a Jane Doe. Both wrists were fractured although one was an older fracture and one is a fresh fracture." The doctor consulted her chart. "She also has a hairline fracture in her right ankle. She probably thought it was only a sprain."

"How was she able to care for herself these past weeks with two fractured wrists? It looks like her other wounds are healing," Steve said.

"Someone did an excellent job of setting the wrists, but she'll need physical therapy and probably plastic surgery on those facial cuts. Whoever set her fractures may not have had the skill set to sew the cuts, so they bandaged her as best they could. Until the antibiotics kick in and she wakes up, we're at a loss as to know what happened. She's a lucky little lady."

"Did you run the kit?" Detective Landers said.

"It was negative," the doctor said.

Steve looked from the detective to the doctor. "What kit?"

Frank intervened and pulled Steve away from the bed. "A rape kit."

Steve choked. "What?"

The detective joined them. "It was negative. Standard

procedure in cases like these. No one took advantage. It's a good thing. We're trying to establish where she flew in from. They keep excellent records and we should know quickly enough."

The detective, the doctor, and Frank left the room so he could have a private moment with his sister.

He touched her fingers. Tears gathered as he gazed at his sister. His stomach churned. Her paleness bled into the sheets. He sniffed and swiped his hand over his eyes. Where had she been? Who had taken care of her? He shook his head. So many questions but, thank God, she's alive.

"Mia. It's Steve. I'm so glad you're back." He massaged her forearm and studied her nails, which were cracked and ragged. How did they get like that? She was so thin and her hair looked lifeless. She needed a haircut. As soon as she came home, he'd make sure she'd be pampered and have anything she wanted.

Thank you, Lord, for bringing her home. Forgive me for not being more appreciative of what she has done for me and the girls. Forgive me for my treatment of Cassie. But most of all, forgive me for my lack of faith and trust in You.

He wouldn't leave the hospital until she did. He'd call...He couldn't. He needed to care for his daughters.

Frank came in and Steve continued to massage her forearm.

"I called Fiona to let her know it is Mia. Why don't we pray for her?" Frank said.

Words died in his throat. Frank put a hand on Steve's shoulder while he prayed. A weight the size of a millstone fell from Steve's shoulders.

For three days, Steve never left the hospital. Between Fiona, the women at church and Frank's wife, the girls were well cared for. He called them before they left for school and when they got home from school while he remained at his sister's side. His secretary brought his laptop and files so he could monitor Mia and still get work done.

The antibiotics had begun their work, so the doctors did surgery on her wrists and now they had to wait for her to wake up. One nurse prompted him to hold her forearm and talk to her. Patients heard conversations even if they couldn't respond.

He didn't know what to say. What could he say? So, he relayed tidbits about Fiona, the girls, their school and activities. He told her about the scheduled fall gym meets and told her about all the cards and flowers that were sent.

He alternated between working on his laptop and talking to her. He had no more breath in his body to wrangle a response. Mired in thought, he stared at his computer screen and hadn't noticed the nurse who came in.

"How long have you been awake?" The nurse said.

"I'm awake," he said, but when he looked up, he saw the nurse had spoken to his sister.

"Mia!" His laptop slid to the floor, and he sprinted across the room to grab her fingers.

With fear in her groggy eyes, she pulled her hand away and whispered, "Who are you? Where's Shannon?" She grabbed the nurse's hand and pleaded. "Don't leave me."

"Honey, I won't leave you." The nurse called the

desk and asked for the doctor. She used code words he didn't understand.

Not only did his sister not know him, she feared him. "Mia…"

The nurse's quiet tone warned him. "I think it'd be best if we waited for Doctor Garrett."

Steve nodded, but his lips formed a straight line.

Mia's eyes darted from the nurse to Steve and back again. "Where's Shannon?"

"Who's Shannon, honey?" The nurse touched Mia's shoulders and focused on her face.

Mia's eyes glistened with tears, and her voice rasped. "Shannon. The guy… The guy who took care of me. He bandaged and took care of me because my wrist and ankle hurt so much. I think I broke my wrist, but I can't remember how."

The nurse smoothed her covers, checked her drips and glanced at Steve. "Why don't we wait for Doctor Garrett?"

Mia's agitation escalated. "Why won't you tell me where he is? And why is that guy in my room? Tell him to leave."

The nurse repeated in a forceful tone. "Doctor Garrett will be here any minute."

When the doctor walked in, he stood by Steve. "You are awake. You're…"

She cut him off with biting words. "Of course, I'm awake. My eyes are open, aren't they? Why won't anyone tell me where Shannon is? Is he hurt?"

The doctor patted her hand. "Now…Now… Don't get upset. We don't know where or who Shannon is. Do you remember anything?" Doctor Garrett said as he took her pulse.

212

This was the Mia he knew. His sister didn't pull any punches and right now the monitor by her bed showed her racing heartbeat.

"Your name is Mia Nardelli. You were in a single car accident. Apparently, Shannon helped you. Do you remember any of it?"

"I only remember waking up in Shannon's cabin and being afraid. He asked me my name, but I didn't know what it was." She pointed to Steve. "Why is that guy here? I don't know him."

The Doctor studied Mia, then peered at her brother. Steve clamped his mouth shut to keep from talking.

"Nurse, bring me a mirror." With a single nod, the nurse left the room.

"Why do I need a mirror? I know my face is all banged up. Why won't you tell me who this guy is and why he's in my room. He looks like he'll cry any minute." She rolled her eyes and turned her face away.

The doctor turned to Steve. "Is she always like this?"

"Pretty much."

Mia shifted her head toward him. "Don't tell me I'm married to him!"

"Ah no." Steve choked and pulled his lips in.

The nurse came in and Doctor Garrett handed the mirror to Mia. "Look at yourself, then look at Steve and tell me what you see."

Mia cast her eyes away from the mirror. "I don't want to and I don't want to see my damaged face."

"If you look in the mirror, you'll know who Steve is."

"Steve, huh?"

She grabbed the mirror from him and her eyes welled up. "I'm hideous. So scarred."

213

Steve squeezed her forearm. "Don't worry about the scars, Mia. We'll find the best plastic surgeon in the country."

She gazed at his hand squeezing her arm and she pulled away. "I still don't know you."

The doctor turned to Steve. "Maybe you should get a cup of coffee while I examine her."

"He's not my boyfriend, is he?" He heard her whisper on his way out.

The next day, Mia yelled at him to leave and not come back until he found Shannon. Heck, he didn't even know who Shannon was or where to find him. Even Dean Landers didn't know who left her at the clinic. In all the accident confusion, no one attempted to get information from the man who left her with them.

Unless the guy came forward, they'd never know. Why hadn't he shown up at the hospital for her? Steve would have liked to thank him. He thanked God Shannon had not taken advantage of her.

When Fiona visited Mia the following day, she sneered. "Who are you and why are you here?"

"Och, lassie. Don't you remember me?"

That was the wrong thing to say, Steve thought. She'd flown off the handle so many times in the past twenty-four hours even the nurses didn't want to come in. He could understand her frustration. Having no memory must be exasperating.

"No. Why should I?" Mia adjusted her covers and a look of boredom crossed her face.

The doctor moved her to a regular room, but her damaged lungs still needed extra oxygen, so a nasal cannula wrapped around her head.

"And what's with the accent? Is it fake? And you, Mr. Steve. Why so quiet? You're always talking. This stranger comes in and you clam up."

Fiona's eyes grew to the size of bowling balls and her lips pursed. Steve could tell she held herself in check, but much more of this and there'd be an all-out brawl. She plopped a container on Mia's tray. "I brought you cinnamon cake."

Fiona turned toward the door. Steve glimpsed the hurt in her eyes and it stabbed him to the quick. Fiona hadn't believed him and she now witnessed it herself.

Steve caught up to her in the hallway, took her arm and turned her around. He wrapped both arms around her as if she had been his mother. "I'm so sorry, Fiona."

"Och. I know she's not herself. I'll keep praying."

Were these his sister's true colors? It couldn't be. He never remembered her being this belligerent. He requested church members not visit because strangers upset her. If he and Fiona, who were her family, distressed her this much, he couldn't imagine her reaction to church members.

When Steve stepped in the room, Mia stuffed a bite of cake into her mouth. "You wasted no time chowing down on the cake."

After she swallowed and took a drink, her face turned red. "It smelled fantastic. I couldn't resist." She shrugged and her eyes narrowed. "Are you going to tell me who you are? And who that lady was?"

The doctor had cautioned him to get to know her again and relay bits of information a little at a time. But darn it, he grew tired of her not knowing him and to hurt Fiona? Disgraceful.

He sat on the lounge chair he'd used for the past week and pressed the bridge of his nose with his fingers. How would Cassie have handled Mia's amnesia?

"I'm your brother," Steve blurted. He hadn't meant to say it quite like that, but there it was.

"We're related by blood?"

"More than that. We shared an amniotic sac."

She shot up and licked her lips again. "We're twins?"

A single nod. She fumbled around in the drawer and pulled out the mirror. She stared at his face and then at her reflection. Tears formed as she touched her face and he rose and stood by her side.

She reached for his hand and whispered. "We *are* twins, aren't we? And that lady, I hurt her feelings, didn't I? I don't mean to be so nasty, but I don't know who I am. Do you have any idea what that feels like?" She sniffed and looked down.

He held her hand. "We know you've had a tough time. That's why we haven't tried to push. I can't even imagine not knowing my name. It doesn't matter though. We know who you are. We've been so worried. The doctor seems to think your memory will return. It merely needs the right information."

"Who else should I know about?"

Steve rubbed his neck. Should he tell her everything? He couldn't ask her about Cassie if she didn't remember him.

"I have two daughters. Stella and Tina. They want to come and see you, but I've been putting them off."

Curious eyes, so like his own, searched his gaze. "Where's your wife?"

"She's dead. You're the closest thing to a mother my daughters have."

She slumped back into the bed and stared at the ceiling. "Stella and Tina. I'm sorry, I simply don't remember."

"The doctor said to try not to force it. You're going to be here till your lungs are clear."

"Then what?"

"Then you come home. You have an apartment over the garage, but sometimes you stay in your old room when I'm out of town or coming home late."

"Where are our parents?"

"Dead. They've been gone a long time."

"I'm tired. I'd like to sleep."

Steve nodded and returned to his chair. He wanted to say more, but her eyes drifted shut. Maybe it was too much for her at once and he should have held back.

Chapter 23

When the call came that Mia had been found, Cassie dropped everything, ready to rush to the hospital, but Fiona said Mia was unconscious in the ICU with no visitors permitted. Fiona promised to keep her updated on Mia's progress. Saddened and angry Steve hadn't called, she remained grateful for Fiona's friendship

When the doorbell rang, Cassie flung open the door and hugged Fiona and they went into the kitchen.

"Mia woke up," Fiona whispered.

Cassie dropped the teapot she had just filled with water, but then snagged it in mid-air. "Thank the Lord."

"But she doesn't know who she is."

She set the kettle on the stove and plopped into a chair. "She has amnesia? Is that common?"

Fiona shrugged. "I dinnae know, lassie. The doctors are scratching their heads and hope she'll remember. She keeps asking for Shannon, but no one knows who he is. Steve's been there since the detective called. When she woke up, she didn't know him and remembered nothing except Shannon's care of her. Steve's beside himself."

"I can imagine," Cassie whispered. "What's the prognosis?"

"Time. The doctors say it'll take time. He wants Steve to relay information a morsel at a time. She's much better and is awake more hours. They moved her out of ICU."

"Should I visit her?"

"That might not be a good idea. I wanted to tell you

218

and came to bring Gabby and Bella's things back."

"Why can't I visit her?"

"Because they're trying to help her regain her memory. Keep praying for her and for Steve. I know the girls want to see Gabby and Bella. Maybe if she regains her memory Steve will soften and allow them to play together again."

"I wish Steve would…" Cassie's voice trailed. "The kids suffer because I told him the dream."

"He's a stubborn one, that boy. The man is steeped in his own misery. He's chewed off the hand that helped him. Things will get better. There's a reason this happened and we'll see God's plan in his timing, not ours."

"Have you seen her?"

"Yes. She didn't remember me either. Doctors say personal things brought from home might help, but she didn't bring much with her when she came home."

"I…I don't understand."

"Not my story to tell, lassie."

Mia never talked about herself and always prodded for Cassie's story. Thank goodness, Steve hadn't exposed her secret writing career. *What is wrong with me? I should be worried about Mia and not my personal issues.*

"I understand. And the girls? Have they visited?"

"No. Steve doesn't want them frightened."

"I can see why he'd think like that. But those girls have been Mia's whole life for years now. Wouldn't they prompt her memory better than personal possessions?"

Fiona's eyes widened. "I've been so worried I never

thought the girls would help her memory. She has awful cuts on her face and arms."

"I figured she got cut, but didn't know the extent of her wounds. Perhaps Steve could prepare the girls."

"Great idea, lassie. I know you'd know just what to say, but he's floundering, the poor lad."

Poor lad, indeed. We're all floundering.

"I have stuff Stella and Tina left, too. Those girls are precious, and they're hurting. Makes me sad."

Fiona hugged Cassie and took the bag with the clothing and toys in her arms.

"Please call when I can visit. I miss her friendship."

Steve pounded his keyboard when Mia opened her eyes later that afternoon.

Her voice startled him. "Are you always on that thing?"

He closed the lid. "Not always, but you do scold me for working all the time."

"I do?"

"Yes. How're you feeling? Doctor Garrett was in while you slept."

"A lot to take in, you know?"

He nodded, but he didn't know. "Ready to see your nieces?"

Mia touched her face. "I don't want to scare them."

"They know you have injuries."

She shrugged, and Steve called Fiona. "Can you bring the girls?" He paused. "No. I'll see you soon."

Mia watched him. "Fiona. Is she a relative too?"

Steve laughed. "No, but she's been a part of our family since long before we were born."

"She looks so young! How old are we, anyway? And who's older?"

"We're thirty-six and I'm your big brother."

"By how much?"

"Two minutes."

She harrumphed. "How long before they get here? I'm nervous."

His smile faded. "Twenty minutes. No need to be nervous. They're your family. And they love you. We all do."

Steve cleared his throat. "Mia, I'm so sorry. I took advantage of your good nature all these years and want to make it up to you."

She jerked and gazed at him with puzzled eyes. "How did you do that?"

"You came home and cared for the girls when Laura died." He hoped she would forgive him. One person had to forgive him. At least he hoped his twin would.

"Laura was your wife."

He nodded.

She cast curious eyes at him. "Came home? Where was I?"

"Someplace back east. I was in so much pain and focused on keeping the business above water instead of on my daughters and you." He hung his head. "By the time the grief dulled and business turned around, you wouldn't talk about it."

"I see."

"Unless you remember, we'll never know."

Doctor Garrett checked her vitals. "You're doing well despite the amnesia. I'm hopeful your memory will return, no reason it shouldn't. The neurologist agreed a traumatic event coupled with a bang on the head could trigger retrograde amnesia."

Steve smiled. "My daughters are coming for a visit and we're hoping seeing them will trigger a memory for her."

"How soon will they be here?"

Steve checked his phone. "Ten minutes."

"In that case, I'll hang around the floor because I'll want to check her again."

Steve gave a single nod and reached for his sister's hand. She didn't flinch or pull away. That was a step in the right direction.

"I'm so glad you're back. We were so worried about you."

Her blue eyes bored into his.

"Here they are."

Fiona breezed through the door with Stella and Tina. They'd never been inside a hospital. He'd not wanted them here now, but his sister's memory depended on it. He cautioned his daughters not to mention her scars when they saw her.

"Aunt Mia?" Stella whispered.

Tina sniffed, but held back her tears and leaped into Steve's arms. Fiona stepped toward the door and allowed them a family moment.

He inched to the side of the bed and shifted Tina to his other arm so she could see his sister while Stella tiptoed to the other side and peered into his sister's face.

Mia shifted her gaze from Tina to Stella and burst into a flood of tears that caused them all to cry. She could barely get the words out. "Don't cry, my darlings. I'm fine. Honest, I am. I'm better than fine. I remember you both. Come here and give your aunt a big hug."

Steve released Tina to the bed, and she snuggled next to her aunt while Stella cuddled on the other side.

Mia drew her nieces closer. "Did you miss me?"

"We missed you so much," both girls said through their tears.

"Maybe now Daddy will let us play with Gabby and Bella again," Tina said.

Steve choked and pursed his lips. He hadn't told them about Cassie's girls. Leave it to Tina to bring up that sore subject.

"I don't...," Mia said as the doctor stepped through the door.

Doctor Garrett strode into the room. "How about that? I didn't think these beds held three people, but we'll make an exception if you tell me you remembered these munchkins."

"I do remember them. Memory's coming back in bits and pieces. Is that okay?"

"Steve, why don't you take your daughters for a drink while I examine Mia."

"Do we have to leave?"

Mia held up her wrists. "If you go with your Dad, I'll let you write your name on my casts."

Steve smirked. "Come on, you heard your aunt." The girls kissed Mia's cheek and dropped to the floor.

Fiona stepped forward. "I can take the girls."

"No. I'd like you to stay," Mia said with forcefulness.

Steve shot Fiona a quizzical look and shrugged.

"Your memory should return in its entirety. Steve should have brought your nieces days ago," Doctor Garrett said after they left.

Her breath whooshed out. "Such a relief."

"I think we'll release you in a day or two after we take another MRI and do more blood work."

"Maybe a seamstress could hire me as a pin cushion."

Doctor Garrett chuckled. "We had to be sure we had all the information we needed to decide what was wrong with you since you couldn't tell us."

"You'll feel much better when you're in your own bed," Fiona said.

"I'll put the orders in and we'll get the ball rolling to get you released."

The doctor left and Fiona gravitated to the bed and clasped Mia's hand.

"Lassie, I'm so glad you're back. You scared this old woman."

Tears streamed down Mia's cheeks. "I'm so sorry. I never meant to hurt you, but I couldn't remember you. It was awful not knowing who I was. My anger got the best of me."

Fiona sniffed. "Och, Lassie…"

"You've been like a second mother to us!"

A look of delight passed over her face. "That I am, lassie."

Fiona hugged her amid tears of relief, laughter and whispered endearments.

"What's this about the girls not being able to play with Gabby and Bella?" Mia said when Fiona released her.

"Och, Lassie… not my story to tell. Ask Steve."

"But…"

Stella and Tina raced in the room, but Fiona held them back. They slowed and stepped to the bedside.

"Aunt Mia, does your face hurt?" Stella said.

"Not now, honey," Steve said.

"But it…" He interrupted her. "What did we talk about before?"

"Oh. Sorry," she said with a contrite face.

Steve drew his arms around his daughters and whispered. "I think Aunt Mia has had a busy day, and she's tired. Why don't you go home with Fiona? I'll be home soon."

When they left, he pulled a chair to the bed and eased himself into it. "Whew! I don't know how you keep up with them. They tired me out."

Mia smirked. "I bet. You've had your hands full these past weeks."

"Just a tad."

She yawned. "Why can't the girls play with Gabby and Bella?"

"You're tired. Why don't you sleep on it and we'll discuss it later? I'd like to go to the firm and get some work done. Will you be okay till tomorrow morning?"

"You're avoiding the question, but I'm too tired to call you on it. I'll nap the rest of the afternoon. At least till they come and bother me."

Steve grabbed his laptop and tiptoed out of the room. He stopped at the nurse's station to let them know Mia slept and he'd be back in the morning.

Chapter 24

When Fiona called with the news, Cassie's heart leaped. She knocked on Mia's door with a soft rhythm. Her eyes remained closed, but they popped open when Cassie tiptoed in.

She hugged her friend, and her eyes moistened. "I'm so glad you remembered. How are you feeling?"

Mia coughed. "I'm okay. I'll need plastic surgery, though."

"Are you in pain?"

"Except for my memory, no, I'm not in pain."

"What do you mean?"

"Some parts I wish I didn't remember."

"Like the accident?"

"Yes. But Shannon took such wonderful care of me. What a gentleman."

"Who is this Shannon?"

Mia shook her head. "He didn't talk much about himself and tried to encourage me to remember things the entire time I was there. According to him, his dog found me. I don't have a clue where the cabin is. He seems to have disappeared into thin air."

Cassie patted her hand. "I'm sure he'll turn up. You can describe him, right?"

"I guess. Let's talk about what's going on with you and Steve."

To evade questions, Cassie pulled a chair closer. "Nothing to tell. I cared for the girls till he no longer needed me."

"No, something more is going on here. Now spill."

Cassie laughed. "One minute I was caring for the girls

and the next I wasn't. You'll have to ask your brother."

Mia harrumphed.

"Tell me about your accident."

"I went to photograph a beautiful area, and the light was perfect, but I was going fast because I wanted a few more shots before I returned when an enormous deer jumped in front of the car. They rarely come out till dusk. I braked, lost control and flew over the road's edge." Mia shuddered.

"Were you in water when you came to?"

Mia shivered. "Water? No. There was a creek, but it was a few feet away when I awoke to a smashed windshield, my head pounding and blood everywhere. I believed I was dying. My wrist hurt so bad I could barely open the door, but I managed somehow. I must have walked for miles along the creek. The gully I was in narrowed and I couldn't go any farther and couldn't return to the car. I tried to climb out and slipped and used my bad hand and fell. I remember my phone flying out of my pocket, then I hit the ground hard and blacked out."

"So sorry you went through that."

"Not your fault." Mia gave her a tremulous smile.

"A dog licked my face and woke me up. I called to him, but he didn't return. I tried to move, got dizzy and blacked out again."

"Oh my gosh!"

"When I woke up, I found myself in a warm bed with the dog's head on the bed. I don't know how I got there, but I was so thankful Shannon found me."

"Me too. Have you told Steve?"

"No. I fell asleep and didn't think to tell him when the

227

girls were here."

"Good. He needs to know what happened."

"According to Shannon, I was out for over twenty-four hours. He didn't have cell service, and the land line was down. A storm dumped so much rain the road to the highway and the bridge to his place washed out, fallen wires and fallen trees kept me there."

"Makes sense."

"But I didn't want to leave because I didn't remember my name or how I'd gotten there. I was safe, but fear crowded into my head and I begged him not to make me leave. He kept trying to help me, but nothing penetrated. Not the accident, the kids, or anything."

"The water finally subsided and someone came to visit him. And he had a horse and chickens he brought with him."

"You wanted to stay?"

"Yes. The day someone came to visit, he was on his horse and I went for a walk. It was stupid, but I was stir crazy. I wasn't paying attention and got lost. Then it rained, and I ran and fell and broke my wrist. I sat in the rain under a tree until Shannon and his dog found me, but I don't remember much after that except that he said the road was clear, and I needed expert medical attention. The next day, I remember he tied my shoes and buckled me into his truck. That's all I remember that last day."

Cassie's face registered her compassion, and she rubbed Mia's fingers. "You've had so much trauma."

"Then I woke up here."

"That's it?"

"Pretty much." Mia glanced the other way.

"Why do I get the sense there's more to the story?"

"You're free to think whatever, but that's the truth."

"I didn't say I didn't believe you. I said there's more you're not saying. Wait. It's Shannon, isn't it? You fell for him."

Mia laughed. "Stop. He took care of me. End of story."

"Okay. I'll let this conversation go, for now. I left my kids with Becka. When will the hospital release you?"

"Tomorrow. What's happened between the girls?"

"Nothing. I'll visit you when you're released."

"You won't tell me?"

Cassie kissed Mia's cheek. "Nothing to tell."

"You'll wear out that stretch of carpet, pacing that way." Steve's assistant said and plopped another cup of steaming coffee on his desk.

"I'm headed to the hospital, they're releasing her. Then I'll work from home the rest of the day."

"Glad to hear she's going home."

He grabbed his coffee and his coat and threw it over his shoulder. "Me too."

At the hospital, he kissed Mia on the cheek. "I found a plastic surgeon. I'll schedule the appointment as soon as you feel better."

"The sooner the better."

He pulled out his phone, and she grabbed his arm. "We need to talk."

He disguised his annoyance. "Let's have it."

"What happened between you and Cassie? Neither she nor Fiona would tell me."

"Cassie came to visit?"

"Late yesterday afternoon. Now quit stalling."

"Let me ask you a question about your accident."

"You're changing the subject. No."

"Yes," he said. "Did Cassie have anything to do with your accident?"

Mia stiffened. "Are you out of your mind? Why would you think such a thing?"

"Calm down. I shouldn't have said anything."

"I won't calm down. This will be a doozy. Out with it."

"She has secrets," he muttered.

"Haven't we been over this before?"

"Yes. But when you went missing, and she couldn't say where you'd gone, I thought—"

"Why would she know? I don't answer to her nor does she answer to me."

"Right. But when she had the dream, I couldn't reconcile that she knew nothing."

Mia looked puzzled. "Dream? What dream? No one said anything about a dream."

He paced the room. "Cassie didn't tell you?" When she shook her head, he rubbed the back of his neck. "I really messed things up, then. I owe her a humongous apology."

"Tell me about the dream and what happened."

"She had a dream. Let her tell you because I don't remember the details. Then I accused her of many things that weren't true."

"Even from the grave, Laura causes trouble."

"Yeah, well. I need to forgive her too, so I can move forward."

"How're you going to do that?"

"Frank has a plan and I need to talk to him."

"He does, does he? I sure hope it works because I'm tired of seeing you always so suspicious of women."

"I'm not suspicious of women."

Mia rolled her eyes. "Only the ones you dated or were interested in."

"We're done talking about this, Mia."

The nurse came in with discharge papers and helped Mia dress while Steve waited in the hall.

Steve carried her to his home office where he had a hospital bed installed and laid her on the bed. Fiona fussed over her and told her to rest.

Later that evening, Steve went to his room and paused before he grabbed the phone. It was do-or-die time. He wanted to right things with Cassie, but he couldn't do it until he got himself right. He had to forgive Laura.

His stomach knotted, but determination stiffened his shoulders. The phone rang once, and he almost chickened out. What was the matter with him? This was Frank, his friend. Why was he being such a wimp?

After the call ended, he wasn't sure if it would work, but he'd try. He'd head over to the cemetery in the morning and then go see Cassie.

Chapter 25

The watery sun provided little warmth and the cold bit into Steve's cheeks, but he focused on what he must do. In the car, he prayed for the right words to say. Laura wouldn't answer. The dead never would.

But Cassie? That was another matter.

Frank inspired him to envision Laura as she was before the hard times. When they loved one another. Then his friend encouraged him to converse with her as if she were still alive. To voice everything he'd never been able to express and offer forgiveness. He realized he could finally come out from under the burden of guilt and anguish he carried and liberate himself. Frank's brilliance astounded him.

Amid all the graves, he regarded the bleak vista. A solitary figure among barren trees. The only sound a slight whistle when the trees swayed.

Steve squatted, placed a bouquet on Laura's headstone and shivered. Everything on his mind and in his heart rushed out at once. Time to heal and move on.

"I forgive you, Laura."

A burden that hung over his head lifted. Not since college had he known such lightness of spirit.

Frank cautioned him those old feelings of mistrust and suspicion could rear up when least expected and he'd need to squash them. Not a simple task, but he didn't want to dwell on such thoughts.

Jogging to his car, he drove straight to Cassie's, but hesitated at her door. Her concern for his family invaded his mind and heart, which already radiated tenderness. To ask her forgiveness would be much harder and he took a deep breath and said a silent prayer about the conversation.

Her shadow graced the narrow sidelight when he rang the bell. When she opened the door, he forced a slight smile. "May I come in? We need to talk."

Cassie stood there and stared for what seemed an eternity. Confusion marred the features he loved and his tentative smile faded.

She gave a tiny nod as she closed front door. "Coffee?" she said, over her shoulder.

"Maybe later."

Cassie led him to the living room and took his coat. Couldn't she help him out and ask what he wanted to talk about? A lead-in would have helped. No matter, though. He stood by the cozy fire and warmed his hands while she hung his coat.

"Have a seat."

He chose the club chair, moved the ottoman, and unbuttoned his jacket as he sat while she dropped on the sofa. His nerves were shot.

"I don't know where to start," he whispered.

Cassie gave a slight smile. "Try the beginning."

He remembered the moment he'd said those identical words. This was more like it. A grin hooked his lips, and he sobered. "I want to apologize...for everything. Every unkind word, every mean thought. Hard to believe, but it has bothered me for some time."

"That *is* hard to believe."

"Well, let's just say I had a come-to-Jesus moment when Mia lit into me for my accusations toward you." She narrowed her eyes, and he wanted to look away, but couldn't.

"I went to the cemetery today." Not what he wanted to say, and confusion once again spread across her face.

His breath whooshed out, and he leaned into the soft cushion and pinched the bridge of his nose. When he looked up, she frowned.

"I want, no, need to tell you why I was a jerk. You told me things about your marriage and now you need to know about mine." He moved to sit next to her.

"When I overheard you on the phone, the first time you came to the house, I panicked."

"You eavesdropped?"

"I went inside to work, remember? The window was open, and I heard your end of the conversation. You were distressed. At first, I thought you might be in trouble. Then I realized you had secrets. My wife had secrets, and that's the reason for my distrustful nature. Mia said I'm too suspicious. Maybe I was."

"Was?"

He nodded and stared into her eyes. "My friend Frank said I was absurd to think you had anything to do with Mia's disappearance, but your dream drove me down that awful path again."

"I understand."

"Do you?"

"People fear what they don't understand. Supernatural things like dreams that foretell events can make a sane person panic."

His eyes watered. "A few months after Laura and I married, my parents died in a car accident. They were headed home from a vacation they had postponed because of the wedding."

"What happened?"

"An eighteen-wheeler lost control. The burden of handling the funerals and taking over the business fell on my shoulders."

"I'm so sorry. Didn't Mia and your wife help?"

"Mia couldn't face the loss. After the funeral, she took off for parts unknown. She called on occasion, but moved around so much I lost track of her. Even if she had stayed, I couldn't depend on her to help with the business. She had no interest."

"And your wife?"

He shook his head. "My wife…was self-centered and needy. I'd walked away from my faith when I met her. Kids do stupid things in college."

Cassie sighed. "That's true."

"Laura was beautiful, fun, and bubbly and I fell hard. She had an agenda, zero business sense, and wouldn't help plan the funerals. Fiona was there for me, despite my catatonic state."

"Fiona's so sweet."

His heart gladdened when he heard her feelings for Fiona. In time, he would share more, but for now he'd only tell her the important things.

"I never realized Laura required constant attention. When she got pregnant with Stella, the business hit the skids and I had no time to coddle her."

"Why did the business flounder?"

His voice took on a hard edge. "I'm embarrassed to say I trusted people I shouldn't have while I juggled my wife's expectations and ran the business. For the past five years, I've worked hard to make the business everything my father wanted it to be. My sister and kids are now secure. My father taught me to provide for the family, but Laura didn't see it that way."

Cassie's sadness almost undid him.

"Laura got pregnant on purpose. Both times. We discussed not having children till the business was on solid ground, but her manipulations meant I'd spend more time with her. I hadn't realized she did it on purpose till after her death. At first, I wasn't thrilled with the pregnancy, but I became overjoyed. A child was coming, and I needed family. With my parents dead and Mia gone, it was just Laura and me."

"Would you like coffee now?"

He needed to think. "Yes."

In the kitchen, he sat at the island and observed her graceful movements. Her presence comforting, but he wasn't sure if he could share the rest. He hadn't told a soul except Frank and not any gory details.

She perched on the other stool. "There's more, isn't there?"

"When Laura got pregnant, she was difficult, not to mention sick during both pregnancies. I admit I wasn't much of a husband or father. After the girls were born, she wanted nothing more to do with them and I had no idea. She used the girls as leverage to get her way."

The situation choked him with fury. But Cassie put her hand on his and gave him the courage to continue. "I didn't know Laura left the girls with Fiona while she went out. She made certain she came home before me and I was never the wiser."

Cassie's lips formed a straight line. "Didn't Fiona tell you?"

He shook his head. "Business decisions took every ounce of my focus that I assumed she cared for them and allowed me to have daddy time in the evenings so she could rest. Fiona didn't want to further burden me with Laura's duplicity. God bless her."

Cassie nodded. "How old were the girls when she died?"

"Stella was three and Tina was almost two. The girls never ask about her, and I don't talk about her. I didn't ask Fiona to help when Mia vanished because she'd already done so much."

He focused on the pattern in the granite counter and remembered.

"Laura died instantly in a head-on crash. The man in the car with her survived. That's when I realized she'd been unfaithful. When the hospital released the man, he sent a letter explaining everything. I burned that letter. I never want my daughters to know their mother's treachery. Her secrets affected my thoughts about you."

Cassie's face depicted the pain in her heart. "I'm so sorry and I agree the girls shouldn't know."

"When you told me you were a novelist and who Phil was, I was ecstatic because you revealed a part of yourself hidden from everyone else. And our situations were so similar I hoped you'd understand when I told you, but there never seemed to be an appropriate time to bring it up. And with Mia missing, my thoughts were always with her." He hung his head in shame then raised his head to see her compassion filled eyes.

"When you had the dream, those wounds opened up again, and the anger rushed in. I couldn't reconcile any of it till I was certain. But that was an excuse. Deep in my heart, I had an awareness Mia's disappearance had nothing to do with you, but Laura's deceitfulness haunted me."

"Forgiveness isn't easy. But if we don't forgive, it hurts us more than it hurts the person being forgiven. You can't change the past. But forgiveness can change the future. When I think what Jesus accomplished on the cross so I could live with him in eternity, who am I to not forgive?"

"You're right."

"We imprison ourselves when we don't forgive. But when we forgive, we set the prisoner free. Does that mean you'll forget? No. But it means you can move on. It's a daily process. Sometimes hourly. And I do forgive you, Steve. My heart told me there was more to your story, and I should wait for an explanation."

His jubilant heart soared. "Thank you. I didn't know if you would. God calls us to forgive one another."

"For sure."

"Since Laura's death, I haven't been a model father. But now that the business is secure, I'm making strides to delegate so I could spend more time with the girls."

She laid her hand on his. "That's wonderful, Steve. I'm so—"

The doorbell pealed and jarred them both. She slid from her perch and stepped through the foyer. The letter carrier took her signature on the registered form and placed a manila envelope in her hand.

When she shut the door, her face turned white.

"What is it?"

"Nico's lawyers."

He escorted her to the kitchen and joined her at the table. He set a fresh cup of coffee in front of her. She dropped the letter and grabbed the coffee. She sipped it as she stared at the thick envelope as if it were a cobra ready to strike.

"Aren't you going to open it?"

"I'm afraid."

He took the cup from her hands. "I'm here and I'm not leaving. Open it."

She lifted the corner of the envelope, smoothed out the pages and read. Tears formed and fell on the pages.

"What is it?"

She shook her head and put her fist to her mouth and continued to cry. "He's… suing for full custody of the girls."

"Don't you already have custody?"

She nodded. "It says he doesn't believe I'm able to financially care for the girls. But that's just what's on this paperwork. Knowing Nico, he had to find a good reason to get his attorney to move forward. I bet Mia's disappearance and you being here that day had an underlying impact for this lawsuit."

Steve's anger exploded. "Preposterous! You had nothing to do with Mia's disappearance."

She gave him a watery smile. "That's an about face."

He pulled her from the chair and hugged her tight. "We'll get through this together."

She nodded and wept into his shirt as he rubbed her back.

"Let's go into the living room and talk about this."

She grabbed the letter, and he threw his arm across her shoulders and leaned her into his side. Her hair tickled his nostrils with the sweet scent of honeysuckle.

After she sat on the sofa, he parked himself next to her and pulled her tight against him.

"Now, let's read this letter from the beginning and come up with a strategy to fix this."

"I don't know if we can. I'll die without my girls." Wracking sobs shook her body.

"Give me the letter."

She handed it to him while she laid in his arms and wet his shirt with her tears. He squeezed her into himself and wanted to punch someone, but he had to be strong for the woman he loved. He couldn't let her ex take away her children.

"How do you think he found out about Mia's disappearance?"

She hiccupped, wiped her tears and shot straight up. "Oh, no. The girls. They must have given him enough information for him to go find the rest. I never coached the girls not to talk about it."

"Are you sure it was the girls?"

"No. But they didn't want to go to their dad's last week."

"Talk to them."

"I know but I don't want this to affect them."

"That horse left the barn, Cassie."

"I need to call my attorney," she said.

"It says you have ninety days to answer the complaint."

"It does? That puts it in January."

He hugged her close and lifted her chin so he could lose himself in the depths of her eyes. "I'll do whatever it takes to help you. I want to be there for you."

She nodded and licked her lips. He groaned and

leaned in to kiss her. This time he couldn't contain his passion and she kissed him with an ardor he hadn't believed possible. He pulled away from her to catch his breath.

"We need to deal with this issue before we can talk about our relationship."

"Uh, huh. What? Relationship?"

"Yeah." He nodded and pointed a finger at her and then himself. "You. Me. Relationship. Starting now."

She gave him a teeny smile and grabbed the phone. "Let me call Blake."

She put her attorney on speaker and explained Steve was with her.

"What's he doing there?" Blake said.

"He came to apologize."

"About time," her attorney said.

His jaw tightened and Cassie hurriedly agreed to scan the letter and scheduled a telephone appointment for the next day and hung up.

"I'll be here for that appointment," Steve said.

"You don't have to."

"Yes, I do. You were always there for me when Mia disappeared. Don't you think I want to be here for you,   too?"

241

Chapter 26

Cassie eased into a conversation with her daughters about Mia's disappearance and visits to their father. She now had a better idea of what transpired. The girls provided the ammunition for the custody battle. There was more to this battle than could be seen on paper. Nico had taken advantage of his own daughters.

She made coffee, reviewed questions for Blake, and waited for Steve. He was a dark horse. That kiss curled her toes. His arms warmed and comforted her like none ever had. Yes, she was in love with him. Had been since he played with the girls in the pool. She shook her head. This custody case would be an uphill battle and she had to remain focused on it for now.

While her brother could stand with her, his hotheaded ways would not be in her family's best interest. She needed cool and collected. That was Steve. He proved it the first time he met Nico. Could she expose Steve to Nico's rants? Would it be fair to him? To his girls?

She wanted Steve. More than she'd ever wanted anything or anyone in her life. But was it fair to involve him in such a volatile situation? He wanted to help now. But what about the future? Would he still be there? His wife was dead and posed no threat. Or did she?

The doorbell rang and Steve stood there in GQ fashion. He removed his coat and tossed it over the stair rail, opened his arms, and she fell into them. How could she resist? Was it the way he cared for his daughters and family? His faith? Or a combination?

He hugged and kissed her. When they parted, she sighed. "Want coffee?"

"I need it after the morning I had."

Her brow wrinkled, and she frowned. "You don't have to be here for this."

"It's nothing to do with this. Well, at least not much."

"Care to share?"

"Minor skirmishes at work, but the biggest headache was my sister with all her questions about forgiving Laura and my meeting with you yesterday. She's regained almost all her memories and demands answers. I could barely escape this morning."

A bubble of laughter escaped Cassie's lips. "Oh yeah, Mia can be daunting."

She poured them both a cup and watched him peruse the paperwork laid out on the table.

"Looks like you're ready."

"As much as I can be. Would you scan the questions and see if I missed anything?"

"I hope you don't mind, but I called my attorney."

Cassie frowned. She was a private person and didn't want her business known. "Why?"

"Because Frank's my friend and knows the situation with Mia and you. His perspective might be better than Blake's because he has firsthand knowledge."

"I see your point. Did you tell Mia?"

"Of course not. Frank is an attorney and is bound by attorney-client privilege. Mia is not. Your decision, if you want to tell her. She and Fiona are already conspiring."

"Funny."

"No, it's not. Too many interfering females in my house."

Cassie stared into her cup and tried not to grin. And there'd be a lot more females in the house with Cassie and her girls around. Seven to one. He didn't stand a chance.

He laughed. "But I love them all and wouldn't change a thing."

The phone pealed and Cassie had no opportunity to respond.

The conversation went as expected and Steve added ideas from his conversation with Frank.

When the call wound down, Cassie's jumpy stomach eased. Even Steve appeared comfortable.

"I'll try to resolve this case without you or the girls having to go to court, but I caution you, it might happen. What's your attorney's contact information? He'll be an excellent resource," Blake said.

Steve blurted the number while he texted Frank to give him a heads up.

"As a friend, Frank had firsthand knowledge. At a minimum, he steered us in the right direction and what questions to ask," Steve said.

"And he did," Blake said. "It's great Cassie has another legal professional in her corner."

After the call was over, they understood the next steps.

"I hope Blake can deliver and get the complaint resolved before the holidays. I don't want it hanging over our heads," Steve said.

"Totally agree."

"Why don't we get lunch?"

Might be the wrong time for her to press the issue but… "I'd love to have lunch but can you pray with me about this?"

A look of dismay crossed his face for a moment, and then gave an imperceptible nod, reached for her hand and closed his eyes.

Father, we come to your feet and ask forgiveness for the many offenses in our lives. We ask that you intervene in this case and look with favor upon Cassie and her daughters. Lord, I pray you give us strength of mind and a peace that surpasses all understanding over this entire situation. Help us be great witnesses of your love and care, in Jesus' name we pray. Amen.

He opened his eyes. "Why are you crying?"

"I'm so thankful you prayed with me, Steve. We can overcome this if we continue to pray for his help and mercy."

"I agree."

"One last thing."

"Can the girls have play time outside school and gym activities again?"

Steve slapped his forehead. "They pestered me for quite a while. Why don't you come for dinner on Saturday and we'll surprise them?"

"That would be terrific. And I'll make a cake and buy ice cream."

He nodded once and rubbed the back of his neck. "One more thing. Mia is still in no shape to care for the girls. Could we share parental duties? Maybe tag-team carpooling the girls from school and their activities?"

"I love it… except with this custody situation, we might want to wait till the court resolves the case. We don't want to give his attorneys any more ammunition."

"You're right. Now can we go eat? I'm starved."

On Saturday, Steve had a wide smile on his face when he retrieved his daughters from the gym. He couldn't stop his constant grin. Despite the custody battle he was certain would be ugly, his joyful heart overflowed.

The surprise celebration to reunite the girls included a Saturday night dinner with a special cake. How much he wanted to tell his family but he and Cassie decided it would be more fun to plan a celebration.

Later that afternoon, when he stepped into the kitchen, Fiona and Mia stilled their conversation. He picked an apple from the tray, bit into it and arched his brow at the silence.

Fiona shrugged and turned away.

"You're happy," Mia said with a dry smile.

He dropped into a chair and munched on his apple.

"I'm dying here. What's happening between you and Cassie."

"Nothing."

"Ha! You've had that smile plastered on your face for days like you won the grand prix or something."

He sighed and put the core on a napkin. "Not going to let this go, are you?"

Mia grinned and peered at Fiona, who held back a grin. "Nope."

"Fiona, you're quiet. Not going to give your two-cents worth?"

"Och, laddie. I figure you'll say what needs to be said when you're ready."

"Thank you. When is dinner?"

Mia jumped from the chair. "Wait. You're not telling us anything?"

She gave him a pout, and he remembered how he

promised to give her anything she wanted. He breathed deep. "Okay. Cassie and I had a discussion. I apologized and asked for forgiveness and she accepted."

"That's it?"

Steve pointed a finger at her. "Yup. And don't grill Cassie, either."

"You're no fun."

Fiona chuckled. "Och, Lass, let the man alone. He still hasn't come to terms with it yet."

He arched an eyebrow, but said nothing. Fiona surmised the situation, but she wouldn't give it away.

"News flash. Cassie and I have planned a celebratory dinner for the girls this evening. Is there enough to go around?"

Mia's shocked look was followed by her usual rant. "What? When were you planning to drop that little tidbit?"

"As soon as you quit pestering me."

"What if Fiona hadn't made enough?"

He rolled his eyes. "Fiona always makes enough. More than enough and we freeze leftovers. Tonight, there won't be enough to freeze. And don't go giving away the surprise to the girls."

Fiona busied herself at the stove. "When will they be here?"

"Soon," Steve said.

He placed flatware, glasses, and napkins on a tray and took them to the dining room. Mia followed him and leaned against the door jamb.

"How're the wrists?" he said.

"They're itchy. The casts come off in a week. And I can't wait, they annoy me."

"And the lungs?"

"They're fine."

Steve set the table while Mia looked on and laughed. "You're pretty domesticated, already. You may not need me any longer."

He stopped. "I'll always need you, Mia. But you need a break and still haven't recovered sufficiently to care for any of us."

"The plastic surgery will happen when the casts come off. Then I'll feel more like myself."

He put his hand on her shoulder. "You'll still need physical therapy for those wrists, and the girls can be a handful. I promised myself, and God, if you ever returned, I wouldn't take you for granted."

Tears clouded her eyes, and she nodded. "I love caring for the girls. You know that, right?"

"Cassie said as much. I was so focused on the business and my own issues I'd forgotten you weren't the hired help." Steve frowned. "I'm sorry, Mia."

"You're my brother, Steve. I love you and I'm glad you are back in church and Bible study. One-eighty-degree turnaround. If Cassie had anything to do with it, I'm forever grateful."

"She did."

"So, tell me, where do you two go from here?"

He turned solemn. "I don't know, yet. It's all so new."

"I think you two have fallen in love and I didn't get to see it happen. The kids adore one another and Tina wants a mommy like other kids."

Steve stopped short. "Tina wants a mommy?"

"Yeah, she does. Cassie would be perfect for the role."

"There are hurdles right now." Steve rubbed his neck.

"What hurdles?"

"Let Cassie tell you in her own time. I'm sure she will."

"Ha! Fat chance."

"Mia, please don't be nosy. Have you located Shannon?"

The abrupt subject change rattled Mia, but she recovered and stared at her hands. "No."

He put his hand on her shoulder again. "You'll find him. When you do, I'd like to thank him."

She nodded, and tears glistened in her eyes. "They should be here in a few minutes. I'll keep the girls occupied."

He nodded and searched for Fiona.

Chapter 27

Gabby and Bella scrambled into the car as the chilly wind whipped their cheeks and turned them a rosy hue. The woodsy fragrance of logs burning permeated the air.

Bella crossed her arms. "We're not going to Daddy's, are we?"

"Did we load your suitcases?"

"No," Bella said.

"So where are we going?" Gabby said.

"Just enjoy the ride, okay?"

When they turned onto Steve's street, Cassie witnessed her daughter's reaction in the rearview mirror. The apprehension on their faces tore her apart. "Are we going to visit Stella and Tina?" Gabby said. A sad frown marred her features. "But their daddy didn't want us to be friends."

Cassie pulled into the driveway, parked by the garage, then turned in her seat. "Steve never said he didn't want you to be friends. He had things to work out and now he wants you girls to spend time outside gym and school again."

A mutinous expression painted Gabby's lips. Steve would be hard pressed to win her back right away. Cassie's breath whooshed out. "Come on, we're having supper here."

Gabby shrugged and unbuckled her belt. Bella responded with a cautious smile. Forgiveness came easy for her baby.

Steve waited at the door and welcomed them. Cassie could see by Steve's wrinkled brow he never expected unhappy faces.

He frowned at her and then at the girls, but took their coats and hung them in the closet. Then he squatted before her daughters and took their tiny hands in his. "I'm sorry if I hurt your feelings."

Cassie stared as he struggled to ask for forgiveness, but realized he had to regain their trust on his own.

"Everything that happened was my fault. There are a lot of reasons. Grown-up reasons. And they were wrong ones. Will you forgive me?"

A slow smile spread across Bella's face, and she gave him a vigorous nod.

Gabby pouted. "What were the grown-up reasons?" She pointed her thumb to her chest. "I'm nine and understand a lot. You thought Aunt Mia got hurt because of my mom, right?"

Steve's face mirrored Cassie's shock over the question. She hadn't discussed the exact reason. This had not gone as they had hoped. Gabby noticed more than she gave her credit for and she'd exercise more caution from now on.

Steve's eyes pleaded for Cassie to intervene.

"Gabby. Steve asked you to forgive him. We talked about this. If someone hurts us, and then asks forgiveness, we need to forgive them because Jesus tells us to do that."

Steve frowned, and extreme sadness filled his eyes. "I am so sorry, Gabby." She glanced at Cassie, pursed her lips and sighed. "All right."

"All right, what?"

"I forgive you," Gabby said with reluctance.

Steve smiled and stood and took each girl's hand. "How about we surprise Stella and Tina?"

Cassie nodded permission when the girls sought her approval. She sighed and went out to the car to bring in bags and her stomach growled with the delicious aroma of Fiona's casserole floating through the air.

When she returned, Fiona stood in the kitchen and wiped tears from her eyes and quick-stepped to Cassie to embrace her. "Lassie, I'm so happy you and Steve made up. Bothered me no end."

"I know. But he had to realize it on his own. I could do nothing except pray."

"Prayer is the best medicine." Fiona gaped at the bags. "What did you bring?"

"A cake and ice cream for starters."

Together they put the items away.

"Go upstairs and call everyone to dinner," Fiona said.

Cassie heard the distant laughter punctuated by Steve's deep rumble as she climbed the steps to the bedroom. Mia hugged her and wiped tears from her eyes. Gosh, how she loved this family.

After they'd eaten a superb casserole dinner and splurged on cake and ice cream, the girls begged for a movie on the gigantic TV screen.

Cassie watched as Steve flipped through the scattered children's DVDs in the cabinet, then opted for a new release from his streaming service instead. "I think I'll sit with the girls a while, if you don't mind."

"I don't mind. I'll help Fiona clean up." She gazed at her girls on one side of Steve and his girls on the other. He promised they could switch places when his favorite scene came up.

Cassie marveled and slipped into the dining room. Mia and Fiona stared at her with sly grins on their faces.

"What?"

"Are you going to give us the juicy details? My brother is tight-lipped and won't utter a word."

Cassie laughed. "If he didn't tell you, why should I?"

Mia's lips thinned. "Because you're my friend and you need to relieve the undue stress this is having on me."

"Lassie, give the gal a bone. Mia's been frothing at the mouth."

"I have not."

Fiona rolled her eyes at Mia.

"Oh, for heaven's sake. Steve stopped by to apologize and told me about his wife and why he didn't trust me. I understood and forgave him."

"Not enough info." Mia huffed. "I want to know how you *feel* about him. He hasn't smiled this much in… wait, I can't remember how long. Can you, Fiona?"

"I cannae. Does a heart good to see him this happy."

Mia's eyes sparkled. "So where do you two go from here?"

Cassie's brows furrowed, and she picked her words with care. "I have a few things to work out."

Fiona stared and placed her hands on her hips. "What things?"

Cassie sighed as she dried the last dish, then set it on the counter. "There's a situation that needs resolution."

"What situation? He loves you and I think you love him. What's to work out?" Mia said.

"I never said I loved him."

"Plain as the nose on your face. His too."

"Lassie, is something else bothering you?"

Sudden tears blurred Cassie's vision.

Mia's two casts made it awkward to give her a hug. "Oh, honey. What is it?"

Cassie sat at the table, and Fiona brought a tray with three mugs of tea.

"My ex sued me for custody of the girls."

A stunned look lingered on both Mia and Fiona's faces. "But why? You're a wonderful mother."

"The paperwork says he doesn't think I can support my children. But I think there's more to it. I think his sister instigated it, but I can't prove it. When we went school shopping, Nico saw Steve at my house and Nico went ballistic. And after you disappeared, the cops questioned me, and it must have exacerbated the situation. And I think the kids gave him a heads up on what was going on, but I'm glad Steve was there when the summons came."

"What's the plan?" Mia said.

"My attorney has it under control. I hope he'll call me next week. He wants to keep it out of court for the girls' sake and I hope he does, but it might come to that."

"What can we do to help?"

"The only thing I would ask for is prayer. Pray it gets resolved quickly without an ugly court battle. That I'll be strong and have peace so I can resume my life with no backlash."

"That's a given. What else?"

"Pray for Steve. He wants to help, but I'm not sure that's wise."

A murderous expression appeared on Mia's face. "Why not?"

"Because it could make things worse. Besides, why should he involve himself in this?"

"Weren't you there for his troubles?"

"Not the same."

Mia face turned belligerent. "Explain how. You stepped in and helped. Why shouldn't he?"

"Because he has a business and this could get ugly."

"I think my brother can handle it. Don't you, Fiona?"

"Aye. Had to care for things much worse than this, he has."

Was Fiona referring to the deaths of Steve's parents or his dead wife's betrayal? Cassie wouldn't ever ask.

Mia brightened. "I'm willing to testify for you. Just say the word."

Cassie smiled and hugged her. "I don't think it'll come to that, but if it does, I'll remember."

"Remember what?" Steve strolled in and snagged a mug and then sat across from her.

Cassie ignored his question. "You tired of that princess flick?"

"No, but it's no fun when the four of them fell asleep and can't laugh at my running commentary."

They all smiled. Cassie's heart swelled for this man who enjoyed a movie with their daughters.

He took a sip and arched his brow. "You didn't answer my question."

"Mia offered to be a witness if I needed it."

"You told them?"

"I did. I'm not sure I should involve you either. It could damage your business."

"Stop right there." Steve's hand went up. "I haven't gotten this far in life without side-stepping a few land mines. I'm a part of it. Mia's a part of it. And we won't back down. Will we, Mia?"

"Nope. Three to one. Right, Fiona?"

"Aye."

"Fabulous. Case closed. Question is, though, do we wake the girls or do we let them sleep here tonight?" Steve said.

"I say, sleep here. You can bunk with me in the apartment," Mia said.

"We can't do that. We have church in the morning and will need our clothes."

"Nonsense. You can borrow something of mine and the girls can wear something from Stella and Tina's closet. They're the same size. Steve will take us to brunch after church. Won't you, brother dear?"

"Absolutely," Steve said.

"Staying the night is out of the question for several reasons," Cassie said.

Steve's lips thinned. "Name them."

"There's the court case. I don't want to tell the children to keep the truth from their father about where they were or what they did. If he finds out we stayed here, it could be detrimental to the case. Even if I'd be willing to coach them, which I am not, I don't know they wouldn't blurt it."

Steve rubbed the stubble on his chin. "You have a point."

"Aye, we dinnae want to be bringing the little ones into the mess, do we?"

"No, we don't," Steve said. "There's nothing for it, then. I'll follow you home and help you put the girls to bed."

"No. That would look bad, too. Who's to say you didn't stay the night?"

"Wow! You have an answer for everything," Mia said.

"Well, I have to be on my guard now, more than ever."

Fiona took her apron off and grabbed her coat. "I'll be praying. I know the Lord will watch over you."

Mia jumped up and hugged Cassie. "Come on brother, let's get our girls into bed and her girls into the car."

Steve took two trips and laid his girls on their beds with a tenderness that melted Cassie's heart. She and Mia dressed Cassie's girls for their trip home.

Mia stayed in the house while Steve helped her put the girls in the car and buckle them in. She was confident things would get better than they had been despite the court case.

Steve leaned into Cassie and stole a sweet kiss. He shivered from the cold and she warmed him with her arms around his neck.

"You need to get inside. It's freezing out here."

"I will. In a minute. I didn't have one moment to spend some private time with you. And I'm not going in yet."

Cassie stared into loving eyes that encouraged her to lean in and receive the kiss she so wanted. When he finally broke the connection, a soft sigh and a tiny smile covered her lips.

"I'll see you at church in the morning." Steve closed her door and waited until she pulled out onto the street.

Chapter 28

Cassie and the girls headed to Rob's home for supper Sunday afternoon, despite Steve's repeated invitations to lunch with them. She believed she had to reveal the court case in person.

"Aunt Becka, guess what?" Gabby said. "We had a surprise party at Stella and Tina's house and Mama and Steve aren't fighting anymore."

Trust Gabby to jump in and give the low-down on what was going on in their lives. It appeared whatever happened in their home was fodder for discussion. Nothing was private with children around.

Becka glanced at Cassie. "That's wonderful, honey. The kids are downstairs. Go play and we'll call you when the food's ready." Both girls scampered through the hallway and slammed the door.

Becka smirked. "You want to explain all that?"

Cassie blew out a breath. "Mia's memory came back."

"I'm so happy for her. Enlighten me about you, Steve and the girls."

"Like Gabby said, the girls had a reunion last night. Steve wanted them to be friends outside the gym again. He struggled to convince Gabby he was sorry."

"About time. I didn't like seeing you hurt, Cass. But I'm glad you two have come to an understanding. Go on."

"The girls watched a movie together and fell asleep. Steve helped me buckle them in the car and we left."

"What changed?"

Cassie's chin lifted. "He told me why he was

suspicious. It appears he'd had a terrible marriage just like me."

Becka reached for her hand and smiled. "I wondered if there was more to his life that no one knew."

"I forgave him despite the hurt he caused. Why should the girls suffer? He treats my daughters better than Nico ever did. In fact, he'll help with the court case."

Becka dropped into a chair and shock registered on her face. "What court case?"

"He was there when the papers arrived and promised to help me."

Rob stepped through the door. "What papers? Who promised to help you?"

Becka shook her head. "Late again, Rob?"

Rob bussed his wife's head and poured a cup of coffee. "Hey, I only caught the last few words. Fill me in."

"Court case with Nico. Cassie was about to explain it."

Rob brought two additional cups to the table. "We're waiting, Cassie."

"He's suing me for custody of the girls."

Rob plopped into a seat across from her. "The court granted you custody. What happened?"

"The lawsuit says he doesn't think I'll be able to provide for the girls on just child support when my alimony payments stop next year. He seems to think with just the child support payments I won't be able to adequately care for the girls. But I think he got wind of me being questioned in Mia's disappearance. Apparently, in his eyes I'm not a fit mother."

Becka drew her hand to her forehead and rubbed.

"Spending time with Steve now might not be the best idea."

An incredulous expression spread over Rob's face. "Is that wise, given the court case? Will your writing for blogs and such be enough to replace the alimony payments?"

The kitchen's temperature chilled ten degrees.

"Now's not the time, Rob," Becka said. "The bigger issue is the court case. Have you spoken to your attorney?"

Cassie squirmed. "Yes. The day the papers came, and he's working on it. Mia and Steve both agreed to testify.

"We'll both be here for you," Robbie said, then sipped his coffee. He flexed his fists. "I would love to pound on Nico. Make him cry." He put his forefinger and thumb together, almost touching. "He cheats on you and now has the nerve to sue you? Lowlife needs my knuckles on his jaw.''

"Rob!" Becka said. Her eyes drifted between Rob and Cassie.

Cassie's face turned white. "You told him?"

"She didn't need to. I have eyes, Cass. Darn good thing he lives three hours away, otherwise, I'd probably be in jail."

Cassie touched her brother's hand. "Thank you, but I've moved on. You need to forget about Nico. Once this court case is behind me, Steve and I can figure out where our relationship is headed."

"Like I said during the summer, I thought you should date again. Plus, I like Steve. I think you two would be fantastic together," Rob said.

The kids barreled up the steps and wanted to eat. Rob

took control. "Go back downstairs. We'll call you when lunch is ready."

Cassie and Becka prepared food platters while Rob got the baby up from her nap. The conversation stilted until Rob returned carrying the two-year-old. "What can we do to help?"

"Blake says neither of you can be witnesses since we're related. But if it goes before a judge, I must appear in court and I may need help with the girls. My hope is a resolution will present itself without the need to drag them to court which Blake is trying to arrange."

"Well, whatever we can do to help, we're here for you," Rob said. Cassie peered at Becka, who turned her back and retrieved utensils from a drawer.

After dinner, the kids raced back to the basement to finish their game.

Cassie and Becka stored the leftovers and relaxed in the cozy family room after Rob lit a fire.

"Nico has not been easy to deal with. Who knows what else he's capable of doing?" Becka sipped her coffee.

"I know. It's just that Nico has moved on and I should be able to as well."

"Agreed. But we both know Nico is a wild card and I'm worried about you and the girls. On the other hand, this will be over soon and you'll be able to move on with your life however you see fit."

"You, the person with tons of faith, worry? I hoped you'd bolster mine."

"You're right. We accomplish nothing by worrying and God doesn't want us to, either. Let's pray while the kids are downstairs."

They had just finished praying when Rob clomped in.

"I need to go. Tomorrow is a school day," Cassie said.

"I'll follow you home, Cass," Rob said.

"Whatever for? Help me settle the girls in the car and I'll be on my way."

"You got it."

After they had belted the girls, Rob hugged her. "Don't worry about the case. I'm here if you need me. Always."

She nodded and whispered. "I know."

Cassie settled herself in the kitchen chair with a hot cup of tea, her notebook and pen. Her attorney called before she found the contact.

Blake got to the point. "I spoke to Nico's attorney and they want the case heard sooner rather than later."

Cassie gasped. "How soon?"

"Before the holidays."

"Thanksgiving or Christmas?"

"In three weeks, Cass. The judge leaves for vacation afterward and won't be back till the new year."

"So soon. Will there be enough time to prepare?"

"If we hustle. And Cass…"

She sensed a hesitation in his voice and could barely get the words out. "What else?"

Blake sighed on the phone. "Nico wants the girls there, and he's questioning your home purchase. He searched public records and knows you have no mortgage. This is not good."

She gave a long drawn-out a sigh and peered at the barren trees in her backyard. She shivered. Her life was falling apart. The candle she lit before he called gave off her favorite fall aroma, but she was oblivious to it.

"What can we do?"

"If we stay ahead of it and figure out what they're up to, we should be fine.

"Tell me what to do and I'll do it."

"What about your house, Cassie? You got half the proceeds when the house in Strickland sold, but with the mortgage there couldn't have been enough to buy the house in Columbus outright. He'll want to know where you're getting your money. I think his rationale is to leverage the information to stop paying the remaining alimony payments. He won't be able to get out of paying child support, regardless."

"Blake, I write for a living, remember? I make a good living. Enough that I bought the house outright. Every penny of child support automatically goes to their college funds along with the alimony payments. I didn't touch a cent of that money."

"Fantastic. We'll keep that jaw-dropper in our arsenal and spring it on them at the hearing."

"Will the children need to hear everything?"

"No. The children will sit with a social worker in a room set up for children while parents work out their details. The judge might want to interview them."

"Understood. Steve plans to come with me. Do you think he should?"

"Sure. Because of these new developments with your income, I don't think it will matter one way or another if he's there."

"Oh. Good."

"We'll need written statements from Mia and the

detective who oversaw her case just as a precaution. Could you get those for me? I'll email you what I want to see in the statement. Then scan them over so I can review them before I put them in the file. Since you're involved with Steve, I don't think he'll be able to testify on your behalf, but I still want to prep him."

"I can do that. How soon do you need them?"

"Tomorrow or the next day."

Cassie's voice wavered. "Not a lot of time. Do you have an exact date? I must speak to Steve."

"Not yet. I hope to have clarification on the hearing date by mid-week. In the meantime, you need to assemble your paperwork. Purchase documents, deed, bank accounts for the college funds and tax returns from the last two years to show your ability to provide for them."

"I'll have everything ready. I also send them to a private school and should probably bring that information."

"Yes. Anything showing you are a responsible adult will help your case."

"Oh. I almost forgot. What do I do about Nico's wife using my daughters as slave labor?"

"What?"

"I have no problem with age-appropriate chores, but I draw the line at them doing housekeeping when they're supposed to spend time with their father."

"You're certain about this?"

"The girls let it slip earlier in the summer when Charlotte was pregnant. I can understand how it might have been convenient to have them help, but I want it stopped or at least curtailed."

"Let's deal with the custody issue first then we'll

tackle that afterward. Agreed?"

"What are my chances of winning?"

"This should be a slam dunk unless they come to court with bombshells, then we scramble. Let me look into it."

After she hung up, tears fell like furious raindrops on a glass pane. She blew her nose and stiffened her back. She would get through this.

Lord, I need your strength. Please help me do the right thing for my daughters. I need you, more than I ever needed you before. Give me wisdom and peace. Your peace that surpasses all understanding. Help the judge to see the truth. Finally, Lord, soften Nico's heart.

She prepared the documents, then called Steve and briefed him on the case. They would meet at the gym. They could talk then.

The next calls would be to Mia and the detective.

She'd need to call her publisher and agent and apprise Blake of her literary agency agreement and pray the judge would keep the information confidential, but that didn't mean Nico would keep his mouth shut. Maybe she could request a court order. Or maybe she should just let those closest to her know her pen name.

Chapter 29

Dressed in her chenille sweats and fuzzy slippers, Cassie plopped into her writing chair. The cold combined with the upcoming court case, caused a sense of dread in the pit of her stomach. But she was strong. Stronger than she imagined. She breathed in and sipped lemon tea.

Cassie used Blake's email as a checklist. The bank's safe deposit box held her deed and purchase agreement. She'd do that today.

Cassie dialed the detective's number, only to find him out until tomorrow. She'd email him with the request and hope he'd get to it quickly.

Next call, Mia. Keeping her on topic would be a monumental task. She picked up on the second ring.

"Hey, Mia. I need you to write a statement and will email you what's needed. Could you return it by Friday?"

"Sure, but why the rush?"

"My attorney wants to review it in case he wants changes."

"I'll handle it. What about you and Steve?"

"We've chatted on the phone and talked at the gym."

"You two need to date, without the kids in tow. I'll babysit."

"Not till I resolve the court case."

"Baloney."

Cassie didn't want to get into it with Mia. "How's the physical therapy on the wrists?"

"They appear to be fine. Pam, my physical therapist, keeps me on track lifting weights and I'm spending a lot of time with her."

"I'm glad. How's the search for Shannon coming along?"

Cassie sensed a coolness over the phone.

"He seems to have disappeared, but my plastic surgery is on Monday. I hope the surgeon can make me better than before."

Mia usually side-stepped any discussion about Shannon, so Cassie dropped it.

"I'm sure he can. He might be a cute, single doctor and you'll turn his head."

Cassie envisioned Mia rolling her eyes. "Please."

The doorbell pealed through the phone. "Pam is here for today's torture. I'll look for that email."

Cassie keyed in the requirements for the statement and then shot off one to Mia and one to the detective. With everything she could do finished, she prepared a casserole and left for the bank.

Cassie struggled to explain the situation to her daughters to prepare them for the trip. Casting Nico in a blameless light took all her storytelling skills. They appeared to understand the situation's gravity with no gory details.

With the hearing date set, Cassie learned Steve cleared his schedule and would leave his girls with his sister.

"Weatherman's predicting snow. Let's take my vehicle. It'll handle a storm better and it'll be more comfortable for the girls," Steve said.

"Sounds good."

"I booked a suite for you and the girls and room for me on a different floor allowing for no hint of impropriety given the circumstances."

"Thanks for taking care of those details. I'm somewhat scattered these days."

"Understandable. Relax, you got this. We'll leave Thursday night after dinner."

He appeared on her doorstep the day before the court case. She noticed he lowered the seats in the SUV so the girls had a make-shift bed and installed a rack on the roof for their luggage.

"Ready to go?"

"Yep. The bags are right here, and the girls are getting their coats, pillows, and blankets. The video games should keep them busy and they're dressed in their warmest pajamas."

Steve looked skyward. "Let's hope the weather holds. If not, at least the kids can sleep. What about snacks?"

Cassie laughed. "Trail mix, homemade cookies and juice boxes."

"What about drinks for the older kids?"

"Thought of that too. Two thermoses of hot coffee."

His teeth gleamed in the starless sky to reveal an enormous smile. "A woman after my stomach. Coffee and cookies. What else could a man ask for?"

Cassie rolled her eyes, but grinned.

The girls settled into the pillows, commented on the trip and settled down with their video games.

Cassie caught Steve steal a glance at her, then in the rearview mirror at the girls. She stared out into the black night and wished this trip was under different circumstances.

She let out another lengthy breath and Steve's hand snaked across the console to grip her fingers. "Everything will turn out okay. Remember, Romans

8:28: All things work together for good to them that love God, to them who are called according to his purpose."

Cassie smiled through her tears and gave a vigorous nod. "Thank you. I needed that."

They arrived later than expected with the girls fast asleep. While Cassie crawled in the back, Steve checked them in and helped her carry the girls to their suite.

"I ordered room service for you and the girls because we're on a tight schedule. I hope you don't mind."

"No, I don't mind. But I need to repay you for the rooms. You didn't need to book a suite."

"Two bathrooms. Makes it easier for you to ready the girls in the morning. I live with three females. Bathroom time is critical."

Cassie laughed.

"No repayment either. You cared for my girls all those weeks. This is not a repayment because I can't repay you for what you did for them, nor would I want to insult you. So don't insult me."

Too stressed to argue, Cassie agreed.

"I'll get the bags. You settle the girls."

Steve didn't linger after he delivered the luggage. Tomorrow would be a grueling day and she needed every bit of sleep she could get. She double-checked her documents before she fell into bed.

When they arrived at the courthouse, Lena, Nico's sister, was front and center and eyed Steve with the girls, but couldn't comment because Blake appeared and ushered them to a private room. "The girls will stay here with Steve and the social worker."

"Mama, why can't you stay, too?" Bella said.

Cassie squatted to eye level. "We talked about this. I have to meet with the judge. I'll be back as soon as I can and we'll go to lunch."

Bella nodded, but tears threatened to erupt when Gabby reached for her sister's hand. "Come on. They have cool toys to play with. And besides. Steve will be with us, won't you Steve?"

He nodded and took their hands in his. Cassie cast worried eyes at him and stepped into the next room with Blake.

"It looks like all of Lena's family showed but, the new wife doesn't appear to be here," Blake said.

Cassie shrugged. "Does it matter?"

"No. The judge will hear the case in chambers."

Her eyebrows rose. "That's fantastic. I worried about Lena. She can be thorny."

"This will be over soon."

Cassie nodded.

Blake's phone pinged, and he read the text. "Let's go. The judge is waiting."

The bleak room matched her emotional state. Dark woodwork and sturdy chairs sat in a semi-circle in front of the massive desk.

The judge, with frizzy hair and a protruding belly, greeted her. "Mrs. Verano. Please sit."

Cassie dropped into the chair farthest from her ex-husband placing Blake between them.

"I don't normally do this, but we'll dispense with a formal hearing and have a discussion. The attorneys will be silent while I speak with both parties."

Nico and his attorney sat on the desk's far side. He glanced her way and said nothing, but ran a finger inside his collar when his attorney laid out his case.

"Mrs. Verano, we want to understand this situation a little better. I understand you were involved in a missing person case. While that has no bearing in this case, it speaks to your character," the judge said.

Cassie nodded.

The judge glanced from her to Nico. "You assisted the police department and stepped in to assist with childcare. Admirable, Mrs. Verano. However, the only item of concern is how you plan to provide for your children after the alimony ends."

She glanced at Blake out of the corner of her eye. His face revealed nothing.

"The child support will remain as is. The amount is barely enough to feed and clothe one child until age eighteen, let alone two." He gave a fierce scowl at Nico, then zeroed in on Cassie.

"Your Honor, I have an income." She opened her briefcase and produced the tax returns. "I can provide my children what they need over and above the child support I will receive. Every child support and alimony payment have been transferred into accounts for the girls' college funds. The account information is under the returns."

His attorney's eyes widened, and Nico's face turned that rusty shade of red. The judge took the proffered papers and placed cheater lenses on the end of his nose. He examined each document.

"Were you aware of this, Mr. Verano?"

"No, Your Honor."

"Did you bother to ask?"

"No, Your Honor."

The judge harrumphed. "Mrs. Verano, I understand from your attorney, the girls attend private school and *you* foot the education bill personally, is that correct?"

"Yes, Your Honor. I have the school's contract and payments made this year."

"Your tax returns are sufficient. May I ask what it is you write that affords you such a generous income?"

"I…"

"She writes?" Nico exclaimed, and his attorney jabbed him in the ribs to quiet him.

"No more comments, Mr. Verano. The hole you're digging for yourself is expanding downward."

"Sorry, Your Honor."

He gave a half smile in her direction. "Mrs. Verano, please continue."

"I wrote a novel series that turned into best sellers. I write under a pen name and prefer anonymity. And I'm not at liberty to discuss other pending projects."

The judge gazed in Nico's direction. "Is there anything you would like to add, Mr. Verano?"

He looked like someone gutted him. "No, sir. I'm confident Cassie can support our daughters." Then he turned toward her. "You should have told me about the college fund, Cass."

Seemed obvious he hadn't expected her to arrive armed like a commando or have bank accounts. Deep in her soul, she had forgiven him. She didn't know when it had happened, but her heart lifted. He no longer held the power to hurt her or make her crazy.

She turned to the judge. "Your Honor, I would like to discuss another minor matter."

The judge's eyebrow shot up. "Go ahead."

Glancing at Blake, he gave the go-ahead nod. "Last summer, it came to my attention, when my daughters visit their father, they are tasked with chores I believe are not age-appropriate."

Nico had turned an awful shade of yellow.

"You seemed to have paled, Mr. Verano. Am I to presume you aren't aware of this?"

"No, Your Honor."

"Considering this recent development, I want to speak to your daughters myself. Blake, please text the social worker and have her bring them here. Mr. and Mrs. Verano, please wait in the lobby with your lawyers. We'll call you as soon as I've spoken with the children."

"She's on her way, Your Honor," Blake said, reading his texts

The judge handed Cassie her documents, and they filed   out.

Chapter 30

Cassie struggled not to squirm under Nico's keen eye. What would the girls tell the judge?

The attorneys left the room, and Nico broke the uneasy silence with a quiet voice. "Why didn't you tell me you saved the payments? When did you start writing for a living?"

"Would you have listened?"

"Probably not." He shifted his eyes toward the door, and then stared at the floor. "I never wanted to file for custody, Cass. Lena coerced me, and I was wrong to listen. Charlotte doesn't want this either. I'm happy and you should find happiness, too."

"Why the change in attitude?"

"Charlotte's pregnancy worried me and I took it out on you. I had no right to judge you."

Cassie nodded. "And the girls doing chores?"

He squirmed and pursed his lips.

"The girls should clean up after themselves, but they are not servants."

"Charlotte needed a little help. I'm sure she thought she could ask them to do chores."

"According to Gabby, they did dishes, swept and scrubbed floors, dusted and cleaned baseboards and even cleaned out the car. These are not age appropriate. Clear off the table, pick up after themselves, make their beds, sure. The rest, no."

"I wasn't home, I was working."

"Apparently."

He flinched.

"We've never been able to discuss our marriage like adults. You mistreated me, but I forgive you. For the girls' sake, we need to act like adults."

"Regardless of what you think of me, I wish you happiness. But what about the writing?"

She could practically see wheels turning in his head, but the attorneys returned.

"The judge is ready for us," his attorney said.

They stepped into the judge's office and took their seats.

"Mr. and Mrs. Verano, your daughters are delightful. Bella was cautious at first but Gabby took the lead. Mr. Verano, you will ensure no one uses these children as servants."

"Yes, Your Honor."

"If you cannot control the situation, the court will advise children's services to make your appointed time with your daughters as supervised visits. Am I clear?"

"Yes, Your Honor."

"I understand your sister, the family matriarch, instigated this custody battle. Be a man, Mr. Verano, and don't allow others to interfere in your personal matters. I don't want to see you in my courtroom or chambers for frivolous reasons again."

Nico had the decency to look chagrined.

"Mrs. Verano, you will retain custody and continue with your visitation arrangement with Mr. Verano. The alimony and child support will continue since the payments fund their college education. Should your daughters appear to be doing more than age-appropriate chores, contact children's services. Your attorney will assist you."

"Thank you, Your Honor."

Relief showed on Nico's face. He and his attorney went down one hallway while she and Blake went in the opposite direction.

Cassie let out a huge sigh. "I'm overjoyed."

"After you sent the tax returns and the bank balances, I figured the judge would rule in your favor."

"How do I thank you?"

"My bill will be in the mail." They both laughed.

Cassie gathered her daughters in her arms and hugged them. Tears threatened to fall.

"Mama, do we live with you?" Gabby said.

"Yes, darling, you do."

She straightened. "I told the judge I wanted to stay with you because I love you. And Charlotte makes us work."

Cassie laughed. "I guess love and not having to do housework goes hand in hand."

Confusion filled Gabby's eyes.

"I told the judge Charlotte was sometimes mean to us," Bella said.

"She is?" Cassie's eyes flashed over Bella's head to Steve whose lips set in a grim line. "We'll talk about that later. How about lunch?"

"This happy news calls for a celebration lunch with a huge dessert," Steve said.

They jumped and hugged him, and Cassie praised God for answered prayer.

Steve adjusted his tie and checked his hair in the hallway mirror. His nerves quivered. Worse than when he closed the Australian deal. His first real date with Cassie. The dinner they had the night the girls had the sleep over didn't count.

Before he rang Cassie's doorbell, he fingered the box in his jacket pocket. Was it too soon?

She looked like a red-carpet movie star. With a gentle hand, he helped her into the SUV. Cassie appeared to be nervous, too.

"You said dressy, right?" Cassie said.

He held her gloved hand. "You'll do. How did the handoff go today?"

"Better than expected. Nico engaged them more, but they were cautious. I sure hope Lena doesn't make overtures."

"Don't borrow trouble. We'll deal with whatever when it hits. Agreed?"

She smiled. "Sounds good."

After they were seated at a swanky restaurant in Columbus, the server brought a bottle of non-alcoholic sparkling wine.

"What are we toasting?"

"Everything."

"Could you be more specific?"

"The custody battle win. That day almost did me in. But the girls needed bolstering and wouldn't leave my side."

Cassie frowned. "I didn't know that."

"I found it endearing."

"You would. You said first."

He struggled with the words. "Over the past six months, I realized what matters in life and you're a big part of what's important. You, your daughters, my daughters, Mia. I fell in love with you when you opened your heart to my girls and loved them like your own." He reached in his pocket. "I hope you care and love me as much as I do you. Will you marry me, Cassie?"

Tears streamed down her cheeks as she gazed at the antique ring he held in his fingers. Other diners' voices drifted away. The remote booth cocooned them.

She raised her eyes and gave him her thousand-watt smile. "Yes. I'll marry you. I fell in love with you the first time you played in the pool with the girls. Then when you watched a princess movie with them, that cinched it."

He placed the ring on her finger and it was like the ring was custom made for her. She frowned.

His eyes turned sad. "What? You don't like the ring?"

"This ring is an antique."

"My grandmother's. My mother wore it when she was young and wanted my wife to have it."

Cassie cast troubled eyes at him.

His brow furrowed. "Don't you like it?"

"It's exquisite. But I would have thought—"

"My mother never offered the ring the first time. My mom and dad would have loved you."

"I'm sorry I never got to meet them and I'll wear the ring with honor."

When her slight smile turned into a frown again, he raised his chin. "There's something else, isn't there?"

The server brought their entrees.

"What about the girls?"

"What about them?"

"We can't spring this engagement on the family so soon after the custody battle."

He passed a hand over the back of his neck, and the heat rose in his face. "I admit I'm selfish. I hadn't thought of anyone except us, but you may have a point. What do you suggest?"

"I need to think about it, but we should wait."

Hesitancy filled his voice. "All right."

"How about I wear the ring on a chain till we decide what to do?"

He took her hand and rubbed the ring.

They continued to eat their dinner. The server brought them a raspberry topped crème brûlée to share.

"Are you writing a lot while the kids are in school?"

"Actually, I wanted to talk to you about that."

He glanced at her. "Go on."

"I told you I'm a novelist, but I didn't tell you what I write—or rather wrote."

"I thought you couldn't say."

"My publisher demanded I have a website, but when I explained my home situation, they reluctantly agreed to wait. Now that things are settled, I plan to move forward with it. I'll occupy myself with that when I'm done with the two books I'm writing. Since the custody case is behind me, I've finally reconciled my past work with my current writing."

"And?"

"It appears I'm your favorite author," she blurted and threw the diamond-ringed hand over her mouth.

His jaw dropped. "*You're* Veronica Cannon?"

She let out a pent-up breath. "Considering the engagement, I want no secrets between us."

"I agree to no secrets. Ever." He shook his head and whistled. "You're Veronica Cannon."

"One and only." A serious look passed over her.

"Fantastic. Why don't you continue to write Jade Parker Adventures? They are awesome and I have every book in the series."

279

"I can't write them anymore. I don't want anyone's faith compromised when reading them."

"Understood. There is a bit of spice, but you made the New York Times best seller's list."

"Mia read the second in the series and said you were dismayed your favorite author pronounced it to be the last one." Cassie put air quotes around favorite author and grinned.

"True. She is and I can't wait to read her new books." He took her hand, touched his lips to her palm and noticed her shiver. "Cold?"

"No. There's more."

He frowned but continued to hold her hand.

"A film company purchased the rights to the Jade Parker series. They want me as a consultant."

"Fantastic. I'm so proud of you, Cassie."

"I told them the spicy parts had to be toned down to a G-rating or I wouldn't sign the deal. They agreed."

"Good for you. You're much stronger than you know."

"I see that now. But we need to figure out what to do about the engagement."

"We could date while we're thinking, right?"

"Great idea. When I think of something, I'll let you know."

Two weeks later, Cassie leaned into him for a warm hug and a lengthy kiss. "Right on time. I like a punctual man."

His stomach growled. She drew back and laughed.

"The best way…"

"Don't even say it."

"Can I help it if I'm hungry and you make the best

smelling pizza in the world?"

"I know what to do about the girls."

"Oh yeah? Lay it on me."

He draped his jacket over the chair. The kitchen table was set, and she placed oversized pizza slices on his plate. He sniffed the pizza and dug in.

"Christmas is less than ten days. Why don't we both get the girls rings and ask them for their hands in marriage?"

He stopped in mid-chew and stared at her, then swallowed and cleaned his mouth. "I'm not sure I understand."

She sighed. "We pick out a ring with each girl's birthstone. You pick out a setting for my girls, and I'll pick out one for yours. I ask your children to be my daughters, and you ask mine. Simple."

Steve stared at her.

She crossed her arms. "You've a better idea?"

"You had time to process it, I haven't."

"While you process, I'll eat."

They ate in silence until Steve said, "It's a great idea. How do we make it happen?"

"Are you available Monday morning to go to the jewelers?"

"I'll rearrange my schedule. Then what?"

"Then we prepare our speeches."

Perspiration beads popped on his forehead. "Oh boy."

"They're little girls who love you already. We'll need to make a lot of decisions."

"Like what?"

"Kids ask a lot of questions. Like when… and where will we live? And we need to be prepared for them?"

"Why not just say we'll decide together, as a family?"

"Perfect." She smiled, and he was happy to contribute something to the idea.

"How about we make the announcement on Christmas Eve? You could come early with the girls and we could talk to them before everyone else gets here."

"Brilliant."

Chapter 31

Steve arrived an hour early on Christmas Eve with his daughters.
None of the girls could contain themselves.

A sternness appeared on Cassie's face. "Girls, we need to talk."

The girls climbed on the sofa, settled into one another and held hands.

"Mama, they're still staying for Christmas Eve, right?" Gabby's lip pouted.

"Yes. Gabby and Bella go into my home office with Steve. I need to talk to Stella and Tina."

Gabby took Cassie's hand. "By why, Mama?"

"Because I asked, and Christmas is tomorrow."

Gabby nodded and grabbed Bella's hand, but cast worried glances over her shoulder to her mother and soon-to-be sisters.

Cassie went to the Christmas tree, and pulled small gift bags and set them on the coffee table.

Stella leaned forward and peeked at the tissue paper. "Are we getting presents from you, Mrs. V.? Is daddy giving Gabby and Bella presents too?"

Cassie laughed and ruffled her hair. "You're way too smart."

She kneeled before them and took each girl's hand in hers and stared at blue eyes so much like their father's. "I want to ask you something important."

The girls' eyebrows crinkled and their eyes became worried.

"I want to ask you if I can marry your Daddy."

It took a half a second for his daughters to

283

understand. They whooped and gave her a tight hug. She hoped her daughters gave Steve the same reception.

Stella leaned back from her hug and her eyes got wide. "We wanted you to marry Daddy. Fiona told us to pray God would make it happen, and he did!"

A wondrous look passed over her face as she realized God answered their prayer, and Cassie's voice wavered. "God answers prayers. What would you like to call me after your daddy and I marry?"

Tina, shy like Bella, blurted, "Can we call you Mama like Gabby and Bella? I don't remember our real Mama and we'd like you to be our real Mama."

Cassie pulled the two girls into her arms and choked. "I'd love that."

"Since you said yes, I have an engagement present for you both."

Each girl received a bag and opened the tiny boxes within.

"Are Gabby and Bella getting rings too?" Stella said.

"We have to wait and see, won't we?"

"It sure smells good in here, Mama." Tina said.

A film of joyful tears threatened to spill as she held Tina and Stella close. Cassie would have never guessed her heart could be so full having four daughters. Two were from her own flesh, the other two a gift from Steve.

When Steve stepped into the room with the girls in front of him, his glassy eyes showed he was just as affected as she was. The girls ran to their respective parent and chattered about their rings amid hugs and kisses.

Cassie motioned for the girls to sit. "When the rest of

the family arrive—"

"Didn't you buy Mama a ring, Daddy?" Tina blurted.

All eyes moved to Steve, who blushed crimson. "I gave your Mama a ring."

"Well, where is it?" Stella said as she held her new Mama's hand.

He raised an eyebrow and Stella backed away. Cassie pulled the chain out from her sweater and showed the girls the ring.

"Aren't you going to put it on Mama's hand?" Tina said.

"Not now, sweetie. She's keeping it on the chain till we tell everyone. But we wanted your permission first," he said.

Steve reached over and held Cassie's hand. "We need you to keep the secret till I officially ask Cassie tonight. I know you'll want to show off your beautiful rings to your new family members, but you must keep the secret. Can you do that?" Steve said.

"We can't wear them?" Gabby pouted.

He pulled out four long boxes and opened one. "We bought you chains so you could wear them around your neck like your mama till we make the announcement."

Cassie locked gazes with each girl. "Can we count on you to help us make this a big surprise? Please?"

"Yes, Mama," they chorused. Steve helped each girl with their necklace while Cassie placed the empty bags under the tree.

"Are you going to come and live with us, Mama?" Tina said.

"When are you going to be our Mama?" Stella said.

Gabby, for once, remained silent while Bella glanced

from Cassie to Steve.

"We'll talk about that as a family," Steve said. "Today isn't the day and tomorrow is Christmas, but I promise the next day, we'll talk about it. Could you wait till then?" Steve said.

All four girls nodded and climbed on Steve's lap to hug and kiss him.

"Why don't you girls go downstairs and play till the others get here," Cassie said and took a finger and thumb to her lips. "Remember, keep the surprise a secret."

"How will we know when we can show our rings, Mama?" Gabby said. "We can't call Steve, *Daddy Steve* till after the surprise, right, Mama?"

Cassie listened in awe at her daughter and glanced at Steve, who cast his eyes away. "That's right, sweetie."

"Same goes for you two," he said, pointing to his daughters. After the surprise, you can call Cassie, Mama, but call her Mrs. V. till we say. Understand?" He waited for their nods. "Now scoot."

When the chattering became muffled, Cassie melted into Steve's arms and let the tears fall. "I'm so happy."

"So am I."

She gazed at the love that shone in his eyes. "Daddy Steve?"

"It was their idea. I told them I would never take their real daddy's place and they could choose what to call me. They wanted a special name just for me so they decided on Daddy Steve and I almost lost it. Never expected them to want to call me that."

When the doorbell rang, Cassie and Steve stepped in

the foyer to answer the door. The cold blew in despite Mia, Rob, Becka and their brood blocking the door.

"Come on in. A fire's roaring in the living room. The kids are in the basement," Cassie said while Steve took coats and stowed them in the sunroom.

"Can I help in the kitchen?" Becka said.

Mia followed them into the kitchen.

They called the kids, and everyone sat in the dining room. Their girls wouldn't last long keeping the secret. She glanced at Steve, who gripped the table. "We have an announcement to make."

Everyone fell silent, and all eyes riveted on him. "I've asked Cassie to marry me. Gabby and Bella have given me permission to marry their mom. We're going to be a family."

Mia crossed her arms. "Where's the ring, Steve?"

Steve turned to Cassie who pulled the chain from her sweater, undid the clasp and handed it to Steve who went down on one knee. "Cassie. You are the love of my life. I can't wait for us to be a family." He placed the ring on her finger and kissed her sweetly amid the claps and hoots.

"Our grandmother's ring," Mia said as she held Cassie's hand. "I finally get a sister."

Becka hugged her. "I'm happy for you, Cassie. I see the love in his eyes and the ring' is exquisite." She poked Rob. "No grunting."

Cassie laughed and allowed Rob to lift her off the floor for his usual bear hug and he shook Steve's hand. "Welcome to the family."

"Now, Mama?" Gabby said. All eyes turned toward Gabby. When Cassie nodded, all four girls pulled the chains from their sweater and asked their new parent to place the rings on their fingers. They passed tissues around because the tears just wouldn't stop.

"Have you set a date?" Mia said.

"We'll discuss everything the day after Christmas," Stella repeated her father's words.

Mia shot a surprised look at her niece. "I guess that answers that. I'm happy for you both. You'll make a wonderful couple and a spectacular family."

Before they ate, Steve prayed a beautiful thanksgiving prayer for Christ's birth and for his new family.

The kids took turns picking board games until it was time for everyone to go home.

Both families spent Christmas dinner at Rob's house after having spent Christmas morning at their respective homes opening gifts. He loved getting to know his future brother-in-law. Frank was the closest he'd ever had to a brother and he couldn't wait to get to know his future in-laws better. The girls begged to go to his house to watch Christmas movies. So that's what they did.

After Cassie and her girls went home, he and Mia carried his daughters upstairs to bed. The girls hadn't spoken of the wedding plans today or this evening, they had been excited to spend the entire day with their best friends. Tomorrow they'd talk about their future blended family, but he didn't know what kind of questions the girls would have.

Chapter 32

The day after Christmas, Cassie and her girls arrived at Steve's ready to discuss the wedding plans.

The girls sat quiet and still at the dining room table. Steve raised an eyebrow, and the silence intrigued Cassie.

When they were all seated, Gabby left her chair to stand next to her mother. "We talked about it yesterday and we want you to get married on Valentine's Day."

The proclamation stunned Cassie, and Steve's mouth dropped open.

Cassie was the first to recover. "That's too soon, Gabby. There might not be enough time to plan."

Mia took out her phone. "Six weeks. I'll help plan. Small wedding, right?"

"We want a Valentine's day wedding." Their little mouths pouted and formed stubborn lines.

Cassie looked at Steve, who gave a slight nod.

"Not a lot of time but we could make it work," Cassie said.

"Valentine's Day is on a Friday next year," Mia said. "Becka, Fiona and I will help in any way we can."

"Valentine's Day it is," Steve said.

The girls cheered and asked to play. When Steve nodded, they scrambled up the stairs.

"So much for planning the wedding." Cassie chuckled.

"Let me get brunch on the table. Stay put, everything's ready," Mia said as she stepped out of the room.

Steve whispered in Cassie's ear. "Valentine's Day can't come soon enough, my love."

He kissed her, and she melted. She couldn't wait either.

The End.

Cassie & Steve's Free Bonus Wedding Story!

Don't you love weddings? What lover of romance doesn't? Do you want to know how Steve & Cassie's Valentine's Day Wedding turns out?

Sign up today for my new release mailing list and you'll receive their wedding story complete with Cassie & Steve's beloved families at www.seralynnlewis.com.

I don't like my email box littered with newsletters and information I don't want or need so I won't burden you with them unless there's something newsworthy for you like cut scenes, character profiles, extended endings, contests, or sneak peaks of covers for upcoming books.

And for a sneak peek at Mia's Irishman, book #2 of the Women of Worthy series, keep reading…

Mia's Irishman

A deer shot out from nowhere and Mia Nardelli slammed on the brakes, but the Honda skidded on wet leaves and pitched down the steep ravine. Her muscles stiffened when she gripped the steering wheel and fought for control. Her terrified scream died in her throat.

The car plowed through saplings and grasses and bounced over rocks. Her arm jammed against the window and her head jerked and hit the headrest as a large branch shattered the windshield before the Honda hit a massive boulder.

Mia's body slammed forward, and she gasped for breath. Rough material smothered her face and knocked the wind out of her. Dazed and disoriented, her head throbbed, and the dust from the deflated airbag clogged her throat, making her cough. When she caught her breath, an eerie silence stretched around her.

With her wrist burning, she pressed her bloody sleeve against the wetness on her face. The metallic taste on her lips made her shiver. Taking deep breaths to calm herself, she shook her head. *How did this happen?*

With blurred vision and wooziness, she fumbled for the door handle. Loud creaking pierced her ears as she grunted and pushed the door open. Struggling, she stepped out, wincing at the throbbing pain in her ankle. Leaning on the side of the car, she cradled her wrist and stumbled to the car's trunk. A wavering creek flowed beyond the car's crumpled front end.

The car hadn't rolled—a miracle that no doubt saved her life.

Blinking several times until her vision cleared, she surveyed the path the car took. She shook her head and peered at the steep ravine. *I have to get to the road and get help.* Tears gathered. She'd never be able to climb those soaring walls with the pain in her ankle and wrist.

Maybe if she sat in the car and waited. Maybe she'd be rescued. She took deep breaths to clear her mind. No one would look for her in this remote area. The tall pines stood sentry overlooking moss-covered rocks and hid her car from view.

Not a sign of life. When darkness came, the late summer air would turn cooler. Even in this isolated West Virginia wilderness, it wasn't uncommon for houses to be built near rivers and creeks.

She checked her cell phone, but it yielded no bars and the battery was getting low. Hopefully, a cell tower could be found nearby. Agonizing wrist pain made carrying camera equipment impossible. Everything went into the trunk along with her bulky purse. With her good hand, she shoved her useless phone into the jacket pocket.

Pain shot from her ankle to her heel and she limped along the creek's edge. She'd been eager to shoot more nature shots for her updated portfolio, and she stressed over having enough time to return home to pick up her nieces on the last day of gym camp.

Thankfully, she'd told her friend to take her nieces home with her in case she'd be late returning and hadn't anticipated an accident that would leave her stranded in the wilds of West Virginia. And worse, her brother was out of the country until Monday. She'd told him the housekeeper would be in town all week, but his housekeeper had been called out of town last night. Getting to civilization was her top priority now. She'd do whatever it took to get herself home, despite whatever injuries she has.

When her sister-in-law died, Mia returned to her hometown of Worthy, Ohio to care for her brother's two children. Her own tragedy buried deep, she dove headlong into caring for the two solemn toddlers while her brother attended to the family business. She dismissed returning to New York and high fashion photography and instead focused on her two nieces— a welcome relief from fashion divas and the pain of loss. The trauma of losing her husband and the realization she'd never have children had gutted her.

For the past five years, she took photos of her family on special occasions. She enjoyed being a doting aunt. Seeing her nieces' animated faces in her mind's eye gave her a reprieve from the intense pain.

The dappled sun dipped behind the hills. The cracked face on her watch read five P.M. Worry about the girls crowded her thoughts and caused her heart to ache. She had mentioned to her friend she might occasionally be out of cell range, but knew her friend would have collected the girls from camp. As each step became more and more difficult, she focused on moving toward her goal of getting home.

Excruciating pain in her wrist pushed her beyond her limits and the sting in her face kept her jaw still. Her ankle ached with every step. She wouldn't be able to go any further when the suffering proved too much. What would happen then? With God's help and her sheer force of will, she plodded along.

She trudged along the creek's edge until it ran into a gully and found a shallow section where she could cross. Focusing on the other side would keep her from thinking about her fear of water. Her mind concentrated on getting across the wide creek rather than on the gurgling water that splashed with every step. Stopping every few steps to maintain her balance on her bum ankle, the chilly water eased the throbbing in her ankle. Her lips trembled and sweat beaded on her forehead as she waded across the broad creek.

The gully narrowed, and she slumped against a rock. A dead end. No ground on either side of the creek for her to continue on and she couldn't walk in the creek. Not happening. Shrubs and trees spilled from the rocky ridge in front of her and the musky scent of wet earth filled her nostrils.

Climbing to the road sounded easier now. No use whining over it. She'd come too far and she couldn't go back now. She'd climb the cliff and hoped to find a house.

A skinny branch dangled overhead. Everything ached as she stretched too far and too fast and then slipped. Her injured hand flew up on impulse, but it wouldn't hold. Sudden pain ripped a scream from her throat. The sound bounced off the walls of the ravine as she lost her balance. The phone flew from her pocket and bounced on the rocks with her tumbling after it as it hit the water and sank before she landed with a thud on the rock-strewn creek bed.

Lord, keep me. Protect me and send an angel to find me.

Then darkness swept over her.

Find all of the Women of Worthy series books at
www.seralynnlewis.com/books

ACKNOWLEDGMENTS

It's been said it takes a village to raise up a child, but it couldn't be truer in the process of creating, writing, and editing a book.

For my wonderful husband, Ted, who has been my greatest supporter and cheerleader. For my daughters, Grazia and Ailene, whose childhood antics gave me great joy and provided ideas for this book.

For my writing partners:

> *Rob McClain, who encouraged and prodded me to be the best writer possible.*
>
> *Cheryl Kramarczyk, who lifted me up with her funny and heartfelt comments.*
>
> *Nanci Rubin, who was always gracious with her comments and suggestions.*

For all my other writer friends who gave words of encouragement and suggestions throughout the entire process. You know who you are! And for my beta readers who gave me crucial feedback in the final phases of editing.

For my editor, Carla Rossi, without whom this book would not have been possible.

For my bestie, Debbie Hnat, who read everything I ever sent her and is proud of me no matter what. I cherish all our years together as friends.

THANK YOU!

Thank you so much for reading Cassie's Secrets. As a voracious reader myself, I know there are tons of books available for you to read so I'm honored you selected my book. I look forward to providing you with more reading pleasure as time goes by.

Building a relationship with you is the very best and most important thing about writing. I occasionally send newsletters with details on new releases, special offers and other bits of news relating to the Women of Worthy series or writing in general.

And I love to hear from readers…what and who they loved, what and who they didn't love…and why. Feel free to contact me at info@seralynnlewis.com or at my website at www.seralynnlewis.com. While you're there, take a peek at my blog *A Woman's Heart.*

If you have a book club or bible study, download the *free* book club and/or bible study questions located under *more* in the menu.

If you enjoyed Cassie's Secrets, I hope you'll consider leaving a review on Amazon or Goodreads which would be helpful to me as an author. I would so appreciate it.

You can also find and connect with me on:

- Facebook
- Twitter
- Instagram
- Pintrest
- Linked In

And, thank you for your support!

Seralynn Lewis
AUTHOR

Dear Reader…

Within the pages of this book, you read about the character's spiritual life. If you were wondering how you could have the same confidence, it's as easy as A-B-C.

Admit that you are a sinner: *Lord, I am a sinner.*
Romans 3:23 For all have sinned and come up short of the glory of God.

Believe that Jesus is Lord, died for your sins and rose from the dead: *Lord, in my heart I believe you died for my sins and rose from the dead.*
Romans 6:23 For the wages of sin is death, but the gift of God is eternal life through Jesus Christ.

Call upon His name: *Lord, come into my life and be the Lord of my life.*
Romans 10:13 For whoever calls upon the name of the Lord Jesus Chris will be saved.

Your salvation does not depend on your good works, or how good of a person you are. You are saved by grace and grace alone!

No one is guaranteed another day. Please don't wait. Follow the ABCs and call upon the name of Jesus today and be saved. And please, contact me at info@seralynnlewis.com so I can pray for you and welcome you into the family of God!

Many blessings,

 Seralynn Lewis

About the Author

Seralynn Lewis was born and raised in a small historical town in northern Ohio. After having lived in various parts of the United States and for a short time in Germany, she and her husband have found their forever home in the Raleigh-Durham area of North Carolina.

She has two grown daughters, two lovely grandchildren, and a husband who supports everything she does no matter what it is.

But it wasn't always like that. A single mom for many years, she put herself through school, but couldn't find a job. Her brother's wife mentioned there were women who met to pray, and would she be interested? It couldn't hurt, and it might help. That meeting changed her life forever.

When the woman asked her, "Where will you spend eternity?" She didn't have an answer and really needed one. That's when her life changed. And she gave her life to Christ.

In those days, romances were mostly sweet romances, but they got increasingly graphic. She stopped reading them because she felt they were a hindrance to my walk with Jesus and learning His word.

Fast forward almost nineteen years later, after many years of prayer, she met a man who loved Jesus and loved her. He is her biggest cheerleader and holds her heart in the palm of his hand. Together they know that without Jesus in their lives they cannot do anything. He is the glue that keeps them strong.

As she dialed back on her formal career, she had

more time on her hands and went back to reading romances for pleasure. As she looked for books, there were wonderful inspirational romances that she enjoyed.

Considering those new romances, and the many scenes that floated around in her head, there was a yearning in her heart to share the truths she learned in her life's journey through romance. And that's where she is today. Writing sweet, inspirational romances.

When she's not writing, thinking about writing, or plotting her next novel, she's busy preparing a telephone Bible Study that's she's been doing for years. A long-time lover of romance novels, she would like nothing more than to sit on a deserted beach somewhere sipping iced tea and reading to her heart's content. She and her husband travel to visit family and friends in her hometown where she browses and delights in her favorite library.

Made in the USA
Las Vegas, NV
09 February 2022

43526549R00177